Stay of Execution

Also by K. L. Murphy

A Guilty Mind

Stay of Execution

A Detective Cancini Mystery

K. L. MURPHY

WITNESS
IMPULSE
An Imprint of HarperCollins*Publishers*

EPub Edition JUNE 2016 ISBN: 9780062491619
Print Edition ISBN: 9780062491718

10 9 8 7 6 5 4 3 2 1

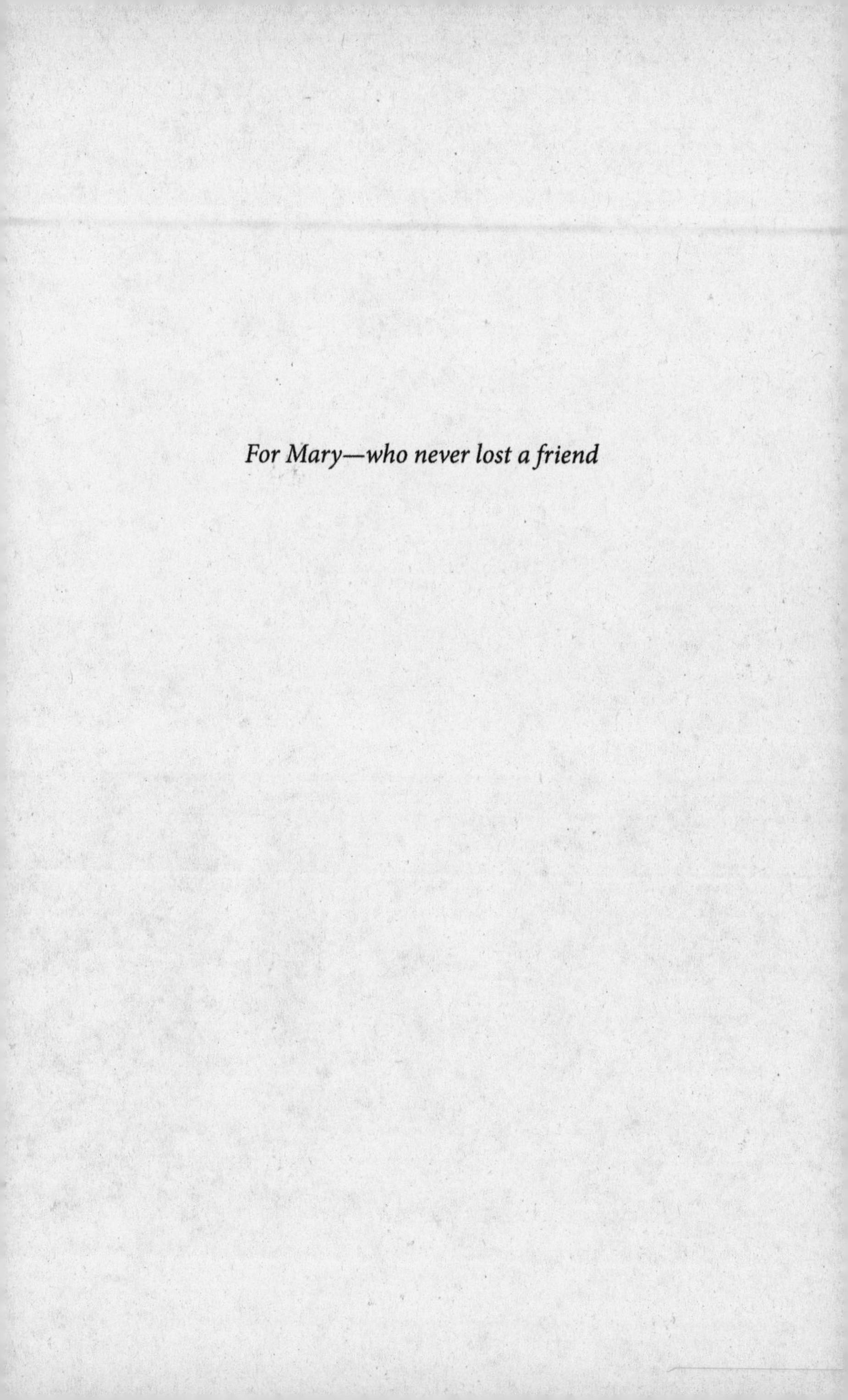

For Mary—who never lost a friend

Stay of Execution

Chapter One

SHADOWS DANCED ALONG the cinder-block walls. A light shone through the tiny window in the door, then moved past as the guard made his rounds. The prisoner lay still while the steps faded, then rolled to a sitting position, rusty bedsprings squeaking under his weight. His head jerked up toward the door. He waited before standing, bare feet hitting the cold, concrete floor.

In a few days, a week, it would all be over. No more guards. No more looking at the same walls twenty-three hours a day. No more crap food. No more of this godforsaken hellhole. He would go home, where he belonged.

On the far wall, a steel container served as his toilet. The stench of old piss stung his nose, but for once, he didn't mind. How quickly things had changed. Maybe he should've been surprised, but he wasn't. Hell, he'd been expecting it for a long time. Some would say he was lucky, might even call his release a miracle. Shit. Maybe it was a miracle. After all, it wasn't every day a man on death row got handed his walking papers. Not that he cared much about cheating death. So what if he wouldn't be executed tomorrow, or next month, or next year? He would still die eventually. Everyone does.

He knew how it would go. The lawyers would show up in their tailored suits and Italian shoes, all smug with their accomplishment. There'd be backslapping, and people he'd never seen before asking what he needed. No one had done that in a long damn time. He ran a hand over his heavy beard. They'd have clothes in his size, a suit and a tie. A barber would give him a haircut and shave. They'd clean him up. It was part of the deal.

He understood his role. His lawyers had shown him the newspapers. The governor himself had weighed in. None of the lawyers could understand why he wanted to go back home. His family was dead. He had no friends. Yet his return would not go unnoticed. There would be a press conference and cameras. It was reason enough.

In the semidarkness, he lay shirtless on his cot. A bead of sweat dripped from his temple to his ear. He'd have to be on his best behavior. Everything he said and did would be watched. Reporters would follow him for a story. The injustice, they'd say. The outrage. An innocent man had suffered, and now his ordeal was over. But they didn't know anything about injustice. They didn't know anything about him. He'd been inside for a long time, and the years had not passed quickly. He had unfinished business now, scores to settle. Everything was about to change.

Chapter Two

DETECTIVE MIKE CANCINI sat up with a start. For the third time in a week, he'd dozed off in the hard hospital chair. He shifted to look at the old man lying in the bed. The rise and fall of his father's sunken chest kept time with his snores. Tubes ran from his arms to the green lights on the monitor. His pulse was steady and his blood pressure read normal.

The television cast a soft light across the room. Cancini stood, stretching his stiff limbs. He used the remote to click to the nightly news. His eyes went back to the old man. His father looked so pale. What little hair remained was snow-white and combed back. Dark bruises dotted the thin skin of his arms where doctors and nurses had poked and prodded. If it weren't for the snoring, Cancini would wonder. He shook away the thoughts. His father had always been stronger than he looked. Strong and stubborn.

"In a surprise move today," a TV reporter said, "the governor has granted a writ of innocence to Leo Spradlin, the man once known as the Coed Killer."

Cancini's head whipped around. He moved closer to the screen.

"Mr. Spradlin, currently housed in solitary at Red Onion State Prison, was convicted of the rapes and murders of five women, all students at Blue Hill College. Sentenced more than twenty years ago, Mr. Spradlin was scheduled for execution later this month." Behind the reporter, a camera panned the dreary prison campus, the highest security facility in Virginia. "A statement from the governor's office and the attorney general indicated that new DNA evidence exonerates Spradlin."

Cancini's temple throbbed. A headshot of Spradlin appeared in the corner of the screen. The man's hair was longish now, not short the way he wore it back then. A heavy beard covered his chiseled face, but his pale blue eyes were the same, clear and cold as a winter night.

"Lawyers working for the newly innocent man had this to say."

The picture switched to an attorney in a gray suit. "Leo Spradlin is a grateful man tonight." The lawyer stood on the steps of the state capitol, microphones shoved under his chin. "He is particularly grateful to the governor for hearing his case. As many of you have already heard, DNA evidence that had previously been used to help convict Mr. Spradlin has been reexamined using more current technology. That same evidence now proves beyond a shadow of a doubt that Mr. Spradlin is not the Coed Killer. Mr. Spradlin is also immensely grateful to the Freedom and Justice Group and men like Dan Whitmore." He paused, nodding at the short, squat man standing to his right. "Finally, he would like me to thank all the friends and family who stood by him through this long ordeal and for their strong faith in him."

"What friends? What family?" Cancini muttered. His long fingers tightened on the remote. No one had stood by the man. Spradlin had alienated anyone and everyone who might once have cared for him. Not just during the original trial. Through countless appeals and hearings, no one ever appeared on Spradlin's behalf. Cancini should know. He'd never missed a single one.

The reporter returned to the screen. She nodded. "The governor's office also issued the following statement: 'In an effort to right this terrible miscarriage of justice, Mr. Spradlin will be granted a full pardon along with his writ of innocence and will be released within a matter of days.'"

A heat rose in Cancini. He'd heard rumblings the DNA evidence was getting another look, but he hadn't given it much thought. It was true some of the evidence in the murder case had been circumstantial, but the DNA evidence—such as it was at the time—had been convincing. The jury had deliberated less than two hours. What had changed?

The newswoman shuffled papers. When she spun to the left, the camera followed. "And on Wall Street today, the Dow Jones took a tumble. Stockholders were warned to brace for another market correction."

Cancini hit the mute button, shaking his head. The sheets ruffled behind him. He squared his shoulders, meeting his father's gaze.

"What does it mean? Is it true?" His father sounded tired, his words barely audible.

The detective swallowed. "How long have you been awake?"

"Long enough. Thought that was your case."

Cancini winced. It wasn't a question. He put the remote back on the nightstand, then tucked the blankets under the old man's spindly arms. His father's hands, blue with puffy veins, lay flat on the bed.

"Well?"

Cancini didn't answer, unable to wrap his head around the reversal. He rubbed the stubble on his chin. How could a man as guilty as Spradlin suddenly be innocent? That case had made his career, started him on the road as a homicide detective. Did that mean everything was built on a lie? If it was, he knew what his father would think. His son was a failure.

"I don't know anything, Dad. I only knew they were looking into old evidence. Not this."

"You said he was guilty. He went to jail."

"He went to jail because a jury convicted him. They thought he was guilty. We all thought he was guilty." He grabbed his jacket and glanced once more at the monitors. Everything appeared normal. "I've gotta go." He started toward the door. "I'll try to come by tomorrow night."

"Michael?"

"Yes, Dad?"

The old man's eyes, still sharp, glowed like shiny coins at the bottom of a murky fountain. "Did you make a mistake?"

The detective swallowed his resentment. His father wouldn't be the only one to ask. Had he made a mistake? The governor seemed to think so. But if Spradlin was innocent, who was guilty? After the arrest, the murders and rapes had stopped. Coincidence? Cancini didn't know if he could accept that.

"I don't know, Dad. I'm not sure."

"Then get sure."

Chapter Three

Julia Manning looked over tortoiseshell readers and peered at the digital clock. After midnight again. She shifted in the worn leather chair, pulling her legs to her chest and resting her head on her knees. It would be another sleepless night. She had no one to coax her to bed, no one to pull her close during the night. She lifted her chin. Damn him.

Holed up in her office, she felt the emptiness of the large house echo throughout the halls. She'd carved out a workspace from the smallest room, barely larger than a closet, but she loved it anyway. Behind her, a wall of shelves overflowed with books and papers. Her collection of knickknacks and pictures from childhood hung on the walls and cluttered the battered desk. It was a mess, but it was hers.

"How can you stand it in here?" Jack had asked one day, leaning in the doorway. His eyes had swept across the room to the furniture crammed in corners and the stacks of old magazines. "Doesn't it make you claustrophobic?"

"No," she'd answered honestly. It didn't and never had. Although the space was small, the window overlooking the backyard made it feel larger, and the light that shone through all day made it bright and warm. "It's comfortable."

Jack had not seemed convinced. "When Marta comes next time, you should have her clean in here." He'd waved a hand toward the junk spilling from the bookcase and said, "It smells." He'd left quickly, as though the foul odor he'd detected might follow. At the time, she'd laughed. Curled up now, she was no longer amused. Then again, blame comes in all shapes and sizes. Laying it all on Jack would be too easy. She couldn't deny she'd begun to spend more time in her office. It hadn't happened all at once, but they had drifted away from each other. Still, she wasn't the one who'd brought other people into it.

Blinking back tears, she picked up the oversized manila envelope perched on the corner of her desk. It was heavy in her hands, thick with the background research she'd requested. A story of this magnitude came with expectations and a whopping amount of history. Julia rifled through her desk for an empty spiral notebook. She pushed up her glasses and studied the first several pages, photocopies of old newspaper articles.

Little Springs Gazette
November 8

Late yesterday, the body of a young woman was found at the edge of the Thompson River. Three hunters, guests of the Powhatan Lodge, discovered the woman's remains. The deceased has been identified as Cheryl Fornak, a sophomore at Blue Hill Christian College.

Julia skimmed the remainder of the article. She picked up her tea, sipping the lukewarm liquid. "Cheryl Fornak," she said out loud. She'd had a friend named Cheryl in college. They'd been close for a while, even sharing an apartment the first few months after graduation. They'd drifted apart when Cheryl got engaged and followed her fiancé to Texas. In her notebook, Julia wrote the number one, and next to it, the girl's name, her age, and the date of her murder. On a separate line, she wrote down the names of the police chief, the town, and the college.

She flipped through the next few pages. After the autopsy, the case had been classified as a rape and murder. Days and weeks had passed with little progress in the investigation when a second girl was found.

Little Springs Gazette
December 5

Early yesterday morning, the body of a second young woman was found nearly ten miles outside Little Springs. A truck driver headed to Blue Hill Christian College spotted the woman, identified as Theresa Daniels, lying on the shoulder of 81 South. The police and a college spokesman confirmed that the young woman was a student at the school, a senior biology major. Authorities revealed that the death would be listed as a homicide. The autopsy is expected to begin as early as today.

It has been almost one month since the body of Blue Hill Christian College sophomore Cheryl Fornak was discovered on the banks of the Thompson River. Dozens of students and local residents have been interviewed in connection with the case. However, the investigation has stalled, and the police have declined to name any suspects in Fornak's rape and murder. Police would not make a statement regarding any connection between the two deaths.

A spokesman for Blue Hill issued this statement, "We are stunned by both murders. Nothing like this has ever happened in the history of our school or in the history of this town. Our highest priority is to protect our students. In light of the second murder, we have instituted a curfew and all school buildings will be locked down by campus security at eleven p.m. each evening. Where it is possible, the faculty will reschedule evening classes."

Manny Fulton, the mayor of Little Springs, attended a town meeting at the high school last night and addressed the murders. "Chief Hobson and the rest of the men are doing their best to find out what has happened to these young women. The best thing we can do is cooperate in any way possible and help them do their jobs so we can all sleep better at night."

Julia shifted in her chair and finished her tea. Her notes were a jumble of names and dates. She drew a line connecting the names of the dead girls, adding the words, "one month." Julia returned to the articles. A third young woman was found just before Christmas break that year.

Little Springs Gazette
December 7

Shocking the town and Blue Hill Christian College, a third victim was found in the early hours of the morning by campus security. The body of Marilyn Trammel, a freshman, was spotted in a Dumpster behind the campus center. Onlookers who saw the naked body pulled from the trash bin reported seeing dark welts and dried blood. Police would not elaborate on the extent of her injuries, only indicating that the woman had probably been dead less than six hours. This murder comes forty-eight hours after the discovery of the slain Theresa Daniels and a month after that of Cheryl Fornak. Although all three victims were students at Blue Hill, there does not appear to be a connection among the three women. They did not share classes, dormitories, or sororities. One source admits that police are stumped. When asked if each of the victims had been raped and how each was murdered, the police spokesman would not comment.

Michael Hudgins, dean of student affairs, announced the immediate cancellation of all classes and exams. "In light of recent events and the ongoing investigation, we are suspending exams until after winter break. Campus will officially close at five p.m. tomorrow, and all students are expected to vacate college housing."

Julia tapped the notebook with her pen. Only two days between the second and third murders and the first body to be found on campus. The first two girls were found miles from Blue Hill. The third was clearly a departure. Was the killer growing bolder or more reckless?

Julia rifled through the next set of articles. Although there were no murders over the Christmas break, there was also no apparent progress in solving the first three cases. The lack of an arrest was bad for the town and worse for the college. Some students—

mostly girls—had applied for deferrals, opting not to return for the spring semester. The town had invoked a curfew of ten p.m. and had brought in additional police from neighboring towns. Still, the killer remained at large.

Julia dropped the pages in her lap, thinking about the dead girls from Blue Hill. No doubt their parents thought they were sending their teenage daughters away to a safe place, a college with strong Christian principles and no city crime, a place where they could grow up and get an education. But Cheryl Fornak, Theresa Daniels, and Marilyn Trammel didn't get to grow up. Head bowed, Julia continued to read. Within days of the students' return, another girl was found, and then another. Five college girls. All raped. All dead. Shivering in the air-conditioning, Julia rubbed her arms.

In an unprecedented move, the college had announced the immediate suspension of the semester. She read the statement from old papers.

> *The safety of our young women and all of our students is at the forefront of this decision. We cannot, in good conscience, ask the students to remain on campus until this situation has been resolved.*

The FBI had been brought in after the fourth murder, spearheading the interviews with every male student enrolled at the college. With a serial rapist and murderer on the loose, the Little Springs town council was forced to invoke "sunset" curfews. The media dubbed the murderer the Coed Killer, a name that stuck. Rumors of vendettas against the college and the town spread like wildfire. Fights broke out among locals as suspicions ran high. Businesses suffered and still, no suspects.

Julia circled the dates of all the murders. The timeline was curious. Had the killer had second thoughts after the first? Why the long gap and then increasingly smaller ones? Over the break, they'd stopped. Did that suggest the killer was also a student? After Christmas, he hadn't waited long to strike again and then again. After the semester was suspended, the murders appeared to stop. Then the police arrested Leo Spradlin.

Julia sifted through the stack of research for pictures of the victims. She placed the photos in a row. Five girls smiling at the camera, all young, all pretty. There was nothing obvious linking them, no common physical traits that she could see. According to the articles, they had different majors and different friends. Yet they'd all known Spradlin—a one-time student at the school—a fact he'd never denied. She set the pictures aside and picked up Spradlin's mug shot. He was young, barely older than college-age himself. Attractive, with dark hair, he had a strong chin and a straight nose. It wasn't hard to see how a young woman might have wanted to be alone with him. She squinted at the black and white photo that was more school portrait than mug shot. His hair was combed and he was neatly dressed. He looked directly into the camera. She held the picture closer, trying to read his expression, but saw nothing. No fear. No anger. No remorse.

Now he would be a free man. His impending release had already made a big splash across Virginia. It was a story that promised to get even bigger, fueling the death penalty debate and causing increased speculation about the governor's political agenda. The release was one thing, the aftermath another. If Spradlin wasn't the Coed Killer, who was? No newspaper could resist this story. The *Washington Herald* was no exception.

Julia turned the page in the notebook and wrote a list of questions. Rereading the short list, Julia hoped she knew what she was doing. She was not the first choice among the staff, and she knew it. Conroy was the star reporter at the paper, and he wouldn't miss this story for the world. But Jack owed her. If he wasn't going to be a great husband, the least he could do was help her rebuild the career she'd let slip from her grasp.

Now that she had the story, she had to do something with it. She picked up the picture of Spradlin again. He'd spent two decades in prison for crimes he didn't commit. Was he bitter? Angry? What would that do to a man? She shook her head, stacking the pages and sliding them back into the large envelope. Spradlin was going back to Little Springs after his release. His lawyers had announced he would hold a press conference the day of his homecoming. The town would be flooded with press, publicity-seekers, and gawkers.

Julia knew a story like this attracted all kinds. She also knew most stories die after a few days. And that was precisely her strategy. She would attend the press conference like the others and position herself for an interview. But when the others were gone, scurrying after the next headline, she would stay. She was in it for the long haul. She was in it for the story of her life.

Chapter Four

THE NIGHT WRAPPED around him like a soft blanket, comforting and soothing. He lay on top of the covers, his body still, letting the darkness seep into his thoughts, his dreams. During the day, he pushed it away, but at night, he embraced it. Eyes wide, he stared at the bare ceiling. After a while, he could see the girls again. He breathed in, nostrils flaring. The memories were all he had.

They'd fought like hell. In vain, of course, but back then, even he hadn't understood his strength or the depth of his needs. The first one, Cheryl, had been especially difficult. He thought most often of her. Swinging her arms and kicking her legs, she'd tried desperately to fight him off, but was the first to learn he was not to be underestimated. What she couldn't have known was that the fear in her eyes only fueled his desire. With each girl, his hunger grew. Their screams and their tears gave him a rush that made him forget everything but the ecstasy of the moment. When they closed their eyes to shut him out, he would jerk their heads, forcing them to watch, to see him as he really was. Since that first night, he'd fallen asleep replaying those beautiful images.

He smiled, his loins hot. It had been such a long fucking time, but now it would be different. The release was big news, and the homecoming was fast approaching. He'd been told there would be press, regional and national. A story of this magnitude was bound to stir controversy. He didn't give a shit. The words "guilt" and "innocence" were thrown around, but few understood how they worked, how closely they were intertwined. One could not exist without the other.

He closed his eyes, holding on to the image of Cheryl. He'd left her in the woods, buried under leaves and sticks, her white skin smeared with mud from the river, her blond hair spread out like a fan around her twisted head. Even dead, her eyes had looked back at him, round and gaping. Nothing could ever erase that beautiful picture. Nothing. And now he'd been given a gift. The Coed Killer would be back.

Chapter Five

"You don't seem surprised to see me," Cancini said, reaching across the desk to shake Derek Talbot's hand.

"I'm not." Talbot stood erect, his dark suit smooth and well fitted. Mid-career, he was still an imposing figure, tall with wide shoulders and a lineman's build. But with his shock of red hair and pale blue eyes, he'd never been a candidate for FBI undercover work. Instead, he'd joined the Criminal Investigation Division early on, where his bloodhound instincts had landed him in violent crimes.

Both men sat. Plaques and framed certificates hung on the wall behind Talbot. It was a sizable office, filled with gleaming cherry and brass furnishings, a leather sofa, and a library of books. A large floral arrangement sat on a credenza. The window along one wall filled the room with enough light that Talbot didn't use the overhead fluorescent or the ornate desk lamp. It was a far cry from the scarred desks and worn-out equipment at the precinct.

"You've moved up in the world."

Talbot waved a hand, frowning. "What do you want, Mike?"

The detective slumped in the chair. Dark circles hung under his eyes, and his pale skin was gray in the bright light. He'd spent most of the night reading his old notes. He rubbed his hand over the faded brown folder in his lap. It was crammed full of papers held in place by thick rubber bands. "You know why I'm here. The Spradlin case." He spoke slowly. "I don't understand. Derek, you were there. We got the right man."

Talbot looked down at his hands and took a breath. When he met Cancini's eyes, he shook his head. "I don't think so."

"But the evidence?"

"I know. The evidence pointed at Spradlin, but the evidence says something else now." The FBI man reached for a slim file on the corner of his desk. "I asked for a copy of the new DNA report. I was as baffled as you. We were sure he was guilty. All of us. No one doubted it."

"And now?"

"And now," he said, then hesitated. He held the file up. "Now I think maybe we all wanted it to be over."

Cancini stiffened, his jaw set. "I see."

"No, Mike, you don't." Talbot opened the folder, his face unsmiling. "This is off the record. Do you understand?"

Cancini wanted to understand, to have someone—anyone—tell him how this could have happened. Spradlin's impending release had haunted him for three nights, the past and present colliding in his mind. It hadn't started out as his case, but it had ended up that way. He'd been so sure, too. He'd never doubted the man's guilt. Not once. Cancini rubbed his fingers across the file again. He'd reread the notes countless times in the past few days and hadn't been able to find a single mistake. He needed to know. He nodded once.

"Good." Talbot cleared his throat. "I don't want to bore you too much, but we both know this case has been in and out of court for years. Spradlin managed to prolong his appeals way longer than most—always with some technicality or legal mumbo-jumbo. Until last year."

"Right. That was the final appeal, and he lost."

"Yes."

"He was scheduled for execution."

"Yes. Around that time, the Freedom and Justice Group came on the scene." Talbot angled his head. "You know what they do?"

Cancini had heard of the group. Similar to the Innocence Project, the organization was dedicated to finding men and women who'd been wrongly convicted. Much of their work focused on older cases, particularly those where the forensic evidence was not as advanced. Cancini couldn't deny that the science used in criminal investigations was vital and continued to improve at a rapid rate. Recently, Virginia had become a leader in using new DNA analysis techniques to clear cold cases as well as overturn dozens more. For Cancini, however, this case seemed different. The DNA evidence in the Spradlin case had been solid at the time.

"Yeah, I've heard, but I still don't get how that matters here. The DNA evidence at trial was the slam-dunk. How could that change?"

The FBI man held his gaze, raising one hand. "Be patient. I'm getting there. It's not clear how Spradlin got on their list of cases, but once they got their teeth into it, they lobbied hard, all the way up to the governor. I'm told they argued that today's testing would be more sophisticated and threw in the stat that fifteen percent of the men convicted in the seventies and eighties turned out to be innocent." Talbot leaned back and kept his voice even. "Spradlin may not go back that far, but the governor isn't a fan of the death penalty. He was probably looking for this kind of case."

Cancini said nothing. Politics only interested him when he was directly affected. He didn't trust either side, so he didn't take one. Still, he didn't like the sound of where this was going.

"They ran the new series of tests on the DNA evidence from the Fornak case. Spradlin wasn't a match."

"That doesn't make sense. What about the forensic testimony at trial?"

"There was a mistake."

Cancini flinched. "What kind of mistake?"

Deep lines creased Talbot's forehead. "It's somewhat technical. Do you want the particulars?"

Cancini's jaw tightened. His experience with the intricacies of DNA wasn't much, mostly limited to finding out whether the evidence gathered was or wasn't a match and praying it was handled properly. "Yeah. Let me hear 'em."

"So, there are several different kinds of DNA testing. Most of the time, we use STR. It identifies short tandem repeats and works best when the evidence is small or degraded. Basically, everyone inherits one copy of an STR from each parent, which may or may not have similar repeat sizes. Since STR testing draws on the genetic code from each parent, it's highly accurate at pinpointing individuals. No two people have the same DNA and all that." He paused, looking down at the file opened on his desk. "Make sense so far?"

"Sure."

"In the original Spradlin case, there was only that one usable bit of DNA evidence, the semen found in Cheryl Fornak. It wasn't much. After that case, there was no semen detected in any of the other victims despite evidence of rape."

"We assumed Spradlin used condoms after the first girl."

"And while there was that partial print lifted from the second victim, it wasn't usable. All the other blood and hair samples collected turned out to be from the victims themselves. But, as I said, we did have that one bit of semen." Talbot coughed, reaching for a glass of water. "In rape cases, DNA evidence is more difficult to define by its very nature. The cells collected tend to be a mix from both the victim, Miss Fornak in this case, and her rapist."

Cancini shivered. The image of the dead girl, lying naked and bruised near the cold waters of the river, felt as close as if it had happened yesterday. He shook away the memory, concentrating on Talbot's words.

"Today, we use a chemical to isolate the sperm for DNA testing, but . . ." He hesitated. "Back then, the labs weren't as sophisticated when working with a sample that small. Because of the seriousness of the case, the lab did something different."

Cancini's eyes narrowed. "Different? What the hell does that mean?"

"They decided to do a Y-chromosome-based test. Since women don't have a Y-chromosome, the idea was that the test would only reflect the male DNA in the sample. It showed what appeared to be a match to Spradlin. It was convincing."

"Appeared to be a match." The words came out slowly. "What does that mean?"

"It's difficult to distinguish between male relatives using Y testing because it doesn't reflect the mother's addition to an individual's genetic code. In theory, using this method, you could say a father and son share the same DNA. Not exactly, of course, but close."

Cancini frowned. "Spradlin's an only child. His dad died when he was a kid. I don't get it."

Talbot sighed. "That's because you're still thinking it was a match. It was similar, good enough to use at the time, but it would never make it into court today. Last month, the lab ran the STR test they weren't able to do back then. The new test isolated the male DNA and unlocked the full DNA code." He paused. "I'm sorry, Mike, but it wasn't a match. Like I said, some of the markers were similar, but the DNA was not Spradlin's. He's not guilty."

Tapping the file with his long fingers, Cancini asked, "Is that common? To share similar markers like that?"

"I guess it happens. In the end, it doesn't matter how similar the markers were. It didn't match."

Cancini leaned forward. "You're sure? What about the evidence being degraded or something like that?"

"Sorry." The FBI man shook his head again. "The governor was taking no chances. It's been checked and rechecked."

He ran his hand over his spiky hair. "I was so sure it was him."

"We all were, Mike. The evidence looked pretty good, and the way he was . . ." His lip curled up in distaste. "Hell, we all thought it was him."

Cancini stared blankly over Talbot's head. The Spradlin case had been his first homicide, and it was still the biggest case of his career. His eyes met Talbot's, disbelief fixed on his face. "But after we arrested Spradlin, there were no more rapes and murders."

"True," Talbot said, shrugging. "The real perpetrator could have taken Spradlin's arrest as his opportunity to get away. Maybe he left town. The FBI is searching for a match in all the state's databases. We might find out he's in prison for rape somewhere else."

Cancini stood up. The rapes had stopped. The day Spradlin was read his sentence, dozens of people in attendance had burst into tears, hugging, gasping with relief. Cancini had left the courtroom bone-tired and mentally exhausted, but the rapes had stopped. He'd walked away from the town then, never turning back.

"It was a good case, Mike," Talbot said, his voice low, serious. "If he hasn't been caught already, isn't already in the system, he will be. I promise."

Cancini looked down at his old friend. There was nothing more to learn. "Already in the system. Sure." Lost in thought, he said, "It just doesn't feel right. It was about that campus, the girls there."

"Maybe. Or maybe he moved to another college?"

Cancini shook his head. "I don't think so."

"Mike, the evidence says Spradlin's innocent. Let it go." He stood, too. "Maybe you should take some time off."

Cancini tucked the folder under his arm. "Teddy Baldwin called me yesterday. Remember him?"

"Sure."

"He's the mayor of Little Springs now."

"Good for him. What did he want?"

"I'm not sure. Rambled on about Spradlin coming back to town. Said Spradlin threatened him. He sounded worried."

Talbot put both hands on the desk, leaning forward. "It's not your problem, Mike. Baldwin is not your problem. It's not your case anymore."

"Maybe not. But I started it, didn't I?"

"What's that supposed to mean?"

"Nothing, Derek. Nothing at all." One side of his mouth turned up. "Maybe you're right. Maybe I do need a vacation. Maybe to a small town."

The words hung there, and Talbot's face darkened. "Little Springs?" Cancini shrugged, his smile gone. "Dammit, Mike. Don't harass Spradlin. Don't make trouble."

"I'm not gonna make any trouble, Derek, but I'm going. I have to be there for that press conference." He glanced away for a brief moment, unease etched in the lines of his face. "I know those people, Derek. They don't want Spradlin back. That's why Baldwin's worried. It was my case. I've gotta see it all the way through. If I did put an innocent man in prison, I need to look that man in the eyes. I need to know."

Talbot cocked his head. "For God's sake. Know what, Mike?"

"The truth."

He slammed a palm against the desk, and the file folder slid to the floor. "Jesus, Mike, weren't you listening? Why do you always have to be so stubborn? You know the truth."

"Maybe," Cancini said. He glowered at Talbot, his eyes steely. "I need to go. Call it closure. Call it whatever you want. I've gotta know."

Chapter Six

JULIA SHADED HER eyes and looked up at the run-down hotel, praying it had hot water and a mini-bar in the room. With time to kill before the press conference, she desperately wanted a long bath and a stiff drink. She ducked out of the blinding sun and stepped into the lobby. Her eyes swept over the heavy furnishings and faded Oriental rugs. She was lucky to have a room at all. Little Springs wasn't a big place, and most of the chain motels dotting the interstate were booked. What this place lacked in amenities, it made up for in convenience, only a block from the courthouse.

An hour later, clean and feeling more like herself, she stood near the window, watching the activity on Main Street. A row of storefronts including a coffee shop, a drugstore, a beauty salon, and a couple of other small businesses lined the picturesque street. The antebellum county courthouse stood at the corner, the planned site of the press conference. A sizable crowd had already formed around a makeshift podium set up behind the sidewalk. The street was closed to traffic. Several policemen moved slowly among the crowd. More were stationed around the perimeter. The tips of her fingers itched, a tic when she knew she was on the verge of a big story. She rubbed them against her shirt.

Julia hoped she hadn't made a mistake, pushing for a story of this importance. She hadn't been able to shake Jack's doubts. She'd read the file twice and pored over everything she could find on the Internet. She'd found dozens and dozens of articles on the case and trial, but surprisingly little about Leo Spradlin. His mother, widowed at a young age, had worked as a maid at the college, and money had been tight. Mother and son had lived on the outskirts of town. A high school athlete, young Leo had attended the same college where his mother cleaned, until he dropped out. And that's where the story ended. What was it about Leo Spradlin that had made him a suspect? What had his life been like for the last two decades? Now that he would be free, how did he feel?

She had no idea how she could write this story better than Conroy or any of the other crime reporters. As a features writer, her expertise in law and crime was next to nothing, but maybe that could work to her advantage. She wouldn't treat Spradlin as a statistic or tabloid story. She wanted the readers to know the flesh and blood of the man, to feel his pain and his joy. She would see where the story took her.

Julia surveyed the street again. Heat rose off the sidewalk, distorting the air. Crowds filled both sides of the street and pressed in near the courthouse steps. Glancing at the old wind-up clock on the nightstand, she grabbed her digital recorder and shoved it into an oversized canvas bag. She swept her auburn hair into a ponytail and hung the press pass around her neck. When she was sure she was ready, she pulled the door shut, skipping the ancient elevator and opting for the stairs. Julia didn't want to be late.

Chapter Seven

He shouldn't have returned Baldwin's call, shouldn't have agreed to meet him. They hadn't spoken in years, not since the original trial, and that was fine with Cancini. He gazed into his empty coffee cup. Damn. Why was he even here? Was it about truth and closure, or was it his own bruised ego? Maybe he was losing it. He sure as hell didn't want to be sitting in this diner, packed with people he didn't know, waiting for a man he didn't want to see. He rubbed his throbbing temples. The diner was crowded and way too hot. It was too hot in the whole town for that matter. He wasn't a small-town guy—wasn't then and wasn't now.

The diner buzzed with locals and a few strays waiting for the big press conference. A quiet simmer, a tension, seemed ready to bubble over at the slightest provocation. The ladies in the booth in front of him wore somber expressions, each of them sipping sweet tea. Others appeared angry, eyebrows and mouths drawn into scowls. He wasn't surprised; Little Springs had been dealt a shocking blow. A few days ago, it was a dot on a map, a tiny college town almost no one knew existed. Today it was swarming with media and spectators. The townsfolk were anxious, many of them angry and frightened, the rise and fall of emotion evident in the diner's rumble. He couldn't blame them. Coming here was probably a bad idea. Bile rose in his throat, and his head pounded.

Cancini fidgeted with his empty coffee cup and tried to focus on the newspaper in front of him.

Reporters are expected to converge on Little Springs, Virginia, today for the homecoming of Leo Spradlin. Convicted in a series of rapes and murders on the campus of Blue Hill College, Spradlin was cleared of all charges when new DNA testing proved his innocence. Spradlin, granted a pardon and writ of innocence by the governor, immediately announced his intention to return to Little Springs. "I'm going home," said the newly freed man, "going back to the only home I've ever known."

Cancini's bony fingers clutched the paper. Spradlin had chosen his words carefully. Back then, he'd kept his razor-sharp tongue and quick mind hidden behind a passive expression and charming demeanor. Some may believe a leopard can change his spots, but not Cancini. Spradlin's public return wasn't without purpose. It wasn't homesickness pulling him back. Spradlin was free and coming home to rub it in, to show them all how wrong they'd been. The townspeople didn't give a damn what science or the governor had to say. To them, the fact was, the day Spradlin was arrested, the murders had stopped. Women in Little Springs were safe again. No one had been more convinced of Spradlin's guilt than Cancini, and no one had been more instrumental in putting the man away.

But Cancini knew it wasn't that simple. The reporters would be fervent in their beliefs, too, particularly when the evidence showed an innocent man narrowly escaping execution. Throw in the lawyers, and it was likely a whole bunch of folks would be wearing righteousness on their sleeves. No matter the reason he'd come, it was a terrible mistake.

"Baldwin." A man's voice rang out. "I wanna talk to you."

The mayor stood near the door, and several diners gathered around him, their voices insistent, demanding. He appeared to listen and nod but offered few words in return. His face was pink, flushed from the heat of a Virginia Indian summer, but he stood patiently, acknowledging each question. After a few moments, the small crowd dispersed, grumbling as they returned to their booths and chairs. The lone waitress, a young woman whose ponytail swung when she walked, waved him in. He smiled at her and scanned the room. Spotting Cancini, he strode over and squeezed into the empty seat at the table.

"Mike. You look good," the mayor said, his blue eyes studying his former friend. "How long has it been?"

"A long time."

Baldwin chuckled, picking up a paper napkin. "We were kids then, weren't we?"

"Yeah, kids," Cancini said. Baldwin, always a big man, had added some girth to his sizable frame, yet still managed to look fit. His face had grown rounder over the years, his skin darker, as though permanently sunburned. His hair was still thick, parted on the side, and brushed back. He wore a starched white shirt tucked into a pair of dark slacks. Gold cuff links flashed at his wrists. "You called me," Cancini said. "What's so important that we had to meet in person?"

Baldwin plucked at the napkin, absently tearing off the corners. Tiny pieces fell to the table. "People are awful unhappy here, Mike. They don't like what's happened."

Cancini sighed. This was not news. "Teddy, why'd you want to see me?"

"It's Ted now."

The waitress refilled Cancini's cup and brought another for Baldwin. "Teddy," he said again, drawing out the name. "What did you need to talk to me about?"

Baldwin's fingers ripped at the napkin. "We were friends once, Mike." Cancini didn't reply. "Well, anyway, after you left, I stayed. Finished law school and worked to rebuild this town and the college. I served on the town council for a while." He paused, dropping the shredded napkin on the table. "I'm in my second term as mayor now. Little Springs is my town. You were here what? A year? I've spent my whole life here. It's my home, and it's important to me." He licked his lips, grabbing a second napkin out of the paper dispenser. Cancini waited. Wiping his brow, the mayor said, "I called you about Spradlin. I figured you'd heard about his release." Cancini nodded. "You thought Spradlin was guilty. You put him away."

"Yeah, I thought he was guilty. The jury thought so, too. That's what the evidence said."

"It was more than the evidence for you. You were always suspicious of Leo, long before anyone else. You followed your instincts."

Cancini flicked the front page of the newspaper. "According to this, Spradlin has spent most of his life in jail for crimes he didn't commit. According to this, I put an innocent man behind bars."

Baldwin's light eyes locked on Cancini's. "Do you believe that? That you made a mistake? That the jury made a mistake?"

"It doesn't matter what I believe."

"It matters," the mayor said. "It matters, or you wouldn't be here."

The men stared at each other. Baldwin might have been half right, but Cancini wasn't about to let him know that. It was true he'd believed Spradlin was guilty, and even in light of new DNA evidence and the knowledge that there'd been a mistake, that belief gnawed at his gut. He needed to witness the press conference for himself. Baldwin didn't need to know any of that, either.

"Look, Teddy, what's done is done. They didn't ask my opinion. New evidence appeared and cleared Spradlin. This isn't my case anymore."

The mayor's fingers twitched, picking at another napkin. "But it should be."

"That's not going to happen. I don't live here. I'm a detective in Washington now and you know that. Besides, there's nothing for me to investigate. The FBI will be handling things." Cancini started to slide out of the booth. "Good luck, Teddy."

Baldwin's hand gripped Cancini's forearm. The pressure of Teddy's oversized hand and the wary expression on his face told Cancini everything he needed to know. "Maybe there's nothing to investigate yet, but there will be."

Cancini looked at the hand on his arm and narrowed his hazel eyes to slits. Baldwin let go. "You don't know that."

"True. Not the way you mean, but you're not the one who spoke to Spradlin. I told you he called me."

"You mentioned that. So? You were always friends."

"Not always." Baldwin's florid face paled. "That was a long time ago, before, you know, he went bad." He paused, his barrel chest rising and falling with each tear of the napkin. "He was all friendly at first, saying he was looking forward to seeing me, seeing old friends, stuff like that. It was weird 'cause he has to know he doesn't have any friends around here."

"He still thinks you're his friend."

"What?" Baldwin's mouth opened. "No. Well, maybe, but that's not the point."

Cancini sat down again. "What is the point, Teddy?"

The man pushed around the small pile of napkin scraps and took a deep breath. "He started talking about how things are gonna change around here, now that he's coming back." He shook his head. "He said . . . he said Little Springs is in for a big surprise."

"A surprise?"

"Yeah. A surprise. Can you believe it? He's got nerve, right? I mean, what the hell?" His voice dropped, forcing Cancini to lean in. "That's why I called you. I haven't told anyone else about this, not even the police." Baldwin swept the paper scraps to the side of the table with his thick hand. "The thing is, he talked like everything was normal until right before he hung up and then, I swear he was threatening me."

"Threatening you?" the detective asked, the hair on his arms rising. "How?"

"He said Little Springs hasn't seen anything yet, that he was calling to give me fair warning."

"Fair warning?"

The mayor stood, his attention drawn to the windows and the growing crowd outside. "I have to get going. The press conference is going to start soon."

"Fair warning of what?" Cancini asked, his voice tight.

"I don't know." Baldwin's gaze shifted back to the detective, his face grave. "All I know is he scared me. His exact words were, 'The best is yet to come.' "

Chapter Eight

OUTSIDE, IN THE blistering heat, the air was thick with humidity and body odor. Threading her way through the crowd, Julia moved closer to the courthouse, where people stood shoulder to shoulder. Having spotted the area designated for the press, she walked in that direction, only pausing to read some of the more colorful signs held high above the crowd. Several folks carried circular-shaped posters outlined in red with "SPRADLIN" written in the center. His name was crossed through in red—the message clear. The townspeople's anger, their animosity, was apparent even without the signs. She frowned and made a mental note to seek out a handful of locals after the press conference.

Julia wore the somber expression shared by most of her peers, some of whom she recognized from other assignments. It was the face they often wore, serious and compassionate, masking the giddy anticipation they felt at the onset of a juicy story. Julia spotted the TV cameras positioned above the crowd, all but one trained on the single podium in front of the courthouse. A lone camera was focused on the crowd, slowly panning the throngs who'd come to witness, or protest, the homecoming of Leo Spradlin.

As the crowd grew, she considered the empty podium. It seemed small and plain to be at the center of all this excitement. Maybe that's what made the story so enticing. It was so big, but happening in such a small town. This was a major story for the national press, but for the locals and papers in this part of the state, it was more than that. It was the biggest news in a decade.

The hours she'd spent researching had not been wasted. She'd done the background, seen the letters of outrage that had been published, read the vitriolic comments on the Internet. The residents of Little Springs didn't seem to care about the truth. It wasn't about right or wrong for them or the miscarriage of justice. As far as she could tell, the facts fell on deaf ears here. In their minds, Leo Spradlin was a guilty man. Maybe the police presence wasn't such a bad idea.

As though on cue, sirens blared in the distance, and a short line of cars pulled up to the end of the block. Two black and whites led, followed by a dark vehicle with tinted windows. Two more police cars brought up the rear. The sirens stopped, and an eerie silence settled over the crowd. All eyes, including Julia's, were focused on the dark car, waiting. A uniformed cop opened the back door. She held her breath, staring when the man slid out. He stood tall in the punishing sun, face expressionless. The cop steered him by the elbow toward the courthouse.

He focused on the path straight ahead, no acknowledgment accorded to the mass of people or the press. Flanked by police, he looked more like a politician or celebrity, someone who required personal security, than a man who'd just been released from prison for a crime he did not commit. Julia was taken by surprise.

Pictures did not do the man justice. He was clean-shaven; the jailhouse beard he'd worn for years gone. His hair had been freshly cut, and he wore a lightweight, casual suit. The man moved at a languorous pace, as though he had no reason to hurry, relaxed and surefooted. Her lips parted. He was as handsome as any movie star she had ever seen. In all the pictures she'd pored over, in all the old stories and articles she'd read, why hadn't she noticed that before? Another man, short and rotund, followed Spradlin as he made his way to the podium. Julia thought she recognized him as one of the lawyers from the Freedom and Justice Group.

A third man dressed in a blue blazer with gold buttons greeted Spradlin near the podium. He said something, reaching automatically for Spradlin's outstretched hand, dropping it almost as quickly as he shook it. He was taller than Spradlin, broader in the shoulders and chest. Turning his back on Spradlin, he moved to the microphone. The man looked out over the crowd, eyes passing slowly over all those who'd come out to brave the additional heat of pressing bodies. He cleared his throat and pulled the microphone close.

"Neighbors and friends, we are a fortunate lot. We live in a beautiful town filled with wonderful people. We live in a town that allows us to raise our families in the best of ways. Little Springs offers a tremendous quality of life, a stable economy, a strong education, and a safe environment."

A rumble rose up in the crowd. Someone yelled out from the back, "You mean we were safe! What about now, Mr. Mayor?"

The man held up his hands as if he could push back on the antagonism. His face was flushed but solemn. "Part of feeling safe is the ability to have faith in the justice system." There were more rumbles from the mass of people, but the man forged ahead.

"More than two decades ago, this town faced a crisis. We were scared and worried for the young women who came to school at our college and for our daughters and wives. That changed when Leo Spradlin was taken into custody. We wanted to feel safe again. We desperately wanted to believe we could feel safe again, and so we did." He paused, wiping his brow with a white handkerchief.

Julia heard the gasps around her. The inflammatory words had astonished the reporters, but the crowd was momentarily appeased. A chorus of "amens" and "hallelujahs" could be heard across the town square. Julia stole a glance at Spradlin. His face was unreadable; his hooded eyes focused beyond the crowd. He stood with his feet spread, his hands thrust in his pockets, the suit jacket pushed casually out of the way. The lawyer stood a few feet behind Spradlin with his chest puffed out. Other journalists snapped pictures or wrote furiously in notebooks. She held up her small recorder, ensuring she did not misquote or misrepresent a single word.

When the crowd quieted, the mayor said, "But the courts have reviewed new evidence, DNA evidence, that says we have lived all these years under a false sense of security. I know this is difficult for most of you to understand." He paused when another angry wave of voices grew louder. Although the crowd was becoming increasingly restless, the police did nothing but stand along the sidewalks, watching. Waiting for the noise to die down, the mayor wiped his brow again. "The evidence, however, does not support Leo Spradlin's conviction. In fact, it proves his innocence." He stopped and scanned the packed street again. His tone remained neutral, as though reciting baseball statistics or reading a news article. "The law is designed to make us feel safe by protecting us from those who mean to harm us, but when a man has been falsely imprisoned for over twenty years, it is also the law's responsibility to protect that man."

Shouts came from the throng. They pushed forward, closer to the podium.

"It's a load of crap!"

"If Spradlin's so innocent, then who killed those girls?"

"It's some damn technicality the lawyers dreamed up!"

Julia craned to pick out the dissenters, but there were too many. Faces in the crowd were flushed with anger, and fists were raised in the air. The mayor's speech was not helping.

"Please," he said, shouting over them. "Let me finish." There were more cries of outrage, but eventually, even those fizzled to muttered cursing and spitting. "The legal system in our great state has declared Leo Spradlin innocent, and his conviction has been overturned. These are the facts." He continued, "As most of you know, he has chosen to return to Little Springs and would like to say a few words." He angled his head slightly toward Spradlin. "Here he is."

Low murmurs gathered momentum when the man stepped to the podium. The mayor moved behind Spradlin, his eyes downcast. Stepping forward, the newly freed man stood tall, his back ramrod-straight, his face pink in the afternoon heat. Julia waited, her curiosity piqued by the man's patient manner in spite of the animosity in the crowd. Several minutes passed. Then the noise seemed to taper off, as though the mob was losing steam, or more likely, wondering what the man had to say. He stood motionless, his hands wrapped loosely around the microphone. Julia leaned forward, standing on her tiptoes. When he spoke, his voice was strong and booming, sexy. She shivered, and goose bumps rose on her neck and arms. His words took them all by surprise, made them stop and wonder.

"I forgive you, Little Springs. I forgive you."

Chapter Nine

THE CROWD RELEASED a collective breath, and the air of hostility evaporated in an instant, swept away by Spradlin's words. Cancini stood at the edge of the crowd, avoiding the fray. He frowned. Spradlin forgave them? The folks of Little Springs stood speechless, but the silence wouldn't last. Cancini knew all too well the backlash the man's words might ignite.

Spradlin stood in front of the very people who'd accused him, hated him, and turned their backs on him, as though he were standing at a pulpit, a holy reverend forgiving his people their multitude of sins. A benevolent smile on his face, he spoke again, his tone soft and inviting. "I have a confession to make."

Cancini squinted in the sun, shading his eyes with his hand, the muscles in his neck and shoulders tightening. He scanned the stunned faces in the crowd, one hand on the pistol hidden under his suit jacket. No one moved. No one spoke. They waited for Spradlin to explain, their anger turning to disbelief and curiosity.

"All those years in prison, all that time on death row, I was waiting for this moment." He surveyed the crowd as his voice grew louder, more insistent. "I am not a stupid man. I wasn't stupid back then, and I'm not stupid now. I made some mistakes, and those mistakes cost me the support of my friends and people who had known me my whole life. I didn't understand back then, but I understand now."

A new restlessness came over some of the locals in the crowd. An angry man, his fists clenched at his side, stood near Cancini. Others were losing patience with the speech. Still others listened, eyes and mouths round.

"I guess I deserved it. I was a jerk. Maybe I made it easy to believe I was guilty." Spradlin hung his head, his voice breaking on the last words. Several moments went by before he spoke again. "The hardest part, and my biggest regret, is that my mother is not here to see my exoneration, to hear the truth from those who condemned me." He sighed deeply. "She deserved better than she got from this town after I was sent away, but for reasons I didn't understand at the time, she refused to leave. She loved this town so much."

Cancini had met Spradlin's mother only a couple of times. He remembered her as a lady with a raspy voice and prematurely gray hair, deep lines creasing the corners of her eyes and mouth. The investigation and the trial had nearly done her in. She'd lost her job. She'd lost everything. Cancini never understood why she'd stayed in Little Springs despite being ostracized, unemployed, and alone.

"Not long before she died, my mom came to see me. She told me she knew I was going to get out and that I would be free someday. She gave me new hope, never losing faith in my innocence. She told me that when that day came, when I walked out of prison, I must return to Little Springs. So, here I am. Like her, I won't run away. God rest her soul, she told me to hold my head high." He paused, bracing both sides of the podium. "She was right. I am free, and I will not run away. This is my home, and you are forgiven."

He spun on his heel and walked to the row of cars, the uniformed police scrambling into position. He halted in front of the press box, the cameras clicking furiously, and then he was gone, ducking into a car and speeding off before the crowd could figure out what had happened.

Cancini's eyes followed the dark sedan until it turned the corner and disappeared from view. The knot between his shoulders hardened, a sign that a full-blown tension headache was setting in. His head throbbed, and the pain began its inevitable movement up from the base of his skull. He needed to lie down in a cold, dark room. Around him, the anger that had defined the crowd earlier simmered again, voices raised in indignation. He ducked his head, moving away from the corner and the crowd, escaping before tempers flared and erupted.

Soon he was stretched out on his bed, an ice pack from the hotel kitchen plastered on his forehead and another propped under his neck. He lay still, his mind preoccupied with Spradlin's speech. He had to give the guy credit. It took balls to show up and stand before a crowd who'd surely stone you if they could, and remain so calm and cool. Then again, Spradlin had always been a cool customer. When they'd first started looking at him for the rapes and murders, he'd seemed unperturbed, amused even. A cocky young man, Leo Spradlin had carried himself with a brash confidence, a combination of youthful ego and innate arrogance. He was tall and handsome with thick, wavy hair, but it was his charisma, an uncommon magnetism, that seemed to draw in both men and women. Naturally athletic, he was the type of guy who might lead a varsity football team or win the title of prom king—or would have if he'd cared. But he hadn't. In fact, Spradlin hadn't seemed to care about much of anything. After a while, those who gravitated toward him fell away.

Cancini took the ice packs from behind his neck and off his forehead. All of that had been a long time ago. It was true he hadn't liked Spradlin, but that wasn't what made him a suspect. The evidence had pointed toward the man. He knew all the girls. But most importantly, physical evidence linked him to the first crime scene, and Spradlin couldn't produce a solid alibi. Cancini sat up and swung his legs around to ease the stiffness in his limbs. What was happening in Little Springs now had nothing to do with him, but he couldn't shake the feeling that he needed to stay. Walking to the window, he pushed aside the worn curtains. The crowds had thinned, but a few folks still lingered on the street. The podium had been taken down, and the press area was now empty. It almost looked peaceful.

Spradlin's words replayed in Cancini's mind, the throbbing in his head intensifying in spite of the ice. Maybe Teddy was right. Maybe Spradlin was up to something after all. That whole bit about forgiveness? The press would eat that up. None of the reporters there today could possibly understand the hysteria that had gripped the town during the weeks and months of rapes and murders. By the time the police had gathered enough evidence to charge Spradlin, the townsfolk would have strung up the college president if it meant an end to the terror. The press from Washington, New York, and the AP wouldn't know any of that. In fact, most of the reporters were only children at the time or weren't from around here.

One thing was for sure. Spradlin was no fool, adept at deception and operating under a smooth façade. Today, he'd played the part well—the victim, the devoted son. Cancini had to hand it to him. But Cancini knew the truth. The late Mrs. Spradlin, the mother Leo claimed believed in his innocence, begging him to return to his hometown, did not visit him before her death. In fact, she had never visited him once in all those years.

Chapter Ten

Squinting, he stared out the window at the setting sun. His body was tired, fatigued after the day's events, but his mind was wide-awake. The day had been a great success, but a sudden pang of loneliness tainted his heady reliving of it. He couldn't remember the last time he'd cared about being alone. Why should this night be any different? Then he remembered the girl and all that she promised.

He'd spotted her in the crowd wearing one of those tight sorority T-shirts, her breasts high and mighty under the thin cotton fabric. Standing on the sidewalk with her back pressed against a storefront, she'd whispered in the ear of a girlfriend. Beads of sweat had glistened on her forehead, and damp blond tendrils had framed her face. He'd known immediately she was more of a curious onlooker than part of the hostile mob. Besides, the sorority girl was too young to remember the old crimes. She'd been there for the show. It was exactly as he'd expected; the news of the release was everywhere.

From under his lashes, he'd watched her wipe her brow and fan her face. The crowd had pressed in, and she'd been momentarily swallowed up. A vein in the man's temple had pulsed, and he'd shaded his eyes from the sun, careful to keep his head steady. He'd been keenly aware of the unfriendly crowd, watching and waiting.

She'd appeared again, a little ways down the wall, farther from the podium. His heartbeat had quickened, and his mouth had gone dry. Without warning, the sight of the pretty coed had brought back all the old feelings, the urges he'd worked so hard to repress. It had been so goddamn long since he'd acted on them, given in to them. Of course, it wasn't as though he'd had much of a choice. His circumstances had made that difficult. His eyes had followed her as she'd pushed off the brick, weaving in and out of the crowd, her friend trailing behind. He'd had only one thought as she moved down the street and out of his view. Her presence was surely a sign.

He'd committed the letters on her shirt to memory. Kappa Kappa Delta. Did she live there? Even if she didn't, she had to go there sometime. His fingers tingled, and he licked his lips. He'd find her when the time was right.

His thoughts strayed to the reporters at the press conference and the row of cameras perched on tripods above the crowd. He'd watched as one lens panned the people with their signs and their small-town attitudes. Uniformed police circled the crowd and stood guard on the steps. He'd suppressed a smile. It was perfect in every way. He couldn't have planned it better if he'd tried.

"So fucking easy," he said out loud. He leaned back, folding his arms behind his head. The stage was set and now that he'd seen the girl—chosen her—everything would fall into place. She didn't know it yet, but soon, she would be famous.

Chapter Eleven

CANCINI SIFTED THROUGH the trial transcript, stopping on the testimony of the forensic specialist. He could recite the questions and answers word for word, but it was moot now. Everything she'd said in the first trial had been wiped away by the new testing. He looked up from the file. The light in the hotel room was fading with the sun. Cancini switched on the desk lamp and read the prosecution's summation. He could still hear the man making his case, his deep baritone laying out the evidence piece by piece until it culminated with the DNA. "How," he'd asked, "can there be any reasonable doubt?"

Cancini flipped back through the file, pulling out his daily reports. Months of investigative work had yielded scraps of evidence, much of it circumstantial but eventually enough for a warrant. That warrant led to the DNA evidence that sold the FBI, the police chief, and the jury. Now that same DNA evidence was the sole reason for Spradlin's exoneration. It made Cancini's head hurt. He gathered the papers, closed the file, and stowed it back in the hotel room safe.

He swallowed some aspirin and stretched out on the bed. The quiet should have made him feel better but instead reminded him he was far from home, far from traffic and horns and weekly homicides. He missed the frenetic pace of Washington life. He missed the job that kept him busy all hours and helped him forget his ex and his empty apartment. Here, the silence stung. The hours crawled by and there was too much time to think, too much time to wonder about things he couldn't change.

Cancini closed his eyes. When the case had gone to trial, Spradlin hadn't helped himself. He'd said almost nothing in the interviews, and the little he had said was oddly incriminating. He'd never denied knowing the victims. He'd never offered an alibi. When the killings had stopped after Spradlin's arrest, even the few doubters were convinced of the man's guilt. Relief had spread among the townsfolk like the smell of summer rain after weeks of dry and dusty weather.

Without the DNA evidence, would Spradlin have been convicted? Cancini couldn't be sure. He relied on DNA—he had to—but knew better than to build a case solely on one piece of evidence. Lawyers used it on both sides of the bench, but it could come back to haunt you. Detectives both prized and hated DNA. Cases turned on it, and now, in the world of ever-evolving technology and science, justice could barely be achieved without it. Even old cases, long forgotten by anyone except the principals, were alive and fresh again, front-page news when a reversal made headlines. The state of Virginia was no exception.

When a former governor ordered old cases be reviewed and any stored DNA evidence be tested, the goal was not to close unsolved cases or seek out the guilty; rather it was to find men and women who had been wrongly incarcerated and grant them the freedom they had lost. Anti–death penalty groups and activists rejoiced, convinced this testing was the first step in eliminating the death penalty altogether.

Conservatives shouted with dismay that juries might be fearful of convicting anyone in the future if mistakes were uncovered and publicized. More than one judge agreed with this assessment, even going so far as to say the standard "beyond a reasonable doubt" was nearly impossible to meet. All of this was relevant in the abstract but took on new significance when the case of the Coed Killer came along. Now, a convicted murderer sitting on death row had been granted a full pardon, his freedom the direct result of DNA testing. What was a small town with virtually no political clout to do?

The jury hadn't needed long to convict Leo Spradlin, deliberating less than two hours and presenting their verdict in front of a packed courthouse. Things in Little Springs had returned to normal. Years had passed. Now old pictures of Spradlin, along with a few from prison, were plastered across the front page and the nightly news. Politicians, civil rights groups, and talking heads all chimed in. No one asked the residents of Little Springs how they felt or what they thought, but Cancini knew and he understood.

He sat up. The pills had reduced the pounding at the base of his skull to a dull ache. He switched on the overhead light and pushed aside the curtains. Outside, the streetlamps illuminated glass storefronts and lit up the courthouse. A couple strolled hand in hand before ducking inside a cafe. Life moved on.

His hand dropped and the drapes fell closed. He paced the room, ten steps toward the door, ten steps back to the window. Coed Killer. Cancini hadn't liked the label then, and he didn't like it now. To him, it trivialized the horror the young girls and the town had endured. With the pardon, the name had no face. The Coed Killer was a phantom.

At the press conference, Spradlin had promised to stay in Little Springs. Yet, after the reporters were gone and the media frenzy had faded, would he? If he did stay, would the townsfolk's antagonism toward him fade, too? Cancini couldn't see how, at least not until another face could be named the Coed Killer. Talbot was right. It wasn't his problem, his case, anymore. The press conference was over. The sun would rise on a new day, and everyone would go about their business as usual. He stopped pacing. So why was he still there, sitting in a bland hotel room, haunting the streets of his past?

After Spradlin's conviction, Cancini had needed to escape, to wash away the horror. He'd spent a month on a Florida beach alone, burning his pale skin day after day, swilling beer from a cooler until he was drunk enough to forget. No one in sunny Florida knew or cared about the Coed Killer, at least not back then, before today's constant barrage of news and tabloid coverage. The days had passed. Restless by nature, he'd wondered idly what he would do with his life. Should he go back to police work? And if he did, would he be destined for the lonely life he anticipated? In the end, he'd had no choice. It was in his soul, in his heart.

Cancini pulled on his jacket and pocketed the plastic hotel key. He switched off the overhead light and closed the door. He didn't have the ability to be anything other than what he was—a homicide detective.

Chapter Twelve

JULIA SAT ALONE, perched on a swivel stool at the diner counter, feet dangling. She pushed aside the meat loaf, dense with peppers and onions, and scooped up a bite of gravy-laden mashed potatoes instead. Shoulders hunched, she ate slowly, eavesdropping on the conversation at the table behind her.

"What's with this guy anyway?" She recognized the man's voice. It was Larry Conroy, the reporter her soon-to-be-ex had sent. "Talk about managing your press. You'd never know this guy's been in jail for twenty years the way he's playing us."

"I heard he's got someone scheduling us in fifteen-minute blocks in order of circulation or TV ratings," a woman said.

Julia smiled. If that rumor turned out to be true, the woman with Conroy would be waiting a long time.

Another reporter from Washington chimed in. "Damn. I hope I get picked. I'd love fifteen minutes. That speech he gave yesterday was like something written for the movies. Beautiful. Only thing is, you kinda picture a gorgeous sunset and a girl waiting at the end, not a mob that seems like it wants to lynch you."

Julia turned at the sound of raised, excited voices. She spotted the mayor, the man who had introduced Spradlin at the conference the day before. Without thinking, she slipped off the barstool, working her way toward him until she stood outside the circle of people surrounding him near the long counter. She tilted her chin to look up at him.

Mayor Baldwin was a big man, well over six feet tall, with broad shoulders and a few extra pounds around his waistline. His age was hard to guess, maybe early forties, and when he smiled, his light eyes brightened. His shirt was open at the collar, his dark tie loose. A matching suit jacket hung over one arm. The mayor glanced down at her, then turned away to nod at an elderly woman clutching his arm. Waiting, Julia kept her position, staying close enough to hear the mostly one-way conversations.

"Mayor, my daughter and my granddaughters are terrified," the older woman said. She held on to his arm with two wrinkled hands. "You can understand. Everyone around here is scared by this whole crazy business. I mean, how can this guy just walk out of jail? All my girls are worried, and I can hardly blame them." She shook her head, pursing her lips. "I remember everything, how afraid we all were." The lady's moist eyes were fixated on the mayor. "You were there, too. I know you remember."

"Yes, Edith, I remember."

The woman opened her mouth to speak again, but a shout from the back of the crowded diner stopped all conversation.

"We don't have to take it," a man said. He raised a finger and pointed at the full house. "None of us want Spradlin here. I say, let's not take it. Shit! Let's force him out. This is our town." A small chorus shouted in agreement.

Baldwin looked at the man, his expression benign. "What's

done is done. The man is legally free. He's entitled to live here if he chooses. We can't make him leave. It would be against the law."

The man scowled. "Fuck the law!"

"Garrett," Baldwin said, casting a look in the direction of a booth filled with gray-haired women, "there are ladies present."

"Sorry," the man muttered, his face sheepish.

Julia's eyes slid from the mayor to the reporters. Conroy struggled to repress his laughter. They weren't in Washington anymore.

"But it's true," Garrett pressed on. "If it weren't for the law, that scumbag murderer wouldn't be free right now." The faces encircling the mayor nodded. Some grew pinched with indignation. Julia glanced again at the reporters who'd been sitting behind her. A few were furiously taking notes now. The others watched the commotion closely.

Raising his right hand, the mayor spoke to the crowd, his tone smooth, controlled. "Look, Spradlin is a free man whether we like it or not."

"We don't!" The man's face was beet-red, his chin jutting forward.

The mayor's right hand dropped back to his side. "Now, Garrett, I don't like it any more than you, but it doesn't matter what we think here. Spradlin has been cleared. Bottom line is, the press, the state, heck, even the nation is watching what this man's gonna do." His eyes swept the diner, landing on the table of reporters. The angry glares followed his gaze. "And what everyone here needs to understand is that means they're also watching what we're gonna do." He smiled. A couple of the reporters ducked their heads. "Of course, they're only doing their jobs, same as we would. It's not their fault. We are a peaceful town, and that's what they're gonna see." He smiled wider, revealing a row of bright white teeth. "Hey Jenna, fill everyone's cups, will ya? It's on me!"

The tension was gone as quickly as it had skyrocketed. The crowd around the mayor scattered. Giggles rose from a booth in the corner, and Kenny Chesney's voice boomed from the old jukebox near the kitchen. Julia exhaled, relaxing her shoulders. It was only then that she noticed the mayor watching her, a tiny smile playing about his lips. He moved closer to her, until they were only inches apart.

"You okay?" he asked. He cocked his head to one side.

Her face grew hot. Had she seemed nervous, afraid? "Kind of an angry group, aren't they?"

The mayor's smile disappeared. He pointed at several tables filled with locals. "These are good people."

"If you say so."

"I do." He raised three fingers in the air, his expression solemn. "Scout's honor."

"Wow. Do people still do that?"

"Do what?"

"That Scout's honor thing?"

"I don't know," he laughed and blushed. "Look, I'm sorry about putting your friends on the spot like that. It wasn't fair."

"They're not my friends," she said automatically.

"Oh." He angled his head, his face serious. "Aren't you a reporter?"

"I am. What I meant to say was I know them, but I'm not with them exactly . . ." Her voice trailed off.

"Oka-ay. Well, I'm sorry anyway, you know, about diverting attention toward them."

"They'll live."

"Good to know."

Julia held his gaze. Fine lines around his eyes and tiny grooves at the corners of his mouth softened his kind face. "I have to say, you sure know how to work a crowd. That free coffee thing was brilliant."

He laughed again. "Comes with the job, I guess." He extended his hand. "Ted Baldwin. I'm the mayor of Little Springs."

"Julia Manning, *Washington Herald*." His large hand covered hers. "It's nice to meet you."

He smiled broadly. "Can I buy you a cup of coffee?"

She shook her head. "Sorry. I've had enough coffee for today."

He blinked, then stammered, "Oh. Okay." His face flushed again. "I understand. Maybe another time then."

She reached out and touched his arm lightly. "I keep saying the wrong thing. What I meant to say was I've got a better idea." She smiled up at him. "Do you know a good place a lady can get a drink?"

Chapter Thirteen

Cancini stood outside the old bar, staring up at the faded sign. Ernie's. Same name. Same place. The siding was peeling, and the torn screens on the second floor windows flapped in the light breeze. If it weren't for the small "Open" sign tacked to the front door, he'd swear the place was deserted, or worse, condemned. Inside, nearly all the stuff on the walls had been there for decades. It was junk mostly, with a few animal heads and rusted metal signs thrown in next to the faded movie posters. All of the memorabilia, even the moose antlers, were covered with a layer of dust, adding to the dingy ambience. Burned-out bulbs dotted the ceiling, casting an uneven light across the bar. Despite the bad lighting, Cancini noticed the rug had worn through, revealing a black, gummy vinyl underneath. The smell of old beer mixed with stale cigarette smoke rose from the mud-colored carpet. Cancini grinned. At least some things never changed.

Ernie's specialized in locals only, a grizzled and loyal clientele. Because of its location in the oldest section of town, college students didn't frequent the place. The stools were filled with solitary drinkers washing away their cares with house liquor or whatever Ernie had on tap. Grey Goose was not popular, and Cancini imagined Ernie had never made a cosmopolitan in his life. Food consisted of burgers and nachos, and if it was the special that night, a loaded chili dog. He wondered if Ernie even knew what a vegan was.

Cancini slid onto a wooden stool, his hazel eyes downcast. The place was mostly empty. A few folks sat at the end of the bar, and a handful more occupied a couple of tables along the far wall. It was early though. In a couple of hours, the regulars would crowd the bar and fill most of the seats. Cancini had always loved Ernie's, a true watering hole where a man could be anonymous yet surrounded by people he knew. The drinks were cold and reliable and, best of all, the owner was a friend. When he'd moved to Little Springs, with only a suitcase and a few references, it was Ernie who'd rented him a place to live, leasing him one of the two apartments over the bar. Ernie lived in the second one.

Rumor had it Ernie opened the bar after his first wife ran off with a traveling salesman. Ernie loved to say, "If I'm gonna spend all my time drinking away my sorrows, I might as well own the place. Makes it a helluva lot cheaper." Nice story, but Cancini knew better. Ernie never drank more than two beers in a day. The bar gave him purpose. Even more likely, owning the bar meant he always had friends, and he would never be alone.

The old bartender worked from one end of the bar to the other. Cancini watched and waited. In spite of his age and a slight stoop, Ernie was still agile, drawing pitchers and wiping tables like a much younger man. His face, pale and heavily lined, was the face of a man who spent most of his days and nights holed up in a dark bar.

Ernie ambled over, a half-smoked cigarette bobbing between his lips. "What can I getcha?" he said, his voice low and hoarse.

The man's faded eyes wandered to a baseball game on an old TV set hanging from the ceiling.

Cancini repressed a tiny smile. "Ernie?"

The old man huffed and wiped his hands on the rag hanging from his waist. He squinted at Cancini. "Who wants to know?"

Cancini chuckled. "You don't recognize me?"

"Oh, for the love of Pete," the old man said under his breath. He reached behind him for a pair of glasses. "Do I look like I have time to . . ." He stopped mid-sentence, breaking into a grin. "Well, I'll be." He shook his head. "Jesus, I can't believe it. Mike Cancini." Reaching across the bar, they pumped hands, smiling at each other. "Goddamn. How long has it been anyway?"

"A long time, Ernie. Too long." Cancini paused. "Since the trial, I guess. I'm sorry about that."

Ernie nodded, his smile gone. "You had your reasons. No one blamed you for not coming back." Cancini was quiet, lost in memories he'd tried once to forget. "Can I get you a beer?"

"I thought you'd never ask. Whatever's on tap." He sat waiting, watching Ernie draw the beer into a heavy mug with a thick handle, an old-style bar glass cloudy with use. Cancini drank slowly until it was half gone. A bowl of pretzels appeared before him. "How are you, Ernie?"

"Never better." Ernie had been saying the same thing for years. After a few minutes of silence, the old bartender spoke again. Although his tone was conversational, his words betrayed his outward indifference. "Shit, Mike, I don't know what they expect us to do. Sit around and wait for the other shoe to drop? You and me, old friend, know the truth, and I don't give a rat's ass who rigged the evidence. Spradlin's guilty. He can't goddamn stay in this town."

Nothing Ernie said surprised Cancini. He understood the town's reaction and would not judge its people. They were not coldhearted or ignorant as so many reporters were already implying. They were just protecting their own. "The law says he can, Ernie. You know that."

Bloodshot eyes searched Cancini's. The bartender nodded. He pulled out another glass, filling it to the rim before taking a sip himself. "What do you want from me, Mike?"

"Nothing, Ernie." Cancini looked down the bar. The stools were half full. He raised his eyes, meeting the old man's gaze. "I don't know. I'm not sure."

Ernie took a long drink. "Are you on the case?"

Cancini almost smiled. He liked the direct approach. In fact, it was the approach he used himself when conducting interrogations. He didn't like games. "There is no case for me, Ernie. Spradlin is a free man. The FBI is investigating now."

"So, why are you here?"

Cancini pushed away the empty mug. "Baldwin called me. Said he was scared."

Ernie snorted. "Of what? His election returns? Probably worried he'll lose his big seat as mayor when everyone remembers how he stuck up for Spradlin at the trial."

Ernie's assessment wasn't entirely accurate, but it was true enough. Baldwin had provided a shaky alibi for one of the murders, but he'd been vague about what time he might have seen Spradlin, discounting his testimony. Spradlin himself offered no alibi. Still, any ill will Baldwin had earned, he'd erased with solid accomplishments since then. He held an important position in town, one he wouldn't give up easily. "Who knows what's going on in his head?"

Ernie's brows furrowed, and he clucked his tongue. "So, then, what're you s'posed to do for him so he won't be such a scaredy cat?"

Cancini raised one shoulder. "Nothing as far as I know. At least I'm not planning on doing anything."

Ernie walked away, tending to other customers. Cancini picked through the pretzels, emptying the bowl. In the last hour, the bar had nearly filled. A waitress wearing a denim dress two sizes too small came out of the kitchen. She glanced at Ernie and then at Cancini, eyebrows arched. He nodded at her once, and she disappeared again.

A fresh mug appeared before him. "If you're not here for Baldwin, then why're you here, Mike?" Ernie asked. He leaned on the bar, his forearms pressed against the dark wood.

Cancini picked up the mug, hesitating. He wasn't sure how to put his answer into words without creating rumors. "I've got some leave coming. I decided to take it."

"Sure, and I'm married to Pamela Anderson." Ernie stood up as straight as his old back would allow, and his tired eyes flickered with amusement. "C'mon, Mike. You're here for a reason, and you walked into my place for a reason." He wore the expression of a man bracing for trouble. "What can I do?"

The detective wiped the beer foam from his upper lip, considering the question. He'd seen the press conference. Spradlin had lied and tensions in town were high. Still, he'd told Ernie the truth. The FBI would handle the case. There was nothing more to see, no real reason not to pack his bags and go home. He'd spent the last day and night wondering why he didn't do exactly that.

A woman's laughter rang out, bubbly and carefree. Cancini shifted on his stool, watching the woman as she joined a table of friends. Two decades earlier, she would have stayed home, afraid to leave the safety of her house. For months, a cloud of fear had hung over this town until Spradlin was arrested. But that was then. Now the deaths of all those girls had been reclassified as unsolved. It burned in his gut.

Cancini's bony fingers rubbed at the nicks and scars in the old wooden bar. He hesitated only a few seconds. He knew he would ask, knew he would start something he'd be obligated to finish. "I was wondering about Spradlin's mother. Did you know her?"

The man nodded slowly. "A little. She didn't come in the bar much, but I saw her at church once in a while. She kept to herself far as I know."

"Do you know anything about her relationship with her son, maybe what her life was like after he went to jail? That kind of thing."

The bartender shook his head. "Nah. I wouldn't know 'bout that." He rubbed his hand over the gray stubble on his face. "I know someone who might though. Want me to have her give you a call?"

"Yeah, sure. I'd appreciate that."

Ernie wiped his hands on the rag again before he took Cancini's card, placing it in the cash register. "Mike, thanks, you know, for doing this, for coming back. I'll sleep better at night jus' knowing you're here."

Cancini looked down at his beer. "I'm not doing anything, Ernie, so don't expect too much. It's follow-up. That's all."

The man stared back. "But you know this is wrong, don't you, Mike? It's total bullshit. You know it is. You put Spradlin away. You know he's guilty, right?"

"I don't know anymore, Ernie." Cancini shook his head. "The DNA evidence is pretty conclusive."

"Conclusive? Ha! It's a crock. I don't know how Spradlin rigged it, but he sure as shit did." Cancini had heard that same sentiment more than once since his arrival in Little Springs. "Besides, you had other evidence. There was that sweatshirt or T-shirt or somethin' and no alibi and I don't know what else. He's guilty. Why else would it have stopped?"

"I don't know, Ernie."

"But you believed he was guilty, didn't you, Mike?"

"I did."

"And now?"

Cancini ran his fingers around the fat rim of the mug. Why couldn't he shake the feeling that something wasn't right?

"I don't know what I believe, Ernie," he said, looking into the old man's eyes. "I wish I did."

Chapter Fourteen

"Hope this is okay," Ted Baldwin said, his voice raised to be heard over the shouting. "You won't run in to any of your reporter friends here."

Shouts erupted in the far corner of the bar and Julia turned in their direction. Several locals cheered and clapped in a circle near a large dartboard. She spotted a jukebox and rusted items hanging from the walls. A musty odor rose from the floor. She blinked several times, her eyes and nose adjusting to the acrid air. "It's fine."

"Good," he said with a smile. He pulled a pack of cigarettes from his pocket. "Do you mind if I smoke?"

She waved a hand. Almost everyone in her business smoked or used to smoke. "Go ahead."

"It's a terrible habit," he said. "It's why I come here. It's the only place I can smoke, and no one notices or cares." He lit the cigarette, inhaling deeply. His shoulders seemed to relax, and the lines between his brows disappeared. "So, tell me about Julia Manning."

She sat back against the wooden chair. The palms of her hands were damp and her heart skipped a beat. The last time anyone had taken a real interest in getting to know her was when she and Jack had started dating, and that was a long time ago. She tilted her head, taking stock of the man seated across from her. It wasn't hard to see how he'd been elected mayor in this town. He was attractive, and his manner engaging. It crossed her mind to ask him if he had bigger political aspirations. Congress? The Senate, maybe? He was young enough and intelligent enough. Julia wondered if there was a wife and kids. He didn't wear a ring, but that didn't always mean anything. She looked down at her own bare left hand, rubbing at the indentation that still marked her third finger, naked and raw. She picked up her shot glass and downed the whiskey in one gulp.

"Wow," he said, sipping his beer. "You weren't kidding about wanting something stronger."

Flushed, she forced a laugh. "Sorry. It's been a strange couple of days. I guess I haven't been myself lately."

"Oh?" He sat forward, tapping his cigarette into a metal ashtray. "Do you want to talk about it?"

"No. I don't think so."

"Are you sure? I'm a pretty good listener. Plus, since I don't know you, I might even be objective."

She smiled. "Thanks, but I'm sure."

He smiled back. "You can't blame a guy for trying, and I do hate to see a pretty lady unhappy. Maybe another drink then?"

Her melodic laugh drowned out the preset oldies playing from the jukebox. His smile broadened. "Are you flirting with me, Mayor Baldwin?"

"Hell, yes," he said with a wink.

She eyed his hand again. "You're not married?"

"No. Almost." The grin faded. "When I was in my late twenties,

I was engaged. About a month before the wedding, Carla—that was my fiancée—was in a car accident." He picked up the mug and took a deep slug of the amber beer. "She was working in Charlottesville for the summer and was coming home for the weekend. The roads were wet and they said she was driving too fast. I tried to tell her all the time to slow down, but she would just laugh at me." His voice shook. "The car must've spun out and she ran off the road into a row of trees. They said it was quick. She didn't suffer." He drained the rest of his beer.

Julia swallowed. "I'm sorry."

"It's okay," he said, his wet eyes finding hers. "It was a long time ago. I came close again a few years ago, but it didn't work out. Guess it wasn't meant to be." He stubbed out his cigarette. "The truth is, I don't date much anymore. It's a small town, and I've known pretty much everyone here my whole life. Makes it harder in a way, and the job takes so much time . . ."

Julia nodded. This was hardly what she'd intended when she suggested they have drinks instead of coffee. She'd hoped to ask a few questions, maybe even score an interview, but not swap sad relationship stories.

"Hey, sorry about that," he said and waved a hand. "I didn't mean to bring any of that up." He motioned to the waitress near the dartboard. "How about another drink?"

"A beer. Thanks." When the waitress was gone, she slid a notepad and pen from her canvas bag. He raised an eyebrow. "Mayor Baldwin," she said, "I was hoping to . . ."

"Please call me Ted."

"Okay. Ted."

The waitress set two mugs of beer on the table and swept away the empty glasses, pausing when her eyes fell on the notepad and pen.

"As I was saying, I was hoping to ask you a few questions."

The waitress moved from table to table. She picked up the empty mugs two at a time, then mopped up any spilled beer. At the bar, she leaned into the bartender, nodded in their direction, speaking in his ear. Baldwin lit another cigarette. He gestured toward the pen in her hand, poised over the open notebook. "They know you're a reporter."

She followed his gaze to the bar. "Is that a problem?"

"Depends. Is that why you agreed to have a drink with me? To ask me questions?"

"No." Her face reddened. "Well, yes and no. I did want a drink, and you seemed nice and . . ."

"And you thought it would be a good chance to get an interview with the mayor?"

There was no anger in his tone, only curiosity, and she breathed a sigh of relief. "Yes. I hope you don't mind. We could start with some background, and then I'd like to ask you about the press conference yesterday. I won't take up too much of your time. I promise."

"I'm not in any hurry, Julia, but I'd rather you put the notebook away." He spoke quietly, his voice gentle. "This is a locals' place, and it's been here a long time, like the people in here. They like their privacy. It wouldn't look good for me to give an interview in here to an outsider. Especially now."

Julia thought of the way the waitress paused when she caught sight of the notebook, how her manner seemed to cool. He was right. She was out of her element, a stranger here, and she didn't need any enemies. Nodding, Julia returned the items to her bag.

"Is that why you brought me here?" she asked, crossing her legs. "So I could see some of the locals?"

"Sort of," he said. "I know you think you saw everything there is to know about this town yesterday, but that's not the whole picture. People will be friendlier toward you if they think you're going to listen, take the time to get know them." He paused, puffing on his half-smoked cigarette. "My advice to you is to keep your notebook and tape recorder inside that bag. The folks around here are going to be turned off if they think you're hanging around so you can write about how Leo Spradlin got a raw deal."

Julia folded her arms across her chest. "What do you think, Ted? Do you think he got a raw deal?"

The mayor shrugged, his bulk shifting with the movement. "Hard to say, but in my mind, he got a fair trial at the time. And from the moment he was arrested, the rapes and murders stopped. When you take that into account, this new DNA evidence is a bitter pill for people around here to swallow." His eyes wandered around the bar. "I don't know about raw deals, but I do know I've got a town full of people who believe a guilty man just got out of prison. The truth is, folks are scared."

Julia sipped the cold beer. She had figured most of this out at the press conference and in the diner. "You talked about justice at your press conference. What did you mean by that?"

He shrugged again. "Only that Spradlin went to prison based on the justice system, and he was also freed based on that same system. We need to respect the law even if we don't always agree with it. Spradlin has every right to live in this town, whether we like it or not."

"Makes sense." She leaned forward, her hands on the table. "But I don't think too many people around here feel the same way. I felt a lot of anger and hate out there yesterday."

He rubbed the back of his neck. "True, but you weren't here

then. You can't understand what it was like. The people who were, they can't accept his innocence. That's why they're scared."

"You were here, Ted. Are you scared?"

"Not the way you mean. Look, the law says he's innocent, so I have to go with that. I may not practice law anymore, but I know DNA evidence doesn't lie. That being said, I also know evidence that's been sitting in a lab or warehouse for years can be tampered with or degraded."

Julia's head jerked back in surprise. "Is that what you think?"

"Not really," he said. "But I know that's what some people think, and I can't blame them. So, yes, I am scared in a way. I'm scared for what Spradlin's presence is going to do to this town. I don't need any trouble, and the college sure as hell doesn't, either."

"No, it doesn't," a voice from behind Baldwin interrupted. A man with dark, cropped hair and piercing eyes stepped from behind the mayor and stood over the table. "At least that's one thing we can agree on. Right, Teddy?" The mayor ignored the man, who reached out and shook Julia's hand. "Mike Cancini."

"Julia Manning," she said, squinting. "You look familiar. Have we met?"

"No." He shifted his attention to Baldwin. "Teddy, I need to have a word with you. Alone."

Cancini wore a brown leather sport coat and rumpled khaki pants. Stylish, he wasn't. Although his build was average, he stood tall, his presence demanding the mayor's attention. His nose was long and narrow, bordering on prominent. But it was his eyes, a dark hazel, almost black in the dim lighting, that drew her to his otherwise ordinary face.

Baldwin fiddled with his pack of cigarettes. "It's not the best time, Mike."

"Mike Cancini. Mike Cancini." Julia said his name out loud, rolled it around on her tongue, and slapped her thigh. "I do know you. You're Detective Mike Cancini. D.C. I write for the *Washington Herald*."

"Figures," he muttered, wheeling around to face Baldwin. "It can wait. I'll be at your office tomorrow morning. Nine sharp."

The mayor slid another cigarette between his lips. "Fine." He focused on his lighter and cigarette, inhaling deeply.

Julia watched the detective walk away. "Well," she said, breaking the silence that had settled over the table, "that might be one of the rudest men I've ever met."

Baldwin blew out smoke. "Might be?" The mayor wasn't smiling. His face was glum, his eyes far away.

"What's he doing here anyway? He's Washington."

The mayor picked at the corner of the cocktail napkin under his empty beer mug. "Mike Cancini lived here for a time. Back then actually."

Her mouth dropped open, and her fingers itched for the second time in two days. "During the investigation?"

"Yeah. He was fresh out of the academy and was a rookie in our department. I was interning there, too, while I was in law school."

Julia's heart thumped in her chest. Damn. It had been right in front of her, in those articles from the town paper. How could she have missed it? "He was working as a Little Springs cop then? Was he on the case?"

"Everyone was. It was his first job as I remember, a training type job." A wry smile crossed his face. "Some training, right?"

She ignored his comment. "I still don't get why he's here now. What's the point? Is he just curious?"

The smile evaporated. "Mike Cancini is never just curious."

He rolled the napkin scraps between his fingers, his lips pursed. "I probably shouldn't tell you this, but if I don't, someone else will." Julia drew in her breath, waiting. "We didn't have many guys in the squad when Mike got here. This wasn't exactly a high crime town, still isn't. Traffic tickets, the occasional drunk and disorderly, stuff like that. Chief Hobson was in charge back then. Passed away now. Mike started out working with campus security after the second girl was found. Reviewed the missing persons reports. Looked for connections in class schedules. Interviewed students. That kind of stuff." He paused, squeezing the ragged pieces of napkin into a ball. "It was terrible. I don't know if you know this already, but my dad was president of the college back then. It was around the holidays. Dad took it hard. Everyone did. Nothing like this had ever happened in the history of this town. No one knew what to do. Chief Hobson did his best, but he was old." His light eyes glistened under the low lights. "After the Christmas break, some kids didn't come back, but a lot did. All of us in the squad pulled shifts working security on campus." Baldwin lit another cigarette, his hands shaking. "It didn't matter what we did. More girls died. Hobson called in the FBI."

Julia rubbed the goose bumps on her arms.

"The feds didn't have much to go on. There just wasn't much evidence. Then Mike discovered Spradlin had known two of the victims. Then it was three. He was like a dog with a bone. He got a search warrant and found a sweatshirt at Spradlin's mother's house. It matched the torn piece found at the river, where the first girl was found." Baldwin sat back. "It was Mike Cancini who broke the case. Not the FBI. Cancini went after Spradlin, built the case against him."

She blinked. "You almost make it sound personal, like he went after Spradlin for a reason."

Baldwin answered sharply. "You don't understand. The murders stopped. It all stopped." He stubbed out his cigarette in the half-full ashtray. "Cancini was a hero around here. He arrested Spradlin, and it stopped. Everything was better then. Everyone was safe again."

She thought about the man who'd left the bar, an experienced detective from a metropolitan city where the number of homicides in a year might outnumber all the homicides in the history of Little Springs. What had he been like when he was young and green? What had it been like to be inexperienced, an outsider in the middle of an investigation as big as this one? He'd come for training and ended up with credit for the biggest collar in this county's history. Baldwin said the young Cancini had been like a dog with a bone. He wouldn't rest until he got his man. Maybe he should have been less single-minded.

"I understand," she said slowly, her voice soft. "I don't know why everything stopped, but it must have been a coincidence. He was wrong about Spradlin. An innocent man spent most of his life in jail because of Detective Cancini. In my book, that doesn't make Mike Cancini a hero."

The mayor stared at her. "I'm sorry you feel that way," he said. He threw some bills on the table.

"Wait, Ted, I—" He cut her off.

"I like you, Julia, I do." His tone was distant. "That's why I'm going to give you a warning. Be careful what you say and to whom you say it. This town is filled with good people, and whether you think it's right or not, they believe Mike Cancini is the reason the rapes and murders stopped. They believed it then, and they believe it now. Don't romanticize Spradlin. You won't win any friends and will probably make a few enemies."

"But—"

"Be careful, Julia. Very careful."

Chapter Fifteen

FADED CURTAINS FLAPPED at the window, rising and falling with the warm breeze. The sweet scent of wild honeysuckle hung in the air. Oblivious to the buzzing of the tree crickets, he stared at the ceiling. Despite the dark and the hum of nature, sleep was proving elusive. It was the girl. He couldn't erase his vision of her bouncing blond ponytail or tight T-shirt. The urges were getting stronger. His fingers twitched, and he curled them into his palms. He shouldn't have gone to the campus. It was stupid, but he'd only gone to look. The sorority house, her house, was the second in a row of ten. The houses were carbon copies, all the same, with their wide porches and huge letters hanging over the front doors. He'd spoken to no one, pulling a baseball hat low over his face. Although he was sure no one had noticed him, it had been damn stupid just the same.

He closed his eyes, remembering the last time. His heart thudded in his chest, and his eyelids fluttered in the darkness. He replayed the shouts, the hysteria, and then the tears that dissolved into whimpers. So friggin' sweet. So fucking powerful. He opened his eyes again putting the memories away, tucking them into the corner of his mind. Patience. He had time, time for new opportunities and new memories. He inhaled, breathing in the sweet smells. Fortune was smiling on him now.

His plan was simple. The Coed Killer would return. Fear would spread like wildfire. If it went the way he figured, shock, outrage, and panic would overwhelm Little Springs. It was such a predictable town. Nothing ever changed here. His lips turned up at the corners. For a college town, a place that claimed to prize education and learning, it was a closed and ignorant place. Of course, that's what he was counting on.

The media, unknowingly, was central to his return. He'd seen the stories leading up to the release, and the governor had played right into his hands. The press conference was the icing on the cake. Poor Leo Spradlin. It was the only story anyone wanted to see and hear. Now that an innocent man had been freed, who would be left to vilify? The rednecks in town? Cancini? Hell, it didn't matter. He'd spoon-feed them what they wanted to hear. It was going to be beautiful.

He grinned in the dark. He couldn't have planned it better if he'd tried. He stretched his arms again and pulled the pillow under his head. He needed to be smart. Patient and smart. If he did things right, if everything went according to plan, the town would be in for a big fucking surprise.

Chapter Sixteen

CANCINI ANSWERED THE phone on the first ring, sitting up straight in the strange bed. Disoriented, he blinked in the pre-dawn light. "Yes?" he answered, his voice hoarse with sleep.

"Is this Mike Cancini?" asked a woman, the twang of her local accent pronounced. "Detective Mike Cancini?"

"Yeah. You got him." He cleared his throat and peered through bleary eyes at the nightstand clock. Damn. He'd overslept. "How can I help you?"

"I'm sorry to call so early." The lady hesitated. "I hope I didn't wake you, but I have to be at work early and, well, Ernie said I should call."

Cancini stood up, pressing the phone closer to his ear. "It's okay, I needed to get up anyway." He moved to the hotel window, pushing aside the heavy drapes. From his room, he had a perfect view of Main Street. It was remarkably empty, unlike the Washington streets where traffic began in the early hours before sunrise and dragged on late into the evening. "I'm sorry, I didn't catch your name."

"LeeAnn Terry," she said. "I don't think we've ever met, but I do remember you. I'm probably old enough to be your mother."

"Well, it's nice to meet you now, Ms. Terry."

"Oh, call me LeeAnn. Please."

"Okay, LeeAnn. How can I help you?"

She was silent only a moment. "Ernie said you wanted to know about Brenda, Leo's mom."

"Yes, that's true. Did you know her?"

"Well, yeah, I knew her pretty well. We go all the way back to grade school, like most folks around here. When we were older, we worked together at the college. That was before she got let go. I always felt sorry for her, unlike most folks, so I stayed in touch. Not that I didn't understand their feelings and all, but I'm a Christian. She wasn't the one found guilty." Cancini walked around the room, flipping on table lamps as she talked. Grabbing his notebook and pen, he sat at the desk in the corner. "The last time I saw her was about a week before she died. The truth is, I got the feeling she didn't have any other visitors. It made me sad for her, but, well, she didn't make it easy, either."

"It sounds like you were a good friend."

"I tried." She sounded pleased.

"LeeAnn, is there anything you can tell me about Brenda's relationship with her son? Do you know what that was like? Were they close?"

"Close?" she repeated, answering slowly, choosing her words. "No-o. I wouldn't say that exactly. Maybe once they were, but that was before, you know . . ." She paused. " . . . before he grew up. When he was little, she used to dote on him, so proud, like all mothers. Carried his picture in her wallet and went to Little League games and stuff."

"But something changed?"

"Yeah, I couldn't tell you what, though. She was pretty tight-lipped about him even before he went to jail." She clucked her tongue. "To tell you the truth, I always thought she was kinda scared of him. Her own son! Can you imagine?"

"No, ma'am," he said. Cancini had met Brenda only a couple of times but thought he understood what LeeAnn meant. A tall woman, Brenda Spradlin had seemed small with her shoulders hunched, her head down, apparently content to stay in the background. When he'd visited the house with Teddy Baldwin, she'd been polite but said little. If Spradlin wanted more coffee or anything, he'd gesture toward her, and his mother would jump to serve him. It had rubbed the young officer the wrong way.

"Some folks felt she had it coming to her, you know," LeeAnn said, the words tumbling out now. "People thought she had a big head and all. See, she was real pretty in high school and smart, but she kept to herself. Didn't date. Didn't go to the football games or hang out. You know how people are, they thought she was snotty." Cancini made a note on the pad, nodding as he wrote. "But she was always nice to me. I had trouble in math, and she stayed after school and helped me a couple of times. That's when I first got to know her. The truth is, I think she was shy. After that, we graduated, and I started working in my father's bakery. Brenda though, she was a smart one. She got some kinda scholarship to Blue Hill. That's where she met William, Leo's father."

She paused to catch her breath. "He was from New York, and the story was he was only at Blue Hill 'cause he couldn't get in anywhere else, but I don't know that for sure. Anyway, they ran off and got married, and then along came Leo. They stayed up in New York for a couple of years, and then William was killed in some boating accident. I guess his family didn't want anything more to do with her, so she and Leo came home. She started working at the college, taking a class at a time when she could. She kept to herself even more after that."

He wrote quickly, making furious notes as she talked. "What about when Leo was growing up? Did she ever say what he was like?"

"Not especially. I know I used to jabber on about my kids and how cute they were and Little League and all that, but she didn't say much. I mean, I know he got to be a big football star up at the high school, but I don't think she even went to a single game. If she did, I never saw her."

Cancini knew Spradlin had played football. He'd been quick and strong. Strong enough to overpower a young woman. "Would you say Leo was popular in school? Did people like him?"

"I s'pose he had a few friends, although I don't know how much people actually liked him. He got his mama's looks, though, and he didn't have a shy bone in his body. I remember I chaperoned at the prom one year, and he was there with a pretty young thing. She kept smiling up at him, and he barely noticed her. It makes my skin crawl now when I think of that and what he did to all those college girls."

Cancini leaned back in his chair, his hand suspended over the page. "You don't believe Leo's innocent?"

"No, sir, I don't," she said, not a trace of hesitation in her voice.

"Okay." He tapped his pen against the hotel's faux wood desk. "What would Brenda have thought of her son being released? Would she have been happy?"

LeeAnn snorted. "Hardly. He may have been her only son, but she wasn't a fool. He was no good, and she knew it. Sure, her life was hard. Money was tight and all, but she didn't want him back. Like I said, I think she was afraid of him. Having him gone was definitely better than having him home."

Cancini swallowed. His own mother had been lost to him at a young age. Leo was lucky to have Brenda, but then again, he was fatherless. They'd both grown up without a parent. Still, no matter how strained Cancini's relationship with his father might be, his father had never been afraid of him. What had happened in the Spradlin house? "Thank you, LeeAnn. You've been very helpful."

"Sure. Anytime." She hesitated. "Detective, Ernie said you were doing some follow-up, asking some questions."

"That's right. Just follow-up."

"Well, if you don't mind my saying, I feel better knowing you're here."

"That's kind of you to say."

"I'm not the only one. Lots of folks would feel that way if they knew you were here." Cancini sighed, sure the word about his return would spread like wildfire. She clucked her tongue again. "No one's sayin' it, but we're all thinkin' it. Lord help us if it starts again."

"There's no reason to think like that, LeeAnn."

"Maybe not, but better to be safe than sorry I always say. If folks are right, and Lord knows I hope they're not, we're gonna need you, Detective. More than ever."

Chapter Seventeen

"YOU GOT THE interview with Spradlin!" Norm Jensen said. Julia's editor's excitement crackled through the phone. "Conroy got one, too, of course, but your story's gonna blow his away!"

She had to smile at Norm's loyalty and enthusiasm. They both knew Conroy was an excellent reporter, the most decorated journalist on staff. "Norm, you're sweet, but maybe you're expecting a tad too much."

"No way. You're the one who doesn't expect enough."

Julia picked at the lint on her pants. Years of writing fluff had dulled her instincts. After last night, after questioning Cancini's hero status, she had no idea if the mayor would even talk to her again. "Maybe."

"Not maybe. You took the initiative to get on this story. You pushed, and you got it. That was you, Julia. Give yourself some credit." He paused, then said, "Don't let him get to you, Julia."

She grinned and bowed her head. Good old Norm. A loyal friend, but maybe he was right. This was her first big story in years. She should never have taken a backseat for Jack, but she couldn't blame him anymore. She could have done things differently, too. This wasn't about him anymore. It was about her. "I promise. I'll do my best."

"Atta girl!"

Her laptop sat open in front of her. The manila envelope she'd brought from home was empty, the photocopied newspaper articles and background spread across the floor. A blurry black and white photo of the young Spradlin lay in front of her on the desk. She traced the outline of the photo. "So when do I get to meet him?"

"Tomorrow morning, nine a.m., in the public library. He'll find you."

She wrote down the time and place. "He's got guts. I'll give him that."

"What do you mean?"

"I'm a little surprised he chose such a public place."

"Why does it matter?"

"People around here don't like him much." She thought of the signs in the street and rose, moving to the window. Main Street was mostly empty. Maybe a dozen cars were parked along the road, and a few people strolled the sidewalk. The makeshift podium was long gone, along with the stage in front of the town hall. The sun blazed, glinting off the storefront windows, casting sparkles everywhere. While it looked like a peaceful town, a quiet and slow-moving place, she sensed something darker here. "No. That's not right. They hate him."

"What? Why?"

It was difficult to explain something she didn't fully understand. "This is going to sound strange, but it's almost like they still think he's guilty."

"That's crazy! The governor himself said the man was innocent."

She closed her eyes, remembering the angry faces in the crowd at the homecoming. "Doesn't matter. They don't believe it. They know the facts. They know about the DNA evidence, but it's like they can't accept it—or won't. I'm not sure which. Either way, I need to be a little careful when I talk to the people around here."

Norm brushed aside her concerns. "Oh, it'll be fine. They'll come around."

"Maybe." He hadn't seen the outrage at the press conference or witnessed the hostile attitudes directed at the reporters. "It would help if they found out who really attacked those girls."

"True. What's the latest?"

"Hold on," she said, scrolling through the notes she'd typed on her computer. "Here it is. The state is testing the DNA from the original case against the DNA of convicted rapists and murderers from the last twenty years. That's the first step. I'm told it could take a while. If that yields nothing, then the FBI will move to surrounding states, start looking for similar cases, blah, blah, blah. Not exactly comforting to the families of the victims or the people in this town."

"But logical."

"I guess. Still, I don't know why they can't reopen the case right away, make a big deal out of searching for the guy. I mean, shouldn't it be more of a priority? It must be hell for those parents." Norm was silent. Julia knew the stony expression that would be on his face, one eyebrow raised in question. "I know, I know. Keep the emotions out of it. I'll try, but we can't all be as unfeeling as you."

"Objective, Julia. Objective," he said. "You can play on the emotions of our readers, but leave yours out of it."

Julia held the phone away, letting him rant. She loved Norm and he was a great editor. Still, she'd heard the speech so many times she could practically recite it. She toyed with the idea of hanging up and pretending they were accidentally cut off, but then she remembered something important.

"Norm," she interrupted, "do you know a Detective Michael Cancini?"

"Cancini? Sure, I've heard the name. Why?"

"D.C. Homicide. Right?"

"Yeah. So?"

"Do you think you could get me some background on him?"

Norm paused, then asked, "Why?"

"He's here. You're not going to believe this, but he's the one who arrested Spradlin. Turns out he was a cop here in Little Springs before D.C."

"You don't say."

"Yep. I saw him last night."

"Odd. His name hasn't been part of any of the stories I've read. Why show up now?"

"I have no idea." She didn't, but she had a funny feeling the mayor did. She would need to mend fences, and soon.

"Well, this could be a fun little twist," he said. "Tell you what. I'll see what I can find out and get back to you. Good?"

"Yeah. That would be great." The conversation was over, and she knew it. Still, she couldn't bring herself to hang up. "Hey, I was wondering how, you know . . ."

Before she got out Jack's name, reliable Norm already understood her unasked question. "He looks like hell, Julia. Spends half the night in his office from the looks of it. He's cranky and a pain in the ass, but that's nothing new."

She exhaled and laughed a little. It was satisfying, at least, to know that the death of their marriage wasn't a piece of cake for him after all. Or maybe his new girl had already tired of him. That possibility was all too real. Still, alone was alone. "Has he asked about me?"

Norm hesitated, and Julia had her answer.

"Never mind," she said before he was forced to make up a lie. "Forget I asked. I'll call you after the interview." Hanging up, she returned to the window facing the street below. Even though Julia had never been to Little Springs before, it had a familiar feel. It was the kind of place Hollywood sets tried to emulate when they filmed small-town America. The people wore their feelings on their faces, and money was for living, not for showing off status or power. Was it backwards or refreshing? She couldn't decide. It might look like Mayberry from TV, but this real-life town had spawned a serial rapist and murderer, and that man was still out there. Somewhere.

Chapter Eighteen

"I DON'T GIVE a damn about helping some reporter," Cancini leaned over the mayor's desk, his voice tight. "No way am I going to be a part of the media circus like the one you orchestrated at that press conference. You're lucky it didn't turn into a full-blown riot."

"You're right," the mayor was quick to agree. "We were lucky. Believe me, it wasn't my idea." He shook his head. "I wish it had never happened."

Cancini straightened. The mayor's discomfort at the podium had been obvious. "Then why the hell did you do it?"

Baldwin shrugged. "I got a call from the governor's office." He imitated the call: "The governor would appreciate a formal press conference allowing Mr. Spradlin the opportunity to speak on the occasion of his homecoming." Cancini folded his arms across his chest. "Look," the mayor continued, "I knew it was PR bullshit and that it could get ugly. But it was still the governor's office, for God's sake. What was I supposed to do?"

"Tell him no."

"Easy for you to say," the mayor said with a huff. "He's the most popular governor this state's had in decades. I'm a simple mayor trying to get by. The media thinks he'll run for president. I've met him, talked to him. He'll probably win." Baldwin spread his hands, palms up. "Little Springs can't be the town that defied the president."

Cancini's hazel eyes darkened to slate-gray. He pointed a finger at Baldwin. "That's a load of crap. You should have told him how it is here, how people feel. You shouldn't have done it. Your job is to look after this town, not bend over for the governor!"

The mayor's ruddy face took on a darker hue. "That's not fair, Mike. You always think you have the answers. I haven't seen you in God knows how many years, and you haven't changed one bit."

Cancini shot back. "Neither have you. Still pandering, worried someone's not gonna like you."

"Dammit, Mike, I'm an elected official," he said, slapping his desk.

"You just proved my point."

The two men glared at each other, Baldwin's face puffy and red. His fingers drummed the edge of the desk, the seconds ticking by until he dropped his gaze and walked to the window. The bright morning sun poured through the large pane of glass overlooking Main Street. Teddy dabbed at his forehead with a handkerchief. "I don't want to argue with you, Mike." Cancini remained silent, hands shoved in his pockets. Baldwin returned to his desk, sinking into the leather chair. "I think this reporter might be different."

"Are we back to that?"

"She might listen if you give her a chance."

Cancini rolled his eyes. "Why? Because she's pretty?" The mayor flushed. "Teddy, you haven't changed at all."

"Maybe not, but I'm not the only one who noticed she was pretty." Cancini's lips clamped shut. Baldwin changed the subject. "Why are you still here, Mike? I'd have thought you'd need to get back to D.C. Isn't that where they have real crimes and real problems?"

Cancini ignored the other man's jab. "I thought you were worried about Spradlin. I thought you wanted me here."

"I thought you didn't take me seriously," the mayor said with skepticism. "Thought I was overreacting."

"Doesn't matter what I thought. I stuck around for the press conference and I saw a town on the brink of imploding. One more word from Spradlin and someone might've gotten hurt. It can't happen again."

The mayor stiffened. "It won't. I already told you that."

"Oh? And what about the first time Spradlin comes to town for a burger? What about when he decides to sit at the bar like a normal person and drink a beer or go to church on Sunday? What are you planning then?"

"You know, Mike. You're a piece of work. You don't give the people of Little Springs enough credit. I do. These are good people, not violent thugs. No one is going to do anything to Spradlin."

"Believe it or not, I do give these folks credit. You're right. They won't start anything. But you can't honestly tell me Spradlin won't. You heard him. That whole speech was a masterpiece, meant to stoke the fire. You think the folks around here didn't go home and let his words rattle around in their heads?" Cancini stood up and paced the office, the muscles in his back tensing. "He forgives them? What kind of crap is that? Is he trying to make them feel bad? For what? Believing the evidence? Believing he was guilty when the crimes stopped the minute he was arrested? Come on!

And that whole bit about knowing he made it easy for them to believe he was guilty. He damn sure did." Cancini stopped. "You remember what he was like back then, don't you, Teddy? Arrogant. Insensitive. Self-centered. Angry."

The mayor gave a shake of his head. "Mike, I think your memory is going. Yeah, Leo was arrogant and selfish, and sometimes he was a real jerk. But angry? I don't remember that. And even if he was, that doesn't make him guilty or mean that people should have believed it."

Cancini's voice softened. "Are you defending Spradlin?"

The mayor flinched and leaned back in his chair. "That's not fair, Mike. I never defended Leo, and you know it. Besides, nobody needs to defend him. According to the courts, he hasn't done anything."

"Yet. Spradlin's not the type of man to let sleeping dogs lie. That's what that speech was about and you know it. It wasn't about forgiveness. He was starting something." Cancini leaned across the desk until there were only inches between them. "I thought you were concerned about him threatening you, threatening this town."

Baldwin opened his mouth, then closed it again. His light eyes flickered in doubt. "I was. I am, but I don't like self-fulfilling prophecies. Just because I don't think he was angry back then doesn't mean I don't think he is now. Hell, wouldn't you be? He wanted to shake me up, and he succeeded."

"And that speech the other day?"

"Okay, he's playing games. I'll give you that, but there's not a damn thing I can do about it. He hasn't done anything wrong."

"Whatever." Cancini straightened. "But you still didn't answer me. What are you going to do when Spradlin shows his face in town?"

Baldwin pursed his lips. "I can't do much, Mike. The man is legally entitled to go anywhere he likes. If I have the police follow him, it could be construed as harassment. The best I can do is ask the police to keep an eye out for trouble. If he comes into town for groceries or hardware or whatever, we'll position a man where he shops. If he gets a bite to eat or a drink, the same. That's the best I can do unless something happens. Satisfied?"

"No. But it'll have to do for now." Cancini's attention wandered to the large window and he squinted at the blinding morning light. "The folks here don't deserve this."

"Maybe not," Baldwin said. "But you can help, you know."

Cancini groaned, tired of Baldwin and his arguments. "No reporters."

"Hear me out. So far, everything the media has reported has been about an innocent man getting out of jail. He's a victim to them. The press sees it as righting a wrong, fixing a miscarriage of justice. The folks here though, and I'm not blaming them mind you, were downright obnoxious the other day. The shouts telling Spradlin to leave. The signs and chants. We looked like a bunch of angry good ol' boys here. I don't want that to be how the story plays out."

"So? I don't care what people say about me. Why should you?'

"Because it affects things like student enrollment at the college. Because our tourism business will drop with bad press about the town. Maybe you don't care about that stuff. You don't live here. Little Springs has been doing okay, but that isn't likely to last with a wave of bad press." He pushed his hair back from his forehead. "If you could make the press understand how it was back then, why the feelings run so deep, what yesterday's reaction was about, it would go a long way in helping the town repair its image."

"Why don't you do it?'

"Because I'm the mayor and clearly biased. You were an outsider when you came here back then, and you're an outsider now."

"I don't discuss cases with the press."

"Jesus, I'm not asking you to discuss the case. No details, but you could at least help explain the hysteria, how all anyone wanted was to feel safe again. One reporter, that's all. For God's sake, it could even be off the record. There's no one better than you to do it."

On the street, most of the parking spaces were filled and light traffic moved steadily through town. A little farther up the road, tucked in the hills, students were eating, studying, and attending classes, seemingly safe in their small academic world. Cancini remembered the faces of the students at the press conference, those who'd been curious enough to come into town. Some took pictures with their phones, openly astonished by the hostility. They didn't understand. They couldn't. He hated to admit it, but Baldwin was right. The news cameras had captured the angry crowd and later broadcast the footage on the nightly news. The town did look bad. "I'll think about it," Cancini said. "That's all."

Baldwin nodded, smiling. "I'll take it. Thanks."

Cancini moved toward the door. "I want to know if Spradlin comes into town. I want to know if he starts anything."

"Sure. I've got your cell. You're staying at the inn?"

"For now."

"How long?"

Cancini paused, his hand on the doorknob. He didn't know why he was staying, but he'd realized one thing. He owed Little Springs. He'd played a part back then, and however reluctantly, he played a part now. He'd never wanted to be a hero. Now he wasn't.

The town and the families were suffering again. He knew all too well what that was like. The pain might lessen over time, but it never leaves. It wakes you up in the night, snaking through your gut to your heart until sometimes you can't breathe. You lie there, waiting for it to go away. You force it from your mind, desperately trying to hang on to the good memories, not the images of your loved one's lifeless and bloody body. Father Joe, the old priest who'd become both a surrogate father and his oldest friend, called it a gift from God, the gift of remembering, but Cancini knew it for the nightmare it was. The grief becomes part of you.

He opened the door and said over his shoulder, "As long as it takes."

Chapter Nineteen

It felt different this time. He didn't know why, but it did. He was older and hopefully a little wiser, but that wasn't it. He possessed a calmness he hadn't before. The need was the same, stronger even, but it didn't hurt the way it had back then. Instead, he relished it, welcomed it. When he was young—the first time—he'd acted on impulse, the need something he hadn't fully understood. After the trial, he was forced to repress that need, that yearning, but now he was free to embrace those urges again. He was smarter now, smarter than the whole fucking lot of 'em.

No DNA this time. Not a hair, no saliva, nothing at all left behind. He couldn't risk it. He'd caught a break once—in such a crazy twist—he wished he could take credit for it himself. Sometimes the gods smiled and handed you a second chance. What could a man do but take it?

The need was the thing. It was like a damn drug, calling to him, beckoning. He used to be afraid of it, disgusted even. He'd resisted as long as he could, but that was ages ago. He'd had years to accept what he couldn't change.

He'd planned the girl and the whole encounter, but he knew better than to rush it. Patience, something he'd learned to appreciate, would serve him well. He closed his eyes and licked his lips. When the media tired of the story, when something bigger and better came along, most of the reporters would move on. It was already starting. He didn't want the barrage of press that had initially swarmed the town, watching and waiting, but he did need some of them. After all, they were part of the story, too. It wouldn't be long now.

The return of the great Cancini completed the scene. The man had known the detective would come, of course. He'd counted on it. The truth was, he'd never liked Cancini, and the way he figured it, once an asshole, always an asshole. The poor guy's ego must be badly bruised, though. Cancini's fumble made the man laugh. They were more alike than the detective realized or would ever admit. Cancini couldn't change who he was, what he was, any more than the man could. The detective would never give up. Something about his presence fit, as though they were playing parts exactly as they were written. Soon, everything would come full circle.

Chapter Twenty

Julia's stomach flipped and fluttered. She sat cross-legged on the floor of her hotel room, back up against the bed. Folders and notes and pictures covered the beige carpet. A notebook open to a blank page sat in her lap. Julia closed her eyes and slowed her breathing. She'd gotten the interview, a coup on the face of it, but a growing unease overshadowed her excitement. Too many years of writing about cuddly dogs and society fund-raisers had made her rusty.

Her eyes snapped open. Damn. What was the matter with her? She was up to this. Norm had faith in her. Her father had always believed in her. There was even a time when Jack thought she could do anything. She raised her chin, uncrossed her legs, and reached for a fat file. Time to stop feeling sorry for herself. Pushing her glasses up on her nose, she opened the file and thumbed through the background Norm had overnighted.

Blue Hill College dropped "Christian" from its name in the late 1990s. In a split vote, the board decided the number of applications would increase without the religious tag. The move was successful. Enrollment doubled. With close to 5,000 undergraduates and 1,000 graduate students, the college now appears on many "best small private college" lists.

Julia looked up from Norm's notes. The stigma of the rapes and murders must have faded. She read on, making notes.

Founded in 1910 by Ted's great-grandfather, the first Theodore Baldwin, the college had only two majors at the time, religion and education. Like many colleges in the South, it only admitted men. That changed in 1950, when Theodore Baldwin the second took over the presidency of Blue Hill.

She took off her glasses and pushed her hair off her face. Ted must have grown up on campus, witnessed college life as a child. Julia frowned. Not for the first time, she hoped she hadn't already lost him as a source. She flipped through several pages of college enrollment statistics, census reports, and business articles.

Little Springs, like many other small towns, had suffered in the last two decades. Most of the agricultural businesses and paper plants had faded away over the years, victims of a struggling economy and increased competition. There were only two surviving industries in Little Springs: the college itself with its growing faculty, administration, and staff, and a small tourism business attracting hunters and fisherman. However, while the town might not have grown, it hadn't seen a decline, either. Julia took off her glasses. Ted had a right to be proud of the community.

She stood, stretching her arms over her head. Julia stepped over the files and flopped backward on the unmade bed. The college and the town shared their history, their triumphs, and their downfalls. Maybe it was an angle she could use. A knock on the door from housekeeping made her sit up again.

Waving the woman in, Julia said, "Let me get this out of your way." She knelt down and swept the files and pictures into her arms.

The woman carried fresh towels into the bathroom before returning to make the bed. Julia sat down in the guest chair, her arms still full.

"You're a reporter?" the woman asked.

Julia stiffened. "Yes."

The maid looked away. With deft hands, she tucked the sheets in at the corners and smoothed the flowery bedspread. She fluffed each pillow one at a time.

"Thank you," Julia said. "That looks nice."

The woman's face crinkled and her tired eyes brightened. "You're welcome." She stepped out into the hall and came back with a trash bag. She emptied the small cans in the room and bathroom. "Do you need anything else, ma'am?" she asked.

Julia shook her head.

At the door, the maid hesitated. "Will you be here long?"

Standing slowly, Julia set the files at her feet. "I'm not sure. A few more days at least. Why?"

"Gotten kinda quiet." The lady lifted her bony shoulders. "Most of the others checked out already. Guess they figure that's the end of the story."

The woman stood with one hand on the doorknob and the other in tucked in the pocket of her uniform. Her drab brown hair, streaked with gray, was pulled back into a hairnet. Julia cocked her head to one side. "How long have you worked here, at the hotel, I mean?"

"As long as I've been workin', I guess. Going on about forty-five years or so. Started right after high school."

"Wow. So, you've probably lived here your whole life?"

"Yes, ma'am." The maid's hand dropped from the doorknob. She leaned out toward the hall, looking in both directions. She stepped back into the room. "Long enough to know about Spradlin—and a whole lot more."

Julia's heartbeat quickened. First the interview and now this. "Do you have a few minutes?"

The lady checked the hall once more and closed the door behind her. "For a nice lady like you, I think I might."

Chapter Twenty-One

WALKING ALONG THE banks of the Thompson River, Cancini breathed in the thick odor of moss and the perfumed scent of wildflowers. Orange and red leaves mixed with green and hung like a canopy over his head. Rainbow trout darted in and out of the crystal-clear water. He knew the water would be cold despite the warm temperatures outside. Flowing down from the mountainside, it bubbled over the jagged rocks, rushing past him. Even after a successful fishing season, the river was still well stocked.

He stepped carefully on the stones in a low spot on the river and crossed over to the west trail, a well-used path that led to the lodge. He continued walking, keeping close to the water. When he got to the place, the spot where Cheryl Fornak's body had been found, he stopped. Crouching, he pushed some dirt aside, picking it up and letting it slip through his fingers. His breath caught in his throat. It had been the first body he'd ever seen in an investigation. He couldn't have known that day how she would change him, how Cheryl Fornak, dead and unable to speak, would alter the direction of his life.

Blue Hill College and the town of Little Springs had tried hard to forget the sordid events of the past. They had locked them away, focusing instead on the small and safe community they had carefully cultivated in the wake of the rapes and murders. Cancini knew what it had been like then, and he had a pretty good idea what it was like now. He, too, had done his best to forget and leave the unpleasant memories in the past, but with Spradlin's release, the memories had come flooding back.

Cheryl Fornak was his first homicide. Before the police had arrived, leaves covered half her body. One young officer had remarked it was almost a miracle the hunters had found her at all. Underneath the leaves, she'd been half naked, her shirt pushed up to her bra, her arms thrown out to her sides. The blue jean skirt she'd worn had been tossed aside, her underwear wrapped around one ankle. The girl's blond hair had appeared almost brown, covered with clumps of mud. Her flawless ivory complexion had been marred by cuts and scratches. One long leg had been bent back in an unnatural manner, bare, dirty, and bruised. Her eyes, the blue of a summer sky, had stared straight out, wide-eyed and big, even after she'd taken her last breath. Cancini recalled how one of the hunters, a man visiting from a small town in the southern part of the state, had described the body. "Like a deer in headlights," he'd said, "like she wanted to run and couldn't get away from a car that was speedin' toward her." His hands had trembled when he'd told the story, and he'd left to go home as soon as the police let him.

Cancini uncurled his body and stood, the memories receding. These woods and this trail offered peace and beauty during the daytime. The sun shone brightly through the thick trees. Sparkles danced across the flowing water, catching the light. Birds called out to one another from the high branches, the only sound for miles. You couldn't hear the rush of traffic from the highway or life from the campus or town. For many an outdoorsman, this place was a sanctuary, perfect for enjoying nature's beauty. But for one night, under a starless sky, a young woman's screams had echoed through the silent trees. For Cheryl Fornak, it had been a living hell.

Chapter Twenty-Two

JULIA WAITED ON the front steps of the library until the doors opened. Inside, she positioned herself at a table with a view of the front door, but not fully visible to anyone who might come in. The town hadn't been media friendly so far, and she already felt like a leper. A public meeting with Spradlin was not going to help. The mayor had been right. Every attempt she had made to interview a town resident—outside of the hotel maid—had been met with unfriendliness and even animosity. One man, looking at her as though she were an alien, responded, "Now why in the world would I want to talk to some danged reporter who wants to make me look like a hick who wouldn't know the law if it kicked him in the ass?" She'd tried softening her approach, expressing sympathy for the families of the victims, speaking about how their loss was fresh again. She was shamed when a woman shot back, "It's always fresh, young lady. If you want breaking news, report that."

Even so, the interview with Spradlin was an accomplishment. He hadn't granted many and was in the process of erecting a high fence around his property. She'd been told "Keep Out" signs were tacked to every tree that lined the dirt road leading up to the three-room house. Conroy had already interviewed Spradlin and left town. Most of the other reporters were in the process of leaving, too. The news had dried up with no one talking, especially Spradlin. With no one talking, there was no story.

Julia needed this interview, and she needed the mayor. He'd called twice, the first time apologizing for his abrupt departure the previous night, intimating she might get to talk to Cancini. She found this possibility not only surprising but also nerve-wracking. The detective's manner had already convinced her he would be difficult. Not her favorite kind of interview. Still, the idea intrigued her. When the mayor called a second time, his tone had been sheepish, almost apologetic.

"I don't want to seem forward," he'd said. "But I'd like to get to know you a little better, and since we both have to eat dinner . . ." There'd been no disguising the man's nervousness. "I haven't had dinner with a woman in quite some time." He'd laughed a bit. "I guess you could say I don't get out much, so I would consider it a treat if you could see your way to joining me."

She'd smiled at the old-fashioned language. It was charming, and so was he. But she didn't know if she was ready to date. Was she even officially separated? She'd touched her ring finger. It felt bare and naked, as though a part of her was missing. She'd expected to feel the indentation from her wedding band, but it was gone. Her skin was smooth and unmarked. Sighing, Julia had realized some separations were official long before sleeping in separate beds, long before the rings were placed in the back of the drawer, and long before lawyers and judges gave speeches and rulings. Besides, wearing a ring—being married—had never stopped Jack. She'd closed her left hand. The mayor was an attractive, kind man. She would be divorced—eventually—and she wasn't dead. She'd accepted.

Julia's thoughts returned to the interview at hand. The library, Spradlin's chosen place, was far less modern than the libraries in D.C. Old steel lights hung from the ceiling, and an antiquated card file stood behind the desktop computers near the wall. Most of the tables and chairs looked exactly like the furniture in the small library of her youth. She'd spent hours in her town library, content with stacks of books in front of her until the six o'clock closing, when she'd walk home to wait for her father to return from work. She still loved the comforting, musty scent of old books.

A tall, slender librarian with dark blond hair moved stacks of books from one counter to another. Her hair was pinned back into a tight chignon, and she wore a floral dress and light sweater in spite of the heat outside. From the librarian's position behind the long desk, she would see Spradlin. Would she be like the others? Unfriendly, bordering on hostile? Julia realized that other than the librarian, she was the only person in the place. It was as close to private as they were likely to get. Maybe Spradlin knew what he was doing after all.

Julia placed her notebook, pencils, and tape recorder on the table. She looked at her watch and her stomach fluttered. Nine-fifteen. He was late. At nine-seventeen, Spradlin walked in, slipping through the front door carrying a small package under his arm. He was taller and leaner than he'd appeared at the press conference. His dark hair was brushed off his face, and salt and pepper stubble had erupted across his cheeks and chin. He wore a polo-style shirt and a pair of khaki pants. It was a far cry from the prison-issued jumpsuit he'd worn for years. He cast an eye over the old tables and dusty bookshelves, the librarian, Julia, and then the librarian again. She watched as he strode toward the front desk. The librarian's face had gone white. Her slender hand rose to her lips, her eyes wide.

Spradlin's back was to Julia. She angled her chair, trying to get a better view, but couldn't see his face. The woman seemed to be listening to Spradlin. Her color returned, and she fingered the pearls around her neck. She nodded a few times but said nothing. Eventually, Spradlin spun around, pointing in Julia's direction. The librarian nodded again. He reached out and touched the woman's shoulder. Julia inhaled. The librarian bowed her head, but not before the reporter saw tears. Spradlin's hand rose to the woman's cheek, and he brushed away a teardrop. He dropped his hand, took a step back, and came toward Julia. He stood, looking down at her, the package still tucked under his arm.

"Julia Manning, I presume?"

"Good to meet you," she said, straightening in the chair. She held out her hand. His was cool and firm. "A friend of yours?" she asked, with a nod in the librarian's direction.

"Yes," he said, without looking back at the woman behind the counter. His eyes, ice-blue and rimmed by dark lashes, were deep-set in his chiseled face. She detected a hint of amusement, not the sadness or anger she would have expected from a man worn down by prison, the victim of a miscarriage of justice. He leaned forward, picking up her tape recorder. "You won't need this," he said, placing it back on the table.

"Oka-ay. I don't have to use it. I don't want you to be uncomfortable, Mr. Spradlin."

"You can call me Leo," he said, smiling. His eyes crinkled at the corners. "And it doesn't make me uncomfortable. I don't get uncomfortable."

"Okay." She waved her hand toward the recorder. "I'll be honest, though. I'm terrible at shorthand. That's why I use the recorder."

"You won't need it."

"Fine. But I'll warn you, you'll have to be patient with me."

"I'm used to being patient." His gaze never left hers. "I've had more practice than most."

"Oh." She gripped her pen, unable to stop staring at the man. "Right. I'm sorry."

"Don't be sorry, Julia." He said her name slowly, his husky voice elongating the syllables. "You had nothing to do with it."

Warmth spread from her chest to her neck. She tried to fight it, flipping to a blank page in her notebook, hoping the flush would pass unnoticed. She waved a hand at the empty chair. "Do you want to sit?"

"No."

She bent her head, focusing on the blank page. It was awkward with him standing and her sitting, but it couldn't be helped. Her questions waited on the tip of her tongue, bursting to be asked. Was he resentful? Was he angry? Did he want restitution? Would he sue? They were all good questions—the kind Conroy would ask—but the ones she was most eager to ask ran deeper. What was he like as a child? How was high school? How hard was it to grow up without a father? What dreams did he have? Why did he think he was a suspect? How had this experience affected his mother? How horrible had it been all those years in jail? How had that time changed him as a person? What would he do now?

This could be her only shot. He'd endured enough, hadn't he? Still, he was to be admired, not pitied. She blinked and raised her eyes to his. "First, let me say how much I appreciate you talking to me. I know it was a short list of journalists, and I'm honored to be among them."

His expression didn't change. "Okay."

"Second, I want you to know that I hope to do more than rehash the old case and the trial. I'd like to write a story that lets people get to know you. I already have most of the facts regarding your background. I would like to learn more about you, as a child, about your teenage years, your hopes, your dreams . . ." Her voice trailed off, her gaze touching briefly on the librarian. The woman pulled the sweater tightly across her chest before disappearing behind a door. Julia licked her lips, her mouth suddenly dry. "I can either ask you questions, or you can start wherever you'd like and tell me about yourself." She put her pen to the page, poised to write. "How does that sound?"

A few seconds passed. "Boring as hell."

Her chin shot up. "I'm sure it's not—"

"Yes it is. Boring as hell." He shifted his weight, moving the package under the other arm. "Look, I don't like talking about myself—never have. Probably why I had a little trouble in the legal department. They want you to talk and I'm not real big on answering questions."

Pursing her lips, Julia put down her pen.

"You're angry," he said, his eyes crinkling again.

"No. Well, yes."

To her complete amazement, he burst out laughing, the sound echoing across the empty library. She glanced quickly toward the front desk, but the librarian was still out of sight. "I admire your spirit," he said when the laughter died in his throat. "I should apologize. I don't mean to be rude. My social skills aren't all that great. Actually, they never were. I can see I've confused you."

"Maybe." It wouldn't do to scare him away. She thought of where he'd been and what he'd had to suffer. She needed to be patient and make it work. "I don't know if I can avoid all questions, but we can freeform it if that sounds better to you. Would that be okay?"

"Are you close to your mother, Julia?"

Her face paled. The old anger bubbled up, and she pushed it down, same as always. It shouldn't matter anymore. The past was dead and buried. After counting to ten, silently, until her pulse slowed, she said, "My mother left when I was five. I haven't seen her since the day she walked out on my dad and me." She kept her tone neutral. "So, you could say I'm not exactly close to my mother. But your relationship sounds different. I heard your speech the other day."

"I know." His eyes followed the movements of the librarian as she returned to the front desk.

Julia cleared her throat. "Uh, it sounded like you and your mother were close."

Leo took the package from under his arm and set it on the table. "This is one of my mother's diaries," he said. "She kept a daily journal her whole life." He pushed the package in her direction. "Go ahead. Open it."

Julia untied the string and carefully pulled off the brown paper. She slid out the book. It was thick with a black leather cover, worn and faded, held together by a large rubber band. A scrap of notebook paper was under the rubber band. She pulled it out, holding it between her fingers. It was blank except for a phone number.

"My cell," he said, looking down at her. "Call me when you've read it." Without another word, he walked out of the library.

Chapter Twenty-Three

"How's my father?" Cancini asked, holding the cell phone close to his ear. A waitress brought him a cup of plain, black coffee. No latte. No cream. No fancy name. The darker it was, the better. He'd long ago traded in a nicotine addiction for caffeine. He took a long, satisfying gulp. "How's he feeling?"

"He's doing well," Father Joe said. "As well as can be expected anyway. He's getting stronger every day."

Cancini closed his eyes and whispered, "Thank God."

"Yes, I agree. Thank God."

"Of course, you heard that."

The old priest chuckled. "Bionic ears with this hearing aid, young man. I might even hear a prayer if you decide to say one."

"Don't get carried away," Cancini said, smiling. Father Joe was the closest thing he had to family outside of his dad, his voice a comfort.

"Michael, the nurses tell me you saved your father's life. If you hadn't brought him in when you did . . ."

"It wasn't that hard to figure out, Father. He was practically coughing up his lungs. Anyone would have done what I did."

"Even so, he's a lucky man," the priest said. "The nurses also told me you'd been spending a lot of hours with him before you left town. They're impressed with your devotion to your father." He cleared his throat. "As am I."

Cancini sipped his coffee, his brows furrowed. "We both know what kind of dad he's been and what kind of son I've been. The nurses might be fooled, but you and I know better."

"Maybe I do, Michael, and maybe I don't."

"Water under the bridge, Father."

"If you say so. How are things in Little Springs?"

Cancini glanced around the diner. The waitresses now wore white polo shirts and pants instead of skirts with aprons. A gluten-free special and a vegan dessert graced the menu. The outside had been painted, but, other than that, nothing much had changed. "The same," he said. "Downtown's been spruced up a little and a few new stores opened, but otherwise, it's still a small town—if you know what I mean."

"I do. How are you, Michael?" the priest asked. "I worry about you. I don't know if it's a good idea you being there right now."

"I'm fine, Father. You shouldn't worry."

"Right. Have you seen Spradlin?"

"Only from a distance."

"Maybe you should keep it that way."

"Maybe. Look, Father, do you think you could go by and check on my dad again tomorrow?"

"Of course. I plan to go every day until you get home, but don't think I don't know when you're trying to change the subject." Strains of organ music played behind the priest's voice. "When do you think you might be home?"

His captain and his partner had asked the same question. He hadn't had an answer for them, either. "I don't know. It depends . . ."

"I see." The priest spoke slowly, his voice soft and low. "Michael, I'm concerned about your well-being. I don't like you being there."

"I'm fine."

"You're not fine. You're getting involved. I have this feeling, one I can't explain . . ." Anxiety shook the old man's voice.

Cancini drank from the steaming cup. "You're making too much of it."

"And you're making too little. You don't always have to be alone." Seconds ticked by in silence and then, "I'm not going to apologize for saying that, Michael."

"Okay."

"Yes, it is okay. Whether you realize it or not, you and your father are more alike than you may think. His inability to deal with your mother's murder was difficult for you." Cancini's shoulders slumped, and he held the phone close. "I know you think he forgot about you, abandoned you, and you had every right to feel that way, but you made choices, too. You shut the world out."

"I was a kid."

"You weren't a kid when you left the church." Cancini flinched. He was eighteen then and unable to reconcile Father Joe's God with the God that allowed his mother to be shot and murdered in a convenience store robbery. "That's not a judgment, Michael."

Cancini bowed his head. The priest had given him solace in the wake of the murder. He'd worked afternoons in the church office, spent Sundays as an altar boy. But none of it had erased the loss of his mother. Almost twenty-five years later, Cancini still had not attended another Mass, but he visited the old priest on a regular basis; their friendship was one of the best things in his life. "I'm sorry, Father."

"I care about you, Michael. Being back there . . . I know what it was like for you. I remember."

"I'm not a kid anymore."

Father Joe spoke again, his tone more insistent. "Maybe not, Michael, but what's done is done. You can't change the past. Maybe you should come home."

Cancini swallowed the lump in his throat. Of course, the priest was right. He couldn't bring those girls back to life or undo his arrest of Spradlin. He couldn't change what happened at the trial or erase the years Spradlin had spent in prison. He couldn't take back the years of peace Little Springs had enjoyed while Spradlin was gone. But if he could do it all over again, if he could change the past, would he?

Chapter Twenty-Four

Dear Diary,

This is the first page of a new book. Can you guess why? It's because today is a special day—a very special day. Today is my first day of college! I'm finally on my own! Dad is spitting mad, but nothing he says is going to make me quit. I'm eighteen, and as long as I can pay, I'm going to college. Thank God Mom encouraged me to take that job at the bookstore last year and work all summer. With my partial academic scholarship, I can swing it. I think Mom was secretly trying to help me so my life wouldn't end up like hers. She told Dad she was trying to teach me responsibility. That's one of his big words. He throws it around as though he knows anything about it. Ha! The only responsibility I've ever seen him keep up with is to drink a fifth of bourbon every night. The only reason he has a job is because of Uncle Jed. I guess I should be grateful. At least he's not mean like Sara Townshend's dad. Everyone knows he hits Mrs. Townshend, but they're too afraid to say any-

thing. They say he keeps a gun under his shirt all the time. I don't know if that's true, but I guess no one wants to find out. Poor Sara. I guess in a small way, I'm the lucky one. Just doesn't feel like it sometimes.

But now I am lucky. I'm in college!!!! My dad thinks it's a waste of time. I'm a girl, he says, and my job is having babies. Then he says something like, "I sure don't see any boys around here, though. Guess you're too stuck-up to attract any." Doesn't matter. I'm here. Not everyone can say they're starting over, but I can. Today is the beginning of the rest of my life.

Julia put down the book, blinking in the bright sunlight. College students streamed past, strolling from class or to their dorm or maybe an early dinner. Some walked in pairs or groups and others alone amid the stately "bluestone" buildings. Old trees and fall flowers dotted rolling lawns. Fragrant pine filled the air. Laughter trilled from a group of students on the lawn. She watched their faces, envied their youthful expectancy, joy, and innocence.

Brenda Spradlin had once been one of these kids, her head full of hopes and dreams. Somehow, Julia didn't think Brenda's life had turned out quite as she expected. The woman who'd written these words had wanted to escape a difficult home life, an alcoholic father, and a future that promised little. She'd worked and studied and made her way to college on her own. The blue ink on the diary's pages might have faded, but the emotions were vivid and real. How did this bright and beautiful young woman end up alone? How did she come to be a cleaning lady at the same college that had once awarded her an academic scholarship? How had she felt when her son was accused and convicted of unspeakable crimes?

Chapter Twenty-Five

THREE MILES IN, only three to go. Geri Hallwell breathed easy, her stride strong. This was her favorite part of the run. She didn't know if she believed in a runner's high, but she did know running was like a drug for her. She ran every day, no matter the weather. Her sorority sisters called her the postal runner. Sweat dripped from her brow and between her breasts. She picked up the pace, her lips moving with the words to a song by Pink, thumping with guitars and drums.

She turned the corner and slowed her pace. Construction had started on the newest Blue Hill academic building. Trailers and equipment filled the adjacent parking lot. She groaned, knowing she would have to pay more attention or change up her route. Trotting in place, she looked behind her, then started forward again. She would stay the course.

As she ran, she appraised the latest expansion project. The new building would be huge. Typical. The sciences always got the best buildings at Blue Hill. Her roommate even told her the school was already lining up high-profile speakers and guest professors for the grand opening. Not that it mattered to her. She would be long gone by the time it was finished. Besides, she was a theater major and would probably never step foot inside. At the moment, it was another big, fat annoyance.

The paved road ended as she approached the site. A light wind swirled, and she breathed the dust of the makeshift road. The site was quiet, the workers already gone for the day. Orange and pink ribbons adorned the early evening sky. She checked her watch. It was later than she thought. If she was going to make it to the sorority house before dark, she would have to pick up the pace. With a flick of her fingers, she changed the playlist and turned up the volume.

The sidewalk and pavement resumed a few hundred yards ahead. Turning in that direction, she noticed the new wooden fence on her right. "Keep Out" and "Construction Only" signs were tacked randomly along the pickets. The song changed and her arms moved in time with the beat and her stride lengthened. She gasped when a man stepped through an opening in the fence, almost knocking her to the ground. She managed not to fall and realized he had caught her, keeping her upright with his arms wrapped around her waist. She pulled her head back to thank him when his arms tightened, pulling her off the ground.

"What are you doing?" she cried out, her arms flailing, punching him. He carried her behind the fence to the deserted construction site, his breathing heavy with the effort. When he reached the wooded area at the edge of the campus, he threw her to the ground, dropping on all fours. Wide-eyed, she screamed, but he stuffed a handkerchief into her mouth. Bathed in sweat, she strained to push him away, to get him off, but he was too strong. He lay flat on her, pinning her arms to the ground, both of them gasping for air. She kicked her legs, but under his weight, it was futile.

"Be still," the man hissed.

When his lips caressed her neck, she bucked, pushing up with all her strength. It was enough, and he let go of one hand. He tried to regain control, reaching for her. She kneed him, hoping she had done some damage, any damage. She scrambled to her feet, pulling the handkerchief from her mouth and throwing it to the ground. She stepped over him, back in the direction of campus, but after only two steps, his hand closed around her ankle and yanked her to the ground. Her body hit with a thud. A bone cracked, and her screams echoed through the empty site.

On the ground, she curled into the fetal position, pulling her broken arm in close. He bent down, tying her hands together with a rope. "Don't fucking scream again," he said. "No one can hear you anyway." Finished with her hands, he tied a single leg to the trunk of a small tree.

Wincing, with tears streaming down her cheeks, she looked into the face of her attacker. In the fading sunlight she recognized the man from somewhere—but where? Then she remembered. But this man couldn't be that man. It didn't make sense. His eyes were wild and his hair flopped down over his brows. Her mind spinning, she thought maybe she was wrong.

He caressed her hair, brushing it off her face. Geri pulled her free leg in tighter, whimpering. He pressed against her, pushing her legs farther apart, using his weight. His hot breath burned her face. He pressed into her, his hands moving from her hair to her breasts and then to her running shorts. He wrapped one hand around the waistband and ripped the nylon shorts from her body in one swift motion. She started to cry.

After, he lay still, the weight of his body making it difficult for her to breathe. Her head lolled to the side, and she stared into the dark forest. Her raw skin stung with abrasions and cuts. Her arm throbbed, her body ached, and her mind was numb. Geri squeezed her eyes shut, willing him off, wanting him gone.

A voice, then another, floated across the empty site, too far away to decipher. Her eyes snapped open as he clamped his hand over her mouth. She waited. There it was again. Closer. She heard snatches of words, no clear meaning. Someone was near. Near enough to hear her if she could get him off. She began thrashing, forgetting the pain in her arm. His hand jerked away just as she was about to clamp her teeth on the flesh of his palm. The voices came again, closer still. It had to be now. She opened her mouth to scream, but the sound died in her throat. She never saw the man pick up the rock and never saw him swing it at her skull. She only felt the blinding pain and the loss of hope in the final seconds before consciousness slipped away.

Chapter Twenty-Six

CANCINI PICKED UP his beer and drained it. Throwing a few dollars on the bar, he stood, following the couple as they left the dining room. Baldwin's hand rested on the small of her back, his touch light. Trailing a few steps behind, Cancini took a position near the desk phones in the lobby, careful to stay within earshot.

The reporter faced the mayor, leaning in to give him a brief hug. "Thanks for dinner, Ted. I had a nice time."

The mayor smiled broadly. "I hope that means you'd be willing to do it again tomorrow night."

"Wow." She looked down at the floor and shifted her weight from one foot to the other.

"Too pushy?"

"Maybe a little."

"I'm sorry. Really," he said, his words rushed. "I understand about your situation and I appreciate you telling me. I do." She smiled weakly but said nothing. "How about if we have dinner strictly as friends? I won't pretend I wouldn't like it to be more at some point, but for now, I think we could both use a friend.

You don't know many people in town, and hell, I know too many."

She laughed. "Well . . ."

"Come on, I promise. Just friends."

"Okay," she said. "Why don't you call me tomorrow?"

Baldwin bowed his head. "Perfect." He backed away with a little wave. "See you tomorrow."

Cancini watched the mayor leave, then intercepted the reporter as she moved toward the elevators. "Can I buy you a drink?"

"Wh-what?" She spun around.

He held out his hand. "Detective Cancini."

"Right." She nodded, taking his hand. "We met the other night."

Squinting, he studied her face. A sprinkling of freckles dotted her nose, and auburn hair complemented wide-set blue eyes. She wore a fitted black dress, light makeup, and glittery, silver hoops. She was barely over five feet, but something in her manner, the way she held her body, told him she was stronger than she appeared. He couldn't guess her age, only that she was younger than he. Pretty in a girl-next-door way, she wouldn't stop traffic or quiet a room by walking in the way his ex-wife did, but he liked her open expression, her direct manner. He dropped her hand.

One hand sat on her hip. "I got the distinct impression you had no interest in talking to me the other night, Detective. To be perfectly blunt, you weren't exactly polite." He said nothing, waiting. "So, what's changed?"

He gestured toward the hotel bar. "How about that drink, and I'll tell you?"

Cancini watched her consider the invitation. It was clear she didn't particularly like him, but he hadn't expected otherwise. "I was thinking of turning in for the evening," she said slowly. "Is this because Mayor Baldwin asked you to talk to me?"

"No." Baldwin hadn't wasted any time cozying up to the reporter.

"Are you willing to answer questions about your role in the investigation?"

He stiffened. "No."

Her hand dropped from her hip. "Then why should I have a drink with you?"

He was surprised by her curiosity, her stubbornness. She needed a reason and he gave it to her. "Spradlin."

Julia inhaled sharply and looked away. He waited, knowing it would be impossible for her to decline now, no matter how much she might not want to sit with him. "Okay," she said.

The reporter followed him back to the bar, where he took the darkest, most secluded booth. She slid opposite him, setting her bag on the table. The waitress appeared, and the reporter ordered a scotch on the rocks.

Cancini raised an eyebrow, then nodded at the server. "Make that two."

They sat in silence until their drinks came. "Okay," she said. "What is it you have to say about Spradlin? I know you were the original detective on the case. I've read the police and newspaper reports." She seemed to consider her words. "I know Spradlin's release can't be easy for you."

"A jury convicted him, Ms. Manning." His long fingers tightened around the glass, but he kept his expression benign.

"They convicted him on the evidence you provided."

"Yes, those seem to be the facts."

"I also know about your reputation in D.C. You've closed more cases that anyone else in the division, but you're not management material. You've had multiple partners. I won't speculate on the reasons. You were married, briefly. Your ex is now married to your captain. You spend a lot of time alone."

He sat back. He hadn't misjudged her. She hadn't wasted any time. "Learned all of that, did you? Your date was your source?"

She picked up her drink and took a slow sip. "It wasn't a date, not that it's any of your business. I do have my own sources, you know."

He shrugged. "If you say so. What would your husband say?"

Her face flushed pink. "That is also none of your business, Detective."

"Have it your way," he said. "If you want to play that game, this is what I know. You were once a sought-after young writer. The *Washington Herald* stole you away from the *Post*. Not long after you moved, you married the boss, and you've written less and less." She bent her head and looked into her drink. "The last couple of years, it's been personality stories and stuff like that. I also know you're separated. Your husband has a certain reputation." He cleared his throat. "I also know Baldwin has a crush on you. Maybe it wasn't a date to you, but it was to him."

"Back to Ted?" Julia's color returned to normal and she stiffened. "This is a waste of time. I thought you brought me here to talk about Spradlin, not Ted Baldwin. Believe it or not, I don't like games." She picked up her bag to slide out of the booth.

"How long did you meet with Spradlin today? In the library?"

She froze. "How did you know about that? The only person who knew was my editor."

He shrugged again. "I have sources, too."

"Good God." She gaped at him. "Are you following me?"

"No."

"You followed Leo?"

"On a first-name basis, are we?"

Julia's eyes flashed. "Did you follow him?"

"No."

She leaned back against the cushioned booth, letting out her breath, and laid her purse back on the table. "Okay. I give up. Do you want to tell me how you knew?"

"No. It doesn't matter. Will you be meeting with him again?"

She folded her hands together. "I'm surprised you're not asking me what we talked about."

"If I were to ask, would you tell me what he said to you?"

"No."

"Right. So, I won't waste your time or mine. Do you plan to meet with him again?"

She frowned. "Why do you want to know?"

"I want you to be careful. You don't know who you're dealing with."

"And you do?" she shot back. "If you know him so well, why did you put him away for crimes he didn't commit?"

"The evidence pointed to him."

"The evidence was wrong."

"I've heard that before."

She toyed with her drink. Pinched lines punctuated her mouth and new frown lines stretched across her forehead. Maybe talking to her wasn't a good idea, but a lot of things he did weren't a good idea—like his marriage. He didn't like reporters on principle, but this was different. When she met with Spradlin, she put herself in a situation she didn't understand. She was strong but not tough. Behind the outward confidence, the persistence, lay something fragile. Maybe it was her separation. Maybe it was something else.

He cleared his throat and spoke. His voice was flat, but his eyes burned with suspicion. "Everything I say is off the record. You cannot use it."

She nodded.

"Although the evidence says Leo Spradlin is an innocent man, you—"

"Although?" she interrupted.

"He's not all he seems. Spradlin's a complicated man. No one who has ever known him would say he was an innocent. He wasn't then, and I'm sure he isn't now."

Julia's brows drew together. "If you're saying he was wild or got into some trouble as a teen, so what? Lots of people go through rebellious stages and grow out of it. Leo Spradlin didn't get that chance."

Cancini leaned in, his tone grave. "Spradlin wasn't rebellious. He didn't have to be. He did what he wanted and got what he wanted."

"That sounds like jealousy, Detective."

"Call it what you want. The man I knew didn't have a conscience. He didn't treat people right. In more conventional terms, you would say he was a taker. There was never any emotion from him—even when he was arrested and then convicted. As though he didn't care one bit about any of it. The girls or being arrested. Nothing."

"No. That doesn't sound like the man I met today, Detective."

"It probably doesn't. Spradlin can say anything he wants because he doesn't care about the truth or what's right. He says and does what he needs to, and that includes lying in that speech he gave the other day."

"At the press conference? What lies?"

"Why don't you ask Spradlin?"

Julia shook her head. "Maybe he was like that once. He was in prison a long time. Maybe he's changed."

"He hasn't."

Julia flopped back against the chair, her expression doubtful.

"If you don't believe me, ask yourself why the people of this town, the people who've known him since he was a child, weren't shocked by his arrest. Ask yourself why he doesn't have a friend left. Then ask yourself why no one wants him back here even though he's an innocent man."

"I already know why they turned on him. It was fear, plain and simple," she said. "They wanted someone arrested. They wanted the rapes and murders to stop. He was the scapegoat."

"Okay. Let's say that's partly true. How about now? He's innocent, right? So, there's nothing to be afraid of, and still, no one wants him here. So, if fear isn't the reason no one wants him here, what is?"

Julia blinked. "I don't know."

"Maybe you should take the time to find out."

She spread her small hands across the table. "Don't you think I've tried? Most people won't talk to me."

"That's not my problem." He glanced toward the bar. Both the waitress and bartender looked away. He gulped the last of his scotch. "Look, I can only warn you to be careful. If you meet with him again, I'll probably know about it, but knowing might not be enough."

"If I didn't know any better, Detective, I'd say you were worried he's dangerous."

He stood, reached into his pocket, and pulled out a card. Sliding it across the table, he said, "My cell phone number is on the bottom. Think about what I said. Think about what the people here are telling you. Think about what made Spradlin a suspect in the first place. Keep your eyes and ears open." He touched her gently on the shoulder. "Sometimes, people aren't what they seem."

Chapter Twenty-Seven

Julia pulled off her glasses and rubbed her eyes. She was tired and it was late, but it was more than that. Why had Detective Cancini felt the need to warn her about a man who'd spent years in jail for crimes he didn't commit? Her head fell back against her pillow and her hands dropped into her lap. He was undoubtedly just a crank and bitter about a case gone wrong. It was all probably some kind of psychobabble scare tactic, and yet he'd seemed dead serious. Shaking her head, she replaced her glasses and sat forward again.

The diary lay open in her lap. She considered putting it aside and getting some sleep, but she was a night owl at heart. Sleep could wait. Brenda Spradlin had written in great detail about life as a college student, yet most of the entries were remarkably similar. Class descriptions. Tests and papers. Praise for her professors. Her social life was virtually nonexistent. The scholarship was an obsession. Terrified of losing it, young Brenda spent most of her free time studying. If she felt as though she were missing out, she never mentioned it. The monotonous entries covered weeks and then months. Julia grew bored. Why had Spradlin given her this? Adjusting the pillows behind her head, she turned the pages quickly, skimming over the remaining repetitive descriptions of the girl's life.

Three classes today. Psychology was really interesting. After class, I approached Professor Bauer about the student assistant opening she had in her office. She said she normally didn't take freshman, but my work was so good she would consider it. Hooray!

Julia yawned. The entry dates were farther and farther apart.

Professor Bauer is letting me work in her office five hours a week, but, for some reason, she doesn't seem happy about it. I don't understand.

Then a few days later.

Professor Bauer left Blue Hill. Dr. Baldwin came to our class today and gave us the news. He said he would be taking over temporarily until a replacement could be found. After class, he asked me to stay on as the student assistant.

Julia traced her fingers over the name, Dr. Baldwin. She had studied up on her history of the college. He was Ted's father and the grandson of the original founder of Blue Hill College. He'd gotten his doctorate in psychology and was the head of the department. Eventually, he would take over as president, a position he would keep until he passed away.

The diary slipped from her knees to her lap, and she leaned back into the thick pillows. She'd told Cancini the truth. Most folks were reluctant to talk to her, suspicious of her motives. Only the maid had been eager to talk—or gossip, if she were more accurate—and Dr. Baldwin, long dead, was an easy target. It made no sense. Credited with building the college's reputation and expanding its student population, Dr. Baldwin had been admired in the academic world. What was it about powerful people that prompted wild stories of debauchery? Spradlin hadn't been spared, either. "Scum of the earth," the maid had said. Norm had loved that one.

With her fingers, she counted the remaining pages. Almost finished. She rolled onto her side and read.

I met a nice boy yesterday in the cafeteria. He told me his name was William Spradlin. Seems nice. He asked me out, but I said no. I'm afraid I hurt his feelings. At first I was afraid he would think I was stuck up like all the rest of the boys do, but he didn't. He said he understood. It's not that I wouldn't like to meet more people, but Dr. Baldwin has increased my hours. Between that and my classes and exams coming up, I just can't.

Julia looked at the date. It was early December when young Brenda had met Leo's father. Clearly, the young girl had eventually found the time. Julia flipped the page.

Exams weren't as bad as I expected. Dr. Baldwin asked me to work on some of his papers and assist him with some research over the break. I was looking forward to some time off, even though it meant going home. But I could use the extra money. I know I should be grateful, but I don't like it when Dr. Baldwin brings up my scholarship. He does it a lot.

Julia set down the book. The girl sounded tired of both the work and her boss. The next entry came two weeks later.

Thank goodness William stayed over the break, too. I don't know what I would have done without him. It's so quiet here without the other students. And so cold! He brought me chicken soup today and held my hand. No one has ever done that before. I didn't know boys could be this nice.

Julia smiled and turned the page. The next entry came after classes had resumed.

The new psychology professor started today. He's old and made it very clear he did not need my help. I don't think he likes me. I'm not sure I like myself.

The next entry was dated a week later.

Stayed up until two last night writing my term paper for freshman English. So tired today and feeling sick. I couldn't eat anything. Also, my roommate asked me if I could ask William to stop coming over so much. I know I should, but he's so nice to me. I don't deserve it.

She looked up from the page. Brenda's self-esteem had slipped to a low level. The only bright spot in her life seemed to be the boy.

I let William kiss me last night. This morning when I woke up, I kept touching my lips with my fingers. We kissed and kissed. They felt swollen, but I liked it. I didn't know I would. I didn't know I could like it. I wonder what he thinks about me now.

Flipping the page, Julia stifled another yawn. Brenda didn't write anything for another four weeks, but when she did, it was brief and to the point.

I'm pregnant.

Julia sat up. She turned the page but there was nothing, the rest of the diary blank.

Chapter Twenty-Eight

CANCINI PRETENDED NOT to see Baldwin. It wasn't hard as long as he kept his nose buried in a newspaper and his coffee cup filled. Baldwin glad-handed his way around the diner, slapping backs and guffawing over twenty-year-old jokes. The detective hoped he could finish his coffee and sneak out before Baldwin saw him. His luck ran out. The mayor plopped into the seat opposite him.

"Cancini, I've been looking for you," he said. Cancini decided the less he said, the sooner Baldwin would leave. "They told me at the hotel I'd find you here." Cancini set his newspaper on the table. "Kinda like old times, I guess." Baldwin's voice faded. He grabbed a napkin and mopped beads of sweat from his wide forehead.

"Why were you looking for me, Teddy?" Cancini's brooding eyes held Baldwin's pale ones.

"I don't want you to overreact," he said. "I wasn't even going to tell you. But I know you. You'll find out anyway and then make an even bigger deal out of something that's most likely nothing."

The detective's shoulders tensed. Pushing his cup and saucer away, he placed both hands on the table. "Spit it out, Teddy."

"It's not official yet . . ." The mayor looked up, his expression pleading. "I pray, I hope this is nothing. God knows there's no one who wants Spradlin's threats to mean nothing more than me. The thing is, it's probably just typical college behavior. I'm sure that's all it is, so please don't jump to conclusions."

With his teeth clenched, Cancini's words sounded clipped. "Jump to conclusions about what, Teddy?"

Baldwin's eyes wandered around the diner. It was packed with regulars, townsfolk who grabbing breakfast or coffee. His fingers twisted a napkin as he spoke. Cancini leaned forward to hear. "Campus security called this morning. Seems some girl didn't make it back to her sorority house last night." Cancini's hands tightened to fists, but he remained quiet. "The roommate said the girl went out for a run and didn't come back. She didn't think much of it though, because the girl has an on-and-off boyfriend and sometimes sleeps there." The mayor stopped speaking when the waitress appeared with a steaming pot of coffee. The two men sat in silence while she poured. When she left, they continued.

"So why did she contact security?" asked Cancini.

"The roommate has a morning class and ran into the boyfriend on campus. He said he hadn't seen the girl all week and had no idea where she was. The roommate also said the girl wasn't responding to texts or answering her phone." The mayor grabbed a sugar packet, dumping it into the steaming coffee. "But it's barely been over twelve hours. There's nothing official. Nothing. I'm letting you know as a courtesy. The roommate admitted the girl could have met another guy and stayed with him. You know how college kids are these days."

Cancini frowned. He didn't know. Still, he couldn't disagree with the possibility that the girl might have spent the night elsewhere. On the other hand, he did know young people and their phones. They never went anywhere without them. "What time is her first class today?"

"Not until eleven."

"Okay. I want to meet with the head of campus security. I want to be outside that classroom to see if she shows up."

The mayor shook his head. "You see? This is exactly why I didn't want to tell you."

"Teddy, if the girl shows up, then what's the harm? I go home happy. We're all happy."

"Damn you, Mike. That's not what'll happen, and you know it. She could be off with some new boyfriend. Her cell phone battery could be dead. She may not be aware everyone is looking for her."

"I hope you're right."

"No you don't. You want this to be something. You want word to spread that a Blue Hill girl is missing, and a D.C. detective is nosing around campus. Folks around here are already anxious. They hear that, and the next thing you know, a mob will go running over to Spradlin's property and string him up in a tree. Then the girl will show up, and all the panic will have been for nothing."

Cancini slid out of the booth and bent toward the mayor. He kept his voice pitched low. "You're wrong, Teddy. I don't want this to be anything. I hope to God it's nothing. But I'm not gonna sit on my hands waiting to find out. It could be the minute that makes a difference in whether she's found alive. If you're worried about Spradlin, put someone on him. If she doesn't show up today, tomorrow, or the next day, then an anxious mob is going to be the least of your problems." Baldwin started to open his mouth, then shut it again. "Call campus security and tell them to expect me in fifteen minutes."

Chapter Twenty-Nine

THE LIBRARIAN LEANED over the front desk, whispering to Spradlin. His face was in profile, her lips near his ear. When she caught sight of Julia watching, she stepped back quickly, her face pink. She grabbed a square of paper, wrote a note, and handed it to the man. He shoved it in his pocket. In a grand gesture, he stepped back, bowing at the waist. He took the woman's hand, kissing it softly. Sucking in her breath, Julia averted her eyes.

A moment later, he stood before Julia, carrying another package under his arm. He pulled out the chair opposite her, sat, and pushed the package toward her.

"Hello, Julia," he said.

"I read the diary. I'm not entirely sure what you expect. Why did you give it to me?"

He leaned back in the chair, rubbing his face, the stubble on its way to becoming a thick beard. He smelled of cigarette smoke and cinnamon gum. "I wanted you to get to know my mother. What did you think of her?"

Julia shook her head. "I'm not sure I'm in a position to think anything. I read a diary that represents one part of her life. I don't know what she was like before or after that period of time."

"Fair enough," he said. "But what kind of person do you think she was at the time she wrote the diary?"

Julia considered his question. What if he didn't like what she told him? Would he leave her without the interview?

"Tell me the truth," he said.

"To be perfectly honest, I thought your mother was sort of lonely. She seemed unhappy at home, and she didn't have many friends at college."

"True." He opened the new package, pulling out a second diary. He pushed it across the table.

"She did have your father, though." She thought his shoulders sank lower in the chair. Her voice was soft. "She commented several times about how nice he was to her."

Spradlin sat up straighter then, leaning back against the wooden chair. "I wouldn't know." He reached across the table and took the first diary. His eyes met Julia's for a moment, then ran over her face and hair. In a voice that caressed, he said, "She would have liked you. I knew you would be the right one to read her diaries."

Stunned, Julia said nothing. He nodded at the book on the table. "I'd like you to take a look at this one tonight. I'll meet you here again tomorrow."

As he started to walk away, she found her voice. "Wait. I wanted to ask you some questions."

He grinned. "Yes. Those pesky questions."

"I am a journalist, you know. It's what I do," she said with a smile. "That's how stories get written."

"Right." He stepped back toward the table but remained standing. "Tell you what, I can do one for today. Tomorrow, maybe more."

"Great," she said, her heart pounding. To steady her nerves, she reached for her pen and notebook. Flipping the pages, she found the list of questions she'd scratched out the night before. None of what she'd written was what she wanted to ask now.

Julia bit her lip and peeked at the librarian. The woman pretended to work at the computer monitor in front of her, but Julia knew she'd been watching them, just as Julia had been watching her and Spradlin earlier. Clearly, this woman was different from the rest of the people in the town. She didn't seem to mind Spradlin's presence in the library and actually seemed to like him. Or was that only her imagination? Either way, Julia's curiosity got the best of her. She nodded toward the blonde. "How do you know her?"

Chapter Thirty

THE BREEZE FROM the open windows ruffled the light sheet. He lay in darkness, the glow from his cigarette the only light in the room. The girl had felt good, but it hadn't gone as smoothly as he'd hoped. He was out of practice; he'd made mistakes. They would find her soon. He didn't feel as satisfied as he thought he would. Or maybe the feeling hadn't lasted as long as he'd hoped. He blew smoke from his nostrils. The girl's hair came fresh to his mind; it had been soft and damp from her run. Sweat had covered her skin, dripping between her breasts. He'd inhaled her scent and allowed himself to run his hands over her body, squeezing her soft, yielding flesh.

She'd fought him, but that was to be expected. Still, he hadn't counted on the advantage of youth. She was strong, and he was older now. Although he'd stayed in shape, the task was harder than he'd expected. Next time would be better. The fighting didn't bother him. It fueled him, gave him power. But he couldn't fucking stand the crying. Why did they always do that? Sure, he wanted them to acknowledge his strength and control, but even more, he wanted them to respect it. He stared out the window into blackness. He'd never really liked death. It wasn't nearly as thrilling as what came before.

He lay back, letting the darkness seep in. He needed to think, to plan his next step. The rock would throw everyone off. He'd meant to break her neck—like the others—but when she opened her mouth to scream, he'd been forced to reach for the stone. Not that it would matter in the long run.

The feds would be called in and the local police marginalized, used only for mundane detective work. He was no fool. In light of the governor's role in the release, that would happen sooner rather than later. Cancini's presence would make things even more interesting. He was such a goddamn do-gooder. No doubt, the public humiliation of making a mistake probably didn't sit too well with a know-it-all like him. Mike Cancini wasn't nearly as smart as he thought he was.

He imagined how the investigation might go. Would the feds try to keep the murder quiet? Some would argue they didn't need the students and the locals erupting into some kind of stupid panic, but the real reason would be far less sympathetic and a lot more strategic. When news of the girl's attack got out, suspicion around town, around the county, would be directed at the man the governor had just declared an innocent man. How was that going to play in the press or in the governor's potential run for president? He smiled.

But word would get out. It always did. Little Springs was a shit small town with a mentality to match. Most everyone knew everyone else's business. They wouldn't be able to keep it quiet once they had a second dead girl on their hands. And that would happen soon enough. Then all hell would break loose. He smiled again.

It would be fucking incredible. When they discovered the next body, the press would return in force. There would be no holding back. He breathed in and out quicker, deeper. Folks would call for a lynching. The law be damned! What a laugh it would be. The feds, police, the townsfolk all running around trying to find him. He'd be long gone. They wouldn't catch him. Not this time. Not ever.

Chapter Thirty-One

JULIA SCROLLED THROUGH her messages and her e-mail looking for a name that wasn't there. She knew she shouldn't care, but she couldn't turn her feelings on and off. She couldn't forgive him—wouldn't—but that didn't mean she didn't want him to care. She rolled over on her side and scrolled through again. There were two messages from Norm, a few from friends at home, and one from Ted thanking her for dinner.

It was nice having dinner with a friend tonight. I hadn't been up to the lodge in months. Thanks again and see you soon. Ted

Julia dropped her phone on the bed and reached for the second diary. She was grateful to Ted. He'd even introduced her to a few locals who'd been willing to speak with her, albeit only a little. They couldn't hide their reticence or their preconceived notions that they would be misrepresented, but at least they'd showed. Even if she didn't fully understand their feelings, she could try to understand their emotional reactions. Ted urged her to be patient and listen. They were quiet and reserved for the most part—maybe a little misguided—but not crazy. She realized after the interviews, Ted's advice was good.

Propping the pillows, she settled back to read.

My mother came to see me today. I almost cried when I saw her on the step; it was such a surprise. She hugged me and almost cried, too, but then she wouldn't come inside. "I can't stay. Your father doesn't know I'm here," she said. "I had to see you and make sure you're okay." I did cry then.

She looked so old. Her hair is completely gray now, and she's gotten so thin. At first I was upset that Leo was taking a nap, and she didn't get to meet him. But then I was glad. When I mentioned it, she said meeting him wasn't necessary. "He can never be my grandson," she said. I'm not surprised, but it still hurts.

Julia laid the diary in her lap. What kind of woman was Brenda's mother? Why the distance? Was it because she left college to get married? Because she got pregnant out of wedlock? The outrage seemed terribly old-fashioned but then, times had changed. Still, what kind of grandmother doesn't want to meet her grandson? Shaking her head, Julia resumed reading.

Then she told me she was dying. Cancer. I didn't know what to say, but it didn't matter. She told me she didn't have long, but she didn't want to die without telling me she loved me. I was completely sobbing then. She let me hold her for a minute and then pushed me away. "I have to go now," she said. I asked if there was anything I could do, and at first she said no. Then she said, "Yes, please don't come to my funeral. Your father will make a scene, and I don't think I want a scene . . ." I can't remember if I said anything, but it didn't matter. She didn't wait for my answer. "Good-bye, Brenda. I'm sorry." And after that she was gone. Maybe coming back here to Little Springs was a mistake after all.

Chapter Thirty-Two

"STUPID BUS!" THE boy yelled, kicking at dirt and pebbles. It was the third time in two weeks it hadn't shown up. His father was out of town—driving a truck—and wouldn't be back until Thursday. Mom had left early for the doctor because his dumb sister had strep, again. That made Mom mad 'cause she was supposed to work the breakfast shift at the Holiday Inn up on the interstate. "This day sucks," he said.

Even at this early hour, the sun was high enough to tell it was going to be hot. "Great," he muttered. He was gonna be late again and probably smell like he needed a shower even before gym. He kicked the dirt again. And his math test was first period. He'd have to stay after again to make up more work. It wasn't fair. He reached into his pocket, pulling out his cell phone. Maybe his buddy Jacob would pick up and could tell Ms. Hopkins about his bus. Maybe then she wouldn't point out to the class how he was late again and that maybe he should find an alternate mode of transportation when the bus ran late. It wasn't like he had a choice. It wasn't like he wanted to walk the stupid five miles to school. The girl who sat behind him, the pretty one with dark, curly hair, had tried not to giggle, but he'd heard her anyway. He didn't blame her. She tried to be nice, but Ms. Hopkins didn't make it easy. That old lady hated him. Shoot, maybe the thing to do was skip today. He could go home, hang out, and when he heard his mom bring his idiot sister home, crawl into bed and complain about his throat. She was always worried about stuff being contagious. The more he thought about it, the more it seemed like a good idea.

He turned his head from the left to the right. No one was coming in either direction. He began to run, heading for the trees, his knapsack banging against his back. He didn't need some nosy lady telling his mom she saw him. If he went through the woods, he wouldn't have to worry. He was glad now he'd been in a bad mood that morning, refusing to get out of bed.

"You care more about Ashley Lynn than me, Mom," he'd whined, pulling the covers over his head.

"Oh, for Pete's sake, Jimmy," she'd said, slamming his door. "I don't have time for this." By the time he'd come down for breakfast, she and his sister were gone.

Reaching the woods, he bent at the waist, coughing, trying to catch his breath. Maybe he really was sick. It was cooler in the woods. He walked slowly toward home, keeping near the edge of the forest. When he was little, he'd been lost there once. He'd come home with scratches and cuts and nightmares. It had been a long time before he played there again. He knew better now but still didn't like it.

The boy looked up at the tall trees, their branches thick and twisted, blocking the warmth from the sun. He pulled the strings of his knapsack tight and walked faster. Feet moving quickly over the slippery ground cover, he tripped, falling forward toward the round trunk of a large oak. “Stupid root. Stupid trees.” Picking himself up, he wiped his hands on his jeans, the brown, wet moss leaving marks on the worn pants. It was only then that he noticed what had caused his fall. Not a root. A leg. He stepped closer to see a bare leg, a woman’s leg, covered in dirt and leaves as though someone had tried to hide her. The boy’s eyes widened, and he screamed. Turning, he ran from the woods toward the first house he could find, still screaming.

Chapter Thirty-Three

JULIA TRUDGED INTO the library, her heavy bag hanging from her shoulder. The overhead fluorescent lights weren't enough to brighten the dark and somber interior or her sour mood. The detective's warning still nagged her. What gave him the right to judge her actions or assume he knew what she was thinking? Irritated, she dropped Brenda Spradlin's diary on the table with a bang. She could feel the librarian watching her. That was another thing. Spradlin had only laughed when she'd asked about his conversation with the woman. "Why don't you ask her yourself?" he'd said.

Flopping down onto the hard chair, heat rose from her chest to her cheeks. Not only had she wasted her one question, she'd looked stupid and immature. The librarian wasn't important. What was important was how Spradlin had gotten in trouble in the first place, the life he'd lost, and how he'd survived. She would not make that mistake a second time.

While she waited for Spradlin, Julia wrote a new list of questions, which she set in the middle of the table.

He stood in front of her, one hand lightly holding the top of the chair, feet spread apart. He glanced at her page of questions. "Did you talk to Shelly?"

"Who?"

"Shelly." She followed his gaze to the librarian. The woman's head was bent over a book, a sweater around her shoulders.

"Oh. No, I didn't." She couldn't meet his eyes.

"My high school girlfriend—at least I guess you could say that. We went to stuff together. She was nice to me then. Still is." Julia waited. It was the most he'd ever said, and she didn't want him to stop. "Not many folks around here are, you know. Not that I blame them."

"Maybe you should." Her voice was soft. "You didn't do anything wrong."

"Depends on how you look at it."

"No, it doesn't. It—"

He waved his hand. "Enough about that. Did you learn anything more about my mother?"

She bit back her words. He should be angry, but now wasn't the time to press the issue. Instead, she touched the diary. "I did. First of all, it wasn't easy for your mother when she came back to Little Springs after your father died. Your dad's parents washed their hands of her, and her own parents disowned her."

"True."

"What I don't understand is why." She hesitated. How much of this bothered him? How much did it hurt to read about how little your family wanted you? But she needed to know. The diaries were only a backdrop. Brenda Spradlin was not prone to spilling her emotions. The majority of her entries were factual and brief.

"You can figure it out, Julia. You're a smart lady."

"That's not what I meant. I realize the pregnancy, your existence, was the source of the problem. I don't think I'm wrong in assuming the Spradlins thought your mother was trash, that she had tricked their son into marriage by getting pregnant. They accepted her while your father was living, but when he was gone . . ."

She watched his face when she spoke but saw nothing, no sign of emotion at all. "Your mother's parents seemed to think the same thing. They thought their daughter had behaved like, um, a slut, and they couldn't or wouldn't forgive her. They believed she had turned her back on God." She paused. Everything she'd said made sense to her and fit with the entries she'd read, but it was still only a guess. "Right so far?"

"More or less."

She tapped the top of the diary with her fingernail. "What happened after your father died? Why did your mother accept such a small settlement? Even if your grandparents hated her, you were their grandson, an extension of the son they had lost."

He stood frozen while she talked, his face placid. He held another package in his right hand, his left still holding the chair.

"And her parents . . . how could they have treated their own daughter that way?"

He shrugged. "I wouldn't know. I never met them, any of them."

"What?"

"I have to go," he said, dropping the package on the table. He was gone as quickly as he'd come, leaving her with a page of unanswered questions and her mouth gaping.

Chapter Thirty-Four

"WHAT'S THE CAUSE of death?" Cancini asked, trailing the red-headed man in a navy suit. A dozen Little Springs police cars were parked on the dirt road along with two nondescript ones Cancini figured were FBI. Yellow tape marked a large section of the dense trees with a small opening for the forensic team. Several police and other folks stood near a small one-story house a few hundred yards from the edge of the woods.

The man stopped, whirling around to face the detective. "How did you find out about this so fast, Mike? Don't you have a job in D.C.?"

"I had some vacation time I needed to use."

Talbot snickered. "Are you kidding?" The detective shrugged but remained silent. "Good God. You're not. I thought you said you would leave after the press conference."

"I changed my mind."

The FBI man pulled out a handkerchief and wiped his brow. "I may regret asking this, but you haven't been stalking Spradlin, have you? He's innocent. There's no reason for you to hang around this town." Cancini shrugged again, his expression stoic. Talbot groaned. "I knew it. Look, you got the wrong guy. It happens. Even to the best of us."

"I keep hearing that," he said. Out of the corner of his eye, he saw what appeared to be a young boy, maybe thirteen or fourteen, wearing a blue T-shirt, jeans, and a knapsack. The boy was being led inside the house, flanked by two local officers. He looked sideways at Talbot. "Spradlin put on quite a show at the press conference. Talked about forgiveness and a bunch of other crap. The media lapped it up. The folks here were more shell-shocked than anything."

"So? I know all that. Hardly seems worth the trip if you ask me."

"And he lied."

Cancini's words landed like an invisible line in the sand. Talbot wiped his brow a second time. "I know that, too. I saw the report. Believe it or not, the FBI does investigative work, too."

"And?"

"Lying about how many times your mom came to visit you isn't a crime."

"He hasn't changed."

"Maybe not," Talbot said. "But as much as you and I don't like it, he's an innocent man. He may be a liar and a manipulator, but he's not the Coed Killer."

"Got it."

Talbot's lips drew into a hard, thin line. "Good. Either way, that press conference is long over. I'll ask you again. What are you still doing here?"

Cancini forced a half smile that didn't reach his eyes. "Like I told you, I'm on vacation."

"Bullshit."

"Maybe." Cancini turned his attention toward the woods, to the place where the boy had found the dead college girl. A handful of officers moved between the trees, visible behind the tape, an indication the body was found not far from the edge of the woods. The campus police had allowed him to wait outside the girl's classroom the morning she'd gone missing. When she hadn't shown at eleven, he'd known. "Maybe not."

Talbot sighed. "What do you want from me, Mike?"

"I want to be a part of it." The detective waited, knowing Talbot was a stickler like him. He would do everything by the book, an FBI man through and through. Even more, he would want to catch whoever had done this. "I need to know if it's the same, how she died, if anything's the same as before."

"Jesus, Mike. Are you sure you're still right? Even after the evidence says you're not? Is this about Spradlin?"

"No, I don't think it is." He paused, unable to put the prickly sensation on the back of his neck and the growing nausea in his belly into words. "It's about the girls. I owe them, all of them." The two men stood for a moment, both quiet and sweating under the blazing sun. "I need to know. I need to see the body."

Talbot's face turned toward the woods and the yellow crime scene tape. "I'm getting too old for this." Cancini waited.

"Okay, but I want you to understand something. You're here only as a favor to me. That's all. No one else is going to think you need to be here. Even I don't know why I'm letting you tag along."

"Because you need me," Cancini said. He wasn't smiling.

"No, Mike, I don't. This is a favor. That's all. You got it?"

"Got it." Cancini couldn't read the man's eyes behind his dark glasses, but he knew Talbot was dead serious. It would be an FBI investigation only. The local police and campus security would be pushed out—if they hadn't been already. They would serve on the periphery at best. That alone made Cancini suspicious. Normally, one dead girl wouldn't get the FBI's attention. But the death of a college girl in Little Springs, Virginia, this particular week, was different.

The governor had declared a convicted man innocent and had pushed him back out into the world. Then a dead girl turns up in the same town where the original crimes had occurred, in the same town where the so-called innocent man is living. Now the governor has asked the FBI to look into it, not to prove Spradlin's guilt but to defend his innocence. Leo Spradlin's name would not be uttered in this investigation if at all possible. They needed to protect their position, their political capital. The detective was convinced they didn't know what they were doing or whom they were dealing with. The governor had better hope he was right, or he'd flushed his political career right down the drain. "Can we see the body now?"

"I must be out of my mind," Talbot said, shaking his head. "Let's go."

The two men walked across the grass field toward the woods. Their steps slowed as they got closer, the smell of dirt and death rising from the ground. The hot sun baked Cancini's skin and beads of sweat dripped from his temple. Spradlin had lied. The FBI knew he'd lied. Knots tightened in the back of his neck. Now they had a body, a dead college girl. He squinted up at the blazing sky and shivered, cold fingers of dread deep in his bones.

Chapter Thirty-Five

DAMN HIM. HE'D left her with another diary and still hadn't answered a single question. Julia didn't know how much longer she could stall Norm. He was losing patience. She hoped he wasn't losing confidence. The new diary was hardly more interesting than the previous ones. It sat open on the library table. So far, it seemed like more of the same. She turned the page.

Leo did something odd today. He doesn't know I saw. I wished I hadn't. I went by the middle school today because Leo forgot his lunch again. After I dropped it off, I saw him and some other kids out on the track for gym class. They were running, not fast, but there was one child who lagged behind the others. To be honest, he was a little overweight and was struggling to run the laps. A group of boys waited at the finish line. They started pushing and shoving him until he fell down. They laughed and pointed at him. Then they started kicking him. By the time the teacher came over to break it up, the kid had a bloody nose, and I don't know what else. I searched the crowd for Leo, hoping he wasn't in the group of bullies, and he wasn't. He was standing a little back from it, watching the whole thing. At first I was relieved, grateful he wasn't part of all that, but then, one of those boys, the one who was kicking the boy on the ground looked over at Leo. Leo nodded at them. The teacher didn't see any of that, but I did. I don't know what to think. I'm worried. Why were they looking at Leo? And why didn't he stop them?

Julia read the passage a second time. Reading ahead several more pages, she saw no more references to the incident. There were no more concerns or worries, only monotonous entries about young Leo's baseball games or the tedium of work at the college. She flipped back to the strange passage and read it a third time. It wasn't hard to figure out what his mother had feared. Was she right? Was Leo the ringleader of the bullies? Was there another side to the story? She opened her notebook to add this to her list of questions. Was this the kind of behavior Leo was referring to at the press conference? How he'd made it easy for people to believe in his guilt?

A shadow fell across the diary. She looked up to find Cancini standing over her.

"Detective Cancini, I wasn't expecting you."

"Has he already been here?" Cancini asked.

She started to ask who but stopped when she saw the expression on his face and the deep lines across his forehead. "Yes."

"How long has he been gone?"

She checked her watch. "An hour maybe."

"Do you know where he went? Where I can find him?" She shook her head. His eyes traveled to the diary. She covered the pages with her arms and pulled it close. "Are you all right?"

Julia's mouth opened. "Yes, I'm fine. Why?"

"You're in over your head."

She pursed her lips. "I can take care of myself."

He smiled briefly and she caught the dark gold in his hazel eyes. "I wasn't saying you couldn't. I'm sorry if that's how it sounded."

Her shoulders relaxed. "It's okay, but what did you mean?"

A shadow passed over his face. "You think you know Spradlin, but you don't. He's using you."

She clucked her tongue. "For what? Publicity? I want the story. I asked for it. If anyone's using anyone, it's me."

He shook his head. "If you hear from him, let him know I need to see him."

"Can I tell him why?"

His eyes were flat and dark, the light gone. "He'll know why."

Chapter Thirty-Six

"IS THERE ANYTHING from forensics?" Cancini asked.

Talbot picked up a folder, shaking it. "We got a preliminary report."

Cancini waited, but the FBI man did not elaborate. "Well?" he asked, finally. "What does it say?"

He dropped the folder back on the desk and sat back in his chair. "Look, Mike, we need to be clear about something. I can't tell you anything, not one word, unless I'm sure nothing will leave this room."

The detective waved a hand. "I know. I know. Courtesy only and all that."

Talbot shook his head. "No. I'm serious, Mike. I'm already getting grief from the brass about why you were even allowed at the crime scene. I explained that I use you from time to time on a consulting basis. But considering your past association with this case . . ." He opened his palms, shrugging. "It didn't fly. Apparently, someone checked with your captain, who was only too happy to share that you've taken an extended leave of absence."

"I told you I had some vacation coming."

"Unofficially, you're a consultant to me and me alone." He folded his arms across his chest. "Mike, I understand your need to know, but I can only pull so many strings. I'm sticking my neck out here."

"So I'm officially out and unofficially still out?" His voice was tight.

"You can call it what you want. You shouldn't even be here."

"I'm not leaving."

Talbot sighed. "I know that. Here's how it goes. You have no authority whatsoever. You are not to flash your badge. You are not to imply to anyone that you are working on this investigation. Most importantly, any information I discuss with you is strictly confidential. Those are the rules."

Cancini ran his hand over his military-short hair. "Sounds like fun," he said.

"Are we clear?"

It was perfectly clear, but that didn't mean he liked it. He wanted to know everything, yet he recognized that would come with a price. "Fine. We're clear." Cancini paused. He also knew without being told that Talbot had done his best. "And thanks."

"Good." Talbot nodded, picked up the file again, and flipped several pages. "The girl appears to have died from blunt force trauma, a blow to the head. She was sexually assaulted, but there are no visible signs of fluid or DNA evidence. It's early though. They're working on unidentified particles in her hair and on her skin." He looked up from the report. "You were right. The body was moved sometime after she was dead. Someone had tried to cover the drag tracks but not well enough."

"Any idea where she was murdered?"

"Not yet. We're hoping what they found in her hair and under her nails might provide some leads."

Cancini thought back to the body. "The cause of death. Blunt force trauma. Are you sure?"

"Sure."

Cancini hesitated. "What about the marks on her neck?"

Talbot sighed again. "The pathologist said her neck was bruised, but barely. The marks were too light to have done any real damage. In his estimation, they most likely occurred after the girl was dead."

Cancini blinked. "After she was dead?"

"Yes." Cancini absorbed the information. "You and I both know this can happen sometimes: the headlines, breaking news on CNN, and all that. The publicity is appealing, and some guy who already has a screw loose gets an idea."

"So, copycat then? That's the theory?"

Talbot nodded. "It makes the most sense."

It did make sense. But that didn't make it true. "Is it possible that the perp planned to strangle the girl but was forced to hit her with something? Maybe he was interrupted, or he couldn't control her."

"Anything's possible, Mike. That doesn't make it probable." The FBI man touched the file on his desk. "This was sloppy. The original murders were efficient. Our profiler has come up with a preliminary description: white male, early to mid-twenties, easily blends in. Probably has difficulties with women, some anger issues, but nothing like this before. She thinks he's a first-timer."

Cancini slumped in his chair. Everything Talbot reported was logical, made sense. There was almost nothing left to say. Then, he asked, "Have you found a match for the DNA from the Fornak case?"

"No, but we've expanded the search to surrounding states."

"Okay," Cancini said, nodding. "Will you let me know if you get anything?"

"Sure."

The detective stood, the meeting over. "Out of curiosity, did you find Spradlin? Did you interview him?"

"We talked to him. We didn't interview him."

"Did he have an alibi?"

"No, but he doesn't have to, Mike. He's not a suspect. And so you know, he was more than cooperative."

"He always was—the absolute picture of cooperation."

"Yeah, I remember." The two men sat in silence for a moment. "Leave him alone, Mike."

Cancini looked across the desk at his old friend. "That would be the smart thing to do, wouldn't it?"

"Yes, it would."

"Problem is, I'm not very smart."

Chapter Thirty-Seven

CANCINI STEPPED ONTO the porch, the knots in his back taut and tender. The front door of the house was splintered, its paint chipped and faded. A gutter hung awkwardly, but the stoop had been swept free of cobwebs and dirt. A single rocking chair sat near the front window, which appeared clean and smudge-free. An old pickup truck was parked around the side of the house, the bed loaded with piles of brush. Squinting, Cancini touched the revolver he wore under his jacket and knocked.

Spradlin opened the door wide, and the light from outside shone into the small front room. "Detective Cancini." His face was impassive as he looked over the detective's shoulder. "Come alone?"

"I just want to talk."

Spradlin gestured behind him. "Come in. I've been expecting you."

Cancini walked through the door into the living area. A threadbare sofa was pushed against the far wall, a hand-knit throw neatly folded and placed over its arm. A round wooden table with four chairs faced the front window and a basic kitchen stood behind it. The detective knew the back of the house: two bedrooms and one bath. Cardboard boxes filled one corner of the front room.

Spradlin's eyes followed Cancini's. "Been going through my mom's things," he said. Without asking, he moved to the kitchen counter, pouring two cups of coffee. He placed them on the round table. "It's not much," he said, nodding toward the back of the house, "but compared to where I was living . . ."

A rectangle of sunlight poured through the front window brightening the room. Cancini remembered being in this house years ago, congregating early for a day of fishing. Spradlin's mother had moved quietly among them, serving eggs and bacon. They'd crowded around the table, eating and talking, refilling their coffee cups. Although Cancini hadn't thought much of it at the time, Spradlin had stood apart that morning, watching. He'd eaten little and said little. He'd said even less to his mother, who'd cleared the dishes and filled the boys' thermoses one by one. That had been a long time ago. Before the girls.

"Sit down, Detective. You've come all this way to talk." He grinned, but his eyes were unreadable. "So, let's talk."

Cancini remained standing. "Where were you last night, Leo?"

Spradlin picked up his mug and took a slow a sip. "I already talked to the feds."

"I know that, but I want to hear it for myself. Is it a hard question?"

"Nope. Not hard at all. I was here. Alone. I'm not exactly surrounded by a shitload of friends and family—in case you haven't noticed."

"Were you here all night?"

"Yep." He cocked his head to the side. "Do you want to tell me why I'm getting the third degree from you and the feds?"

"No."

"That's what I thought." He stood up, carrying his cup to the counter. "Why don't I take a guess, and you tell me if I'm right?" He walked back to the table, his cup refilled. "A girl, a college girl from Blue Hill most likely, is missing, maybe worse than missing. The feds and the big D.C. cop come looking for the man they put away once before to see if he's been up to no good. They ask where I've been. Was I alone? They look around my yard and house. Is there anything out of sorts? Is good old Leo doing something he shouldn't be doing?" He looked up at the detective. "How'm I doing so far?"

Cancini said only, "Have you, Leo? Have you been doing something you shouldn't?"

Spradlin smiled. "That's what you want, isn't it, Mike? It's killing you that I'm out. You can't stand that the law declared me an innocent man."

Refusing to rise to the bait, Cancini asked, "Why are you meeting with Julia Manning every morning at the library?"

"Have you been following me? You know I could charge you with harassment." Leo shook his head. "Shame on you, Mike. Your ego is bigger than I thought, stalking an innocent man to save your reputation. It's pathetic."

The detective kept his voice low, matter-of-fact. "I haven't been following you, and neither has anyone else as far as I know. They don't have to. When you come to town, people notice. They don't like it, and they talk. I listen."

The man grunted, his tone biting. "Oh, that's right. I'd forgotten again. No friends. No family. No one wants me here."

Cancini said nothing for a moment, then asked what he'd been wondering since the press conference. "Why did you come back?

It wasn't that bullshit about it being your mother's dying wish, and it wasn't because you have a desire to be a part of this town again. Why?"

Spradlin's gaze wandered around the cabin, settling on the pile of boxes. "I have my reasons." He faced Cancini. "But I don't feel like telling you."

"That's too bad," the detective said. He went to the door and hesitated, his hand on the knob. "What did you mean you'd been expecting me?"

Spradlin finished his coffee, then set the cup on the table. "Do you remember that time we went hunting over at Spruce Valley Mountain? We took Hal's old dog with us because Hal swore he could sniff out anything. But Hal was always a damn idiot. That dog couldn't find a bowl of dog food without a guide. Still, the dog was persistent. He could keep at it for hours even when he couldn't stay on the trail of a herd of deer or anything else for that matter."

Cancini swallowed. He remembered. It was his one and only experience hunting. "Hal's dog was shot that day accidentally by another hunter."

A slow smile spread over Spradlin's face. "That's right he was." Then his expression hardened, the smile gone. "I've been expecting you, Mike, 'cause you're like that old dog. You may not be the best hunter, following the wrong scent, but you are persistent." He folded his arms across his chest. "Be careful, Mike. Persistence could get you in trouble. Killed even."

A cold chill ran up Cancini's spine. "Is that a threat?"

Spradlin gave a laugh, arms unfolding. "Hell no, Mike. It's only friendly advice. You're the one who came into my house asking questions. We both know what that means. The feds wouldn't be here if something bad hadn't happened. Neither would you."

"I didn't say—"

"You didn't have to. I'm not stupid. There's a girl for sure. For all I know, maybe more." Clouds covered the sun, and the light in the cabin faded. "Take it however you want. Just remember, I warned you."

Chapter Thirty-Eight

NIKKI STEPHENSON HATED Blue Hill College. She hated the classes and the boring professors. She hated her part-time job at the Campus Grounds Coffee Shop, and most of all, she hated the stupid town of Little Springs, where absolutely nothing ever happened. The only interesting thing had been the press conference where the guy who'd been in jail for years stood in front of all those rednecks and told them he forgave them. She smiled at the memory. All around her, people had been grumbling and talking about running him out of town. Then he came out and shut them up. She had liked him immediately.

Hurrying across campus, she glanced at her watch. Late again. Not that it mattered. Not many coffee drinkers showed up in the middle of the afternoon anyway. Mornings and nights were busy, but she tried to avoid those shifts. The less she had to deal with customers, the better.

She strode through the door and pretended not to see the annoyed expression on the baby-faced boy behind the counter.

"Hey," he said. "You were supposed to be here a half hour ago."

She shrugged and went to the back of the store, grabbed an apron off the hook, and tied it around her waist. She logged in on the computer, pulled her hair off her face, and moved back to the front.

The boy shot her a nasty look. "I ought to report you, you know. This is the third time you've made me late for class."

"So report me."

He followed her to the register. "You think you're so much better than the rest of us? You're not."

Pink spots appeared on her pale cheeks, but she refused to let him get to her. Instead, she counted to ten, concentrating on her breathing. It was so tiresome. There wasn't a single person on campus who didn't know who her father was. Not just a politician, Senator Connor Stephenson was also a nationally known evangelist. He'd pushed her into this school. "Strong Christian principles. Good foundation," he'd said. And he'd held the checkbook. Still, she'd mistakenly thought getting away, even to Blue Hill, was better than staying. Ha!

She forced a smile to her lips and took a step backward, putting space between them. "Leave it alone, Jake. I won't be late again."

"You'd better not. I happen to know you need this job."

She glared at him, the smile gone. "That's none of your business."

He laughed, a hollow, bitter sound. "Yeah, well if you don't want everybody knowing your business, Miss Virginity, then tell your big-shot dad to keep his big mouth shut."

She groaned. "Old news, asshole."

"Yeah? Well, tell the boss how much you need your paycheck for tuition after you get fired."

Nikki's head whipped around. "What are you talking about?"

His eyes danced over her, his expression a mix of disbelief and glee. "You don't know."

Her stomach fluttered and rolled. "Oh, for God's sake. Know what?"

His smile broadened. He reached under the counter and pulled out a national news magazine. Her face, smiling in a cap and gown, stared back at her from the cover. The headline read, "Is This the Face of a New Generation?"

She sucked in her cheeks, the color drained from her face.

"What's the matter, Miss Fancy Pants?" She pushed past him, knocking him in the shoulder. "Don't you want to read it?"

"What for?" She struggled to keep her voice from shaking.

He threw the magazine on the counter. "Why're you always such a bitch?"

When he was gone, she picked it up and turned to the cover story, her stomach churning. Inside were several pictures of her and her family. She swallowed hard and read. After two readings, she tossed it in the trash.

"Hypocrite," she said under her breath.

"Excuse me?"

Nikki's head jerked up.

"Is this a bad time?" A small woman with reddish-brown hair stood at the counter holding a cup.

"No, sorry," Nikki said, her cheeks hot again. Seemed everything she said and did was wrong. "A refill?" The woman nodded. Nikki set the machine in motion, watching the coffee drip into the cup.

"You're the girl on the cover of *NewsWorld*, right?"

She looked past the woman to her table. On it sat a laptop, a notepad and pencils, a black book, and a large canvas bag. A reporter. Nikki had seen a few in her day and recognized the gear. They were always around her father, and he loved it. He had a personal trainer now and a stylist, too. It was disgusting.

"So?"

The woman apologized. "I don't mean to be nosy, and I promise I'm not asking for a story." Nikki pushed her hair behind her ears, one hand on her hip. "Although it's a shame you were only quoted once. Something tells me you might have had more to say." Nikki bit her lip. "That wasn't a story," the woman said. "It was a campaign speech." The woman's voice was gentle. "Was the article a surprise? I know it's none of my business, but I couldn't help overhearing."

Nikki nodded once. Shock was more like it. She wondered how many other kids found out they would be paying their tuition—with no help—in a magazine. Was it true? She had no idea. The only thing she knew for sure was he'd made her the poster child for hardworking, Christian children. The media would lap it up. His constituents and followers would hold him up as an example of solid parenting. It was a joke.

"I'm sorry," the reporter said. "Look, I've taken enough of your time." She nodded at a waiting customer.

Nikki poured coffee and wiped the counters. Her face burned when she heard the whispers.

"Did you see her? It's Senator Stephenson's daughter."

"I'll never get my parents to pay for spring break now."

It was a nightmare. She'd become part of his stump speech. Dropping out was not an option. Her mother and sister—they would pay the price. She hated her father and everything he stood for. He knew it, too, but didn't give a damn.

Her eyes wandered back to the woman. Nikki was rarely allowed to speak to reporters. Her presence was required for family pictures, but after that, she was nothing but a convenient statistic and sound bite. Even though she'd always hated the press, she was starting to be intrigued by the idea of journalism. Reporters might not make the news, but they did have the ability to shape it. Maybe writers were in the background, but at least they were heard. Somehow, she didn't think her father would approve. She smiled and tossed her dishtowel onto the counter. Within seconds, she stood in front of the red-haired reporter.

The woman looked up from her laptop, fingers frozen over the keys. "Hi," she said.

Nikki's mouth went dry. "Hi," she said back. "I was wondering if I could ask you a few questions." The woman leaned against the back of the booth, hands folded in her lap. Nikki's words tumbled out. "About being a reporter. What that's like. How you do it. Do you even like it?" When the woman laughed, her blue eyes sparkled, and Nikki began to relax. "Sorry. That part is probably none of my business."

The reporter laughed. "Then we're even." She waved a hand at the other seat. "Actually, if you're thinking about journalism, that's the first question you should ask." Nikki sat down, nodding. "I do like it. Not every day but most of the time. Sometimes it's hard, but I wouldn't trade it. I wouldn't want to do anything else."

Nikki nodded again. "So, you don't mind my asking you some questions?"

The lady smiled. "Not at all. I'll be on the other side of the interview for a change." She stuck her hand out across the table. "You can call me Julia."

Grinning, she took the reporter's hand in her own. "I guess you already know my name, but it's nice to meet you. I'm Nikki."

Chapter Thirty-Nine

FROM A BENCH across the street, he peered over the newspaper at the two women. They stood on the sidewalk outside the campus coffee shop. As they talked, the younger woman wiped her hands across her red apron. Julia hooked the straps of her bag over her shoulder, talking as she handed the woman a card. The girl took it, nodded, and smiled. He was too far away to hear their conversation, but he could see they liked each other. He didn't like complications. Julia reached out and gave the girl a hug, her auburn hair catching the sunlight.

"Well, well," the man said out loud. Julia gave a wave and strode off. The young woman stood a moment, watching Julia's retreating back, a half smile on her face. After a moment, she went back to her job in the coffee shop.

Setting aside the paper, he strained to make out the younger woman through the large glass window, but all he could see were shadows in the afternoon glare. Irritated, he scratched at the dark wig. Under the hat and wig, his head was slick with sweat. Precautions were necessary now. He'd seen the police and the FBI on campus. The girl had been found, and while it might not be public knowledge yet, he had no doubt they were already looking for him. Not that it mattered to him too much. They were stupid and incompetent. Looking wasn't the same as finding.

From behind the sunglasses, he scanned the street. On the next corner stood an FBI man, propped against the brick exterior of a sandwich shop. The lawman, in his dark suit and sunglasses, garnered far more curious looks than he did. After all, who would notice a dark-haired man of indeterminate age, wearing a hat, sunglasses, and the rumpled tweed blazer adopted by so many Blue Hill professors? An empty attaché case was propped at his feet. The FBI man, though, stuck out like a fucking sore thumb. It took all his self-control not to laugh at the absurdity of it all.

The laughter died in his throat when he saw the young girl come out of the coffee shop. The apron gone, she hurried down the street toward her dormitory. His heart pounded, but he stayed on the bench, resisting the urge to follow. Later. He knew where she was going anyway—straight across campus to her dorm, same as the other times. Her room was on the third floor. The shade would be drawn until the girl yanked it up and threw open the window. She'd climb out, perching on the windowsill, knees pulled up to her chest, and stare out into the distance. Sometimes she'd stay like that for an hour, sometimes longer. He wondered what she thought about, what she dreamed about. Maybe, when the time came, he'd ask her. Maybe not. He didn't care that much.

From under his hat, he peered at the FBI man again. Pathetic. The police, the FBI, even the school had acted exactly as he'd anticipated. So predictable. They were confused, and that was good. They were anxious and aware. It wasn't enough, though. He wanted more. It was time to do something bolder, louder. It was time to make believers out of doubters. He was back.

Chapter Forty

THE TWO YOUNG men trudged across campus, shivering in the early morning chill. The taller one pulled the hood of his jacket around his ears. They walked along the tree-lined street, kicking at the leaves dotting the sidewalk.

"That test on Monday was a bitch," the tall boy said.

"I know," Jackson said, shaking his head. He was shorter by almost a foot and craned his head to look up at his friend. "If I don't do well on the final, I'll be lucky to pass this stupid class. I don't know why we have to take math anyway when we're both English majors."

"Yeah. Dumb." They cut across a courtyard, taking the shortest route to the cafeteria. The sidewalks and park were still empty. That would change in another hour.

"Thanks for grabbing breakfast early today," Jackson said. "I wanna try and catch Professor Morris before class."

"Sure. No problem." The tall boy slowed, elbowing his friend. He nodded toward a bench across the courtyard, near the largest oak tree. "Look, some girl is sleeping it off."

"Damn. Must've been some party."

The other boy laughed. "How come I never get invited to any of those?"

" 'Cause you're a dork. That's . . ." The words faded. Both boys froze. The girl's bare feet hung off the edge of the bench. They looked at each other. "Do you think she's okay?"

The tall boy shrugged his shoulders and scanned the empty park. "Who knows? We should probably wake her up before she gets in trouble." He walked toward the bench.

Jackson nodded, glancing once at the cafeteria, then back at the sleeping girl. "Yeah, okay," he said, following at a distance.

"Holy shit!" The tall boy stopped, stumbling backward. His face blanched. He bent over, arms folded across his stomach, and vomited.

Jackson sprinted forward. Stopping short, he gasped, his eyes wide. "Jesus Christ." He pulled his phone from his pocket, fingers fumbling as he dialed. "This is bad," he whispered, backing away from the body. "Really bad."

Chapter Forty-One

"GODDAMMIT!" CANCINI GLARED at Talbot and slammed the car door. "What are all these kids doing here?"

"I've got a team working to secure the perimeter now," Talbot said. He nodded toward a handful of agents and Little Springs cops pushing the gawking students from the courtyard.

Cancini followed his gaze. Several of the young people held up phones, snapping pictures of the crime scene. "They're taking pictures."

Talbot stopped as they reached the tape. "Mike, we'll take care of it." He put a hand on Cancini's shoulder, leaning in close. "I know I don't need to remind you, but this is not your investigation."

"Right," Cancini muttered. Groups of students were herded away, and police cruisers stood ready, stationed at every corner. It would have to do. The kids were the least of his concerns. The fact that another girl was dead was all that mattered. The short amount of time between the two murders sent cold chills up and down his spine. Someone—Spradlin, a copycat, or someone else entirely—was clearly trying to make a statement. No matter which turned out to be the case, a murder scene was no place for college kids. "Got it."

"Good."

"Who found the girl?"

"Couple of students on their way to breakfast, a little before six. One of them called 911. We've taken them in for questioning and confiscated their phones."

"Photos?"

"I don't think so. I actually think those boys were too traumatized to snap any, but we're taking every precaution." Talbot paused and motioned toward the bench. "It's not pretty," he said, his tone somber.

The detective sighed. He recognized the defeated slope of Talbot's shoulders and the troubled expression on his face. "It never is."

Talbot lifted the tape, and the two lawmen ducked underneath. A forensic team had arrived and was waiting for Talbot to give them the go-ahead. He held up a hand indicating they should wait. Cancini pulled on a pair of gloves, the rubber snapping at his wrists. Talbot led the way. "Early estimates place time of death between midnight and this morning when the body was found. Appears to have been sexually assaulted. She was beaten, her neck snapped." Talbot's straightforward report couldn't disguise his sadness.

Cancini stiffened as he approached the girl. She was naked from the waist down, a dark piece of clothing tossed across her bruised legs. He crouched by her feet. Barely touching the toes, he pulled them apart and angled his head to look at the soles of her feet. "She was forced to walk somewhere without her shoes. Clay soil, some cuts, dried blood."

He stood and moved toward her head; it hung awkwardly from her neck. Cancini bent at the waist, his face close to the girl. He inspected the bruises that covered her shoulders and upper torso, pushing aside the thin fabric of her shredded blouse with the tips of his gloved fingers. He looked at her swollen face, one eye already dark with pooled blood. He picked up a hand and, one by one, opened the clenched fingers. The hair on the back of his neck rose. There, in the palm of that dead hand, lay a single button with several blue threads. Like the others, she had fought hard. Unlike them, she'd done something no one else had been able to do. She'd brought them evidence. Careful not to disturb that evidence, he folded her fingers and let go of her hand. "Get the photographer. She got a button from the perp."

Chapter Forty-Two

THE INSISTENT KNOCK on the door jerked her awake. Rubbing her eyes, Julia struggled to make out the numbers on the wind-up clock. "Ugh," she groaned. It wasn't even seven in the morning. No one she knew would bother her at such an ungodly hour. She pulled a pillow and the covers over her head. A few minutes passed before the pounding started again. "For God's sake," she muttered, throwing off the pillow.

Sliding from under the sheets, she shuffled to the bathroom, grabbing her robe from the hook on the door. Her face in the mirror reflected puffy eyes and creases along one cheek. The annoying presence at the door knocked again. "Okay, okay," she grumbled, "I'm coming." Julia ran her fingers through her hair and slipped on the robe.

She opened the door and inhaled sharply. Fingers shaking, she pulled her robe tighter.

"Sorry to wake you," Spradlin said. He brushed by her, carrying a stack of diaries. He dropped the books on a pile of folders and papers on the desk. Arms folded across her chest, she watched, saying nothing. "These are the rest of the diaries," he said.

Julia eyed the books and sighed. "Why don't you just tell me what you want me to know?"

His eyes wandered to the unmade bed and pile of clothes strewn across the chair near the window. "I can't do that."

She started to protest, then noticed the dark circles and sunken cheeks. His shirt was rumpled, as if he'd slept in his clothes or not at all. Her face softened. "It would save time if you could. Tell me, I mean."

"You have to read them to know. Right away."

"Right away?" She bit back on her irritation. Norm was already pressuring her to come up with something more, something different. That wasn't going to come from the words of a dead woman. Julia needed an interview with the man standing in front of her.

"Yes. As soon as possible actually. Things are happening fast."

She shook her head. "I don't know. I've got a deadline. It would be helpful if I could ask—"

"It has to be today." His tone was strained. He walked toward her and placed both hands on her shoulders. She breathed the musky scent of his soap. "It can't wait."

Julia hesitated. She'd never seen him show any emotion. Maybe pushiness didn't qualify as an emotion exactly, but something was going on. "Leo, what's wrong?"

He looked down at her, his blue eyes soft. He tucked a lock of auburn hair behind her ear. His finger trailed down the side of her face, tracing her cheekbone. He dropped his hand, and his face was once again unreadable. "Read the diaries," he said. "Please." And then he was gone.

Chapter Forty-Three

THE RISING SUN brought clarity after the confusion of the night. The man had done things he'd never done before, things he didn't even know he had in him. He'd been the aggressor plenty of times, but he wasn't cruel by nature—only when necessary. This time, though, he'd become something more, someone he hadn't recognized. It was the girl. She'd provoked him, hurling vile words and accusations. He'd hit other girls before, to shut them up, but he'd never before beaten a woman to death. It was her fault, though. The bitch had asked for it, and, once he'd started, he'd been unable to stop. It was odd. He'd never felt so fucking strong, never more invincible. He wasn't sorry. Not one damn bit.

He'd wanted to be there when the body was discovered, but he knew that was just ego. This girl would make the news for sure. It wouldn't be a little boy the police stifled. Dozens of kids would know about this girl in minutes, thanks to social media.

He fumbled with the top of the medicine bottle and shook one single pill into the palm of his hand. His body and hands hurt, but he needed to stay alert. He couldn't afford to sleep or lose focus. The FBI, the police, and Cancini would hunt him with renewed intensity. The media would again descend on the small town. He smiled. He would not be afraid. He wouldn't hide, and he wouldn't run. Not yet. He still had work to do.

Chapter Forty-Four

"WHERE THE HELL are you?" Norm demanded.

Julia rolled her eyes. Absently flipping through the diary in her lap, she held the cell phone to her ear, wishing she'd let it go to voice mail. She didn't have the energy to hear that she needed to get more from Spradlin. Norm wouldn't be thrilled about the stack of diaries sitting in her lap. "I'm in my hotel room."

"Have you been out? Heard anything?"

"What? No." The most she'd managed was a large cup of coffee from room service and a little reading. Curled up in a chair near the window facing Main Street, she pulled the soft robe around her legs. She stifled a yawn and started to tell him about her morning visitor. "Listen, I—"

"Tell me later," he said, breathless. "Get over to the campus right away. If you can, get your mayor friend or even Cancini to make a statement. Conroy is on his way back to Little Springs. Until then, you're our man on the ground."

She stood up, diary dropping to the floor. "What's going on,

Norm?" She pushed the drapes aside. An increased police presence stirred on the street below.

"Jesus, Julia, they found a dead girl right in the middle of the campus. There might even be two; I'm not sure. Anyway, it looks like the girl they found was raped and murdered—like the girls from before."

"What?" Her hand went to her throat.

"Crazy, right? It just came over the wire, a brief statement about a girl being found dead on the campus and that the FBI has sectioned off the area. No one will comment, but I've got a guy who says she was half naked and beaten pretty bad. Here's the real kicker: I've got a couple of unconfirmed reports that she's not the first. I'm still working on that lead, but I'm told the FBI has been in Little Springs for two days. Two days!"

Julia's eyes wandered to the diaries piled up on the floor next to the chair. What had Spradlin said? *Things are happening fast.* The tips of her fingers tingled and her heart thumped, almost hurting her chest. What did that mean, and why was it so important that she read the diaries right away?

"Julia, are you there?"

"Yeah," she said, shaking off the questions. She shed her robe and grabbed a button-down shirt from the closet. "Norm, I'm on it. I'm going up to the college now. Call you when I get there." She searched her contacts for Ted Baldwin and pushed the call button.

Chapter Forty-Five

BALDWIN PACED THE floor of the college president's office. His head swung from Talbot to President Sinclair to Talbot and back again. "When are you bringing him in?" Baldwin asked, his voice unnaturally high-pitched. Cancini sat on the guest sofa, silent.

"Who? Spradlin?" Talbot asked.

"Who else? Jesus," the mayor said. His hands were balled into fists. "This is a goddamn disaster. What am I supposed to tell the people now? Don't worry, folks. I know I told you not to worry before. I stood on the steps and told you we had to welcome the man back. Welcome him! What a joke! I told them we have to follow the letter of the law and all that. And now . . ." He paused, his voice shaking. "Jesus. Now we've got not one, but two dead girls. It's happening all over again." He slumped into a chair.

Talbot, leaning against the wall, folded his arms across his chest. He shifted his gaze from the mayor to the college president. "We'll have a statement soon. Don't tell anyone anything. We stick to the statement."

"Fine," the president said. He looked at Baldwin. "Ted?"

Baldwin opened his mouth to say something, then nodded glumly. "Okay, fine. But please tell me you're bringing him in for questioning. You're doing that at least, right? I've gotta have something." His eyes searched their faces.

"Spradlin will be questioned," Talbot said. "I've dispatched two men to bring him in." He rubbed the bridge of his nose. "The governor has been apprised of the situation and will be kept in the loop."

Baldwin raised a hand, pointing at Cancini. "I told you something bad was going to happen. I prayed he was just blowing smoke, but I knew it. I told you . . ." His voice trailed off.

Talbot cleared his throat and shifted his focus to President Sinclair. "I know you were considering sending the students home for a few days, but I need to do some interviews first. I need to talk to anyone who might have seen Ms. Thompson in the last few days. We've already established her schedule and habits. I need to talk with anyone who had classes in common with the girl, sorority sisters, anyone who might have something to offer."

Sinclair picked up a file folder and handed it to Talbot. "Here are both girls' schedules as well as all classes they've taken since they enrolled. Ms. Hallwell was a senior and in a sorority. Ms. Thompson did not go through rush as far as we can tell. Ms. Hallwell ran cross-country, and I've been told she spent most of her time outside of schoolwork training. Ms. Hallwell lived in her sorority house; you have the list of the girls who live there. Ms. Thompson was a freshman, so she lived in one of the freshmen dorms, Heather House. It's coed, houses close to a hundred kids. The list of residents is in the folder." He paused. "It's possible they knew each other, but I haven't seen any evidence of that yet."

Talbot took the folder. "We have a few names of students

who've been in trouble of one sort or another. We'd like to interview them as well."

The president agreed. "Whatever you need." He walked over to a large table crowded with drawings and building models. "What about the construction on campus? Williams Construction?"

"They've been cooperating. We're still running the names they gave us. It's my understanding they've agreed to halt all work until the campus is cleared for break." The president nodded. "Good. Today is Thursday. I'll try to finish all my interviews by tomorrow afternoon. We'll issue a press release and increase security around campus. I need you to cancel classes for Monday and Tuesday. Sending the students home Friday night is best."

"Agreed." The president cleared his throat. "There is the matter of the families. When should I speak to them?"

"I'm going to handle that myself," Talbot said.

Cancini shifted on the sofa. He didn't envy Talbot this part of the investigation. Speaking with the families, doing your best to console them while also seeking any pertinent information, was the hardest part of the job. Talbot would try to learn everything he could from the girls' loved ones. When had they spoken to them last? Had they had any problems with anyone? Had there been any threats? The questions would be difficult, and some would come close to crossing the line. That was the job. Cancini shifted, restless. They'd already spent too much time in the president's office. They needed to get back to the investigation.

The president's face sagged with relief. "Thank you for doing that."

Talbot slipped the folder under his arm. "The official statement from the college, until I tell you otherwise, is to refer to the FBI press release. It should be ready shortly. You are not authorized to make any statements beyond that. Understood?"

Sinclair frowned. "I'd like to add something about our condolences to the families."

"That would be fine," Talbot said, giving Cancini a nod toward the door. Cancini stood.

Baldwin sat with his head in his hands. He looked up, his eyes glistening in the fluorescent lighting. "This is a nightmare." He brushed away the unshed tears, his voice pleading. "You've got to stop this, Mike. For good this time."

Chapter Forty-Six

"DAMN," JULIA MUTTERED, her cell phone jammed against her ear. Traffic slowed as she approached the campus, and she could see streets blocked off up ahead. She hit end and redial. She'd already called the mayor at least a half-dozen times, but he couldn't or wouldn't pick up. She'd tried Spradlin, too, but he wasn't answering, either. She'd placed a single call to Cancini, not expecting any response. It didn't matter. She already knew what he'd say if he did bother to answer. "No comment."

The Campus Grounds was packed with students and the noise they brought with them. The air crackled with tension. The young men's and women's faces looked anxious, their voices tinged with worry and fear. Julia ordered a latte and found an empty seat where she could work.

"I heard she was mutilated," a girl at the next table said, her shoulders shuddering. "I heard they cut off her head."

Julia slid her chair closer to the couple's table. She pretended to be absorbed by her computer but listened to every word.

The boy at the table snorted. "That's not true. Jason knows one of the guys that found her."

"But I heard—"

"Her neck was broken, but I know for a fact her head was still there. It was not cut off." The girl's lips clamped shut. "Jason said she was beat up pretty badly. Her face was smashed to a pulp is the story." He paused, then said, "I wish I'd seen it."

The girl's head shot up. "What? How can you say that?"

He shrugged. "Amy, you know I'm pre-med. I have to look at stuff like that."

"You're sick," the girl said, pushing her hair behind her ears. He grunted and looked away. After a moment, she leaned in toward the boy. "I think I know who it was. I mean, I don't actually know her, but Sarah does. You know Sarah, right?"

"Yeah, but how could she know? Jason said the guys that found her didn't recognize her, and they haven't released any names," he said doubtfully.

"Sarah lives in Heather House, and she said this girl named Amanda Thompson didn't come back to her room last night. Sarah said Amanda's roommate was completely hysterical this morning when she heard a dead girl was found in that courtyard by the cafeteria. It has to be her."

Julia typed the names in her computer as they spoke, not daring to look in their direction.

"Please. Not coming back to your room doesn't mean anything." His tone turned suggestive. "You didn't go home last night."

The girl ignored him. "Sarah was pretty sure."

Neither said anything for a moment, then the boy said, "I heard there might be another girl."

"No way!"

"I've got a pretty reliable source."

"Yeah? Who?"

"My friend Martin works in the campus police building. He said some of the cops were saying a sorority girl went missing a couple of days ago. She was found somewhere off campus. Dead."

The girl pushed her plate away, her breakfast sandwich untouched. Her face was pale. "This gives me the creeps."

The boy's phone vibrated on the table. "It's a text from the dean. Weird."

The girl leaned in to see, her long hair falling across her face. "What's it say? My phone's dead."

"Hold on. I'll read it to you." His right index finger swiped across the screen. "It says: 'Fall break has been rescheduled, and classes will be canceled this Monday and Tuesday. Campus will be closed beginning Friday at five p.m.' That's it."

A murmur buzzed in the small coffee shop as students received and read the same text message. Julia returned to her keyboard, typing as fast as she could.

"Oh my God. This is worse than creepy," the girl said.

"I don't know if I'd say creepy. To tell you the truth, it's the first exciting thing that's ever happened on this campus."

"Jesus, you're sick, you know," she said, her voice high and tight. "You wouldn't be talking that way if you knew one of those girls."

He raised his palms. "Okay. You're right. Exciting is the wrong way to put it. You don't have to freak out."

"Why not freak out? The dean is. Why else would they be sending us home?" She rubbed her arms. "If there really was a girl missing already, and they didn't tell us, that makes it even worse!

Are we supposed to feel safe here?" She leaned toward the boy. "I'm glad we're going home."

Julia looked up from her keyboard. Voices were raised in disbelief. The kids' faces wore expressions of confusion and doubt. Like the girl at the next table, most seemed afraid.

Julia's phone pinged and she snatched it off the table. "Ted?"

"Yeah," he said. "I guess you've heard?"

She pulled her chair toward the window, turning her back on the students. Hunching over, she kept her voice low. "Some. Bits and pieces. The story hit the wire earlier, but it didn't say a whole lot."

"I can't say a whole lot, either, Julia. There's an investigation and all." He sounded like he'd been crying. "The official statement will come from the FBI."

She took another tack. "The college is going to send the kids home tomorrow. Did you know that?"

"Yes. I'm on the board."

"Oh. Right. Maybe I could ask you a few questions about how the college will handle this situation?" She checked the time. It was nearly nine. "Are you on campus?"

"Yes. I'm leaving the president's office now."

"Great. Why don't you meet me at the Campus Grounds? I'll buy you breakfast. You probably haven't eaten."

He was quiet a moment and then said, "I can't talk about it."

Julia again saw the concern and fear on the faces of the students. Some of them would find out today they knew the victim, lived in her dorm, or shared a class with her. They would have to talk with their parents. The administration would have to answer to those same parents. Baldwin would have to answer to everyone. She spied Nikki behind the counter, her dark eyes wary. Nervous energy filled the small shop. Her mind flashed back to the decades-old newspaper articles. The fear had started slowly, spreading like a slow-growing cancer, eating at the college and then the town itself. "It's okay. I know this is a difficult time. Come anyway, and I'll buy you breakfast. As a friend. No questions."

"As a friend?" His voice brightened.

What would Norm say to that? What would her get-the-story-at-all-costs, soon-to-be-ex say? To hell with it. Julia didn't care. She liked Baldwin, even if she wasn't interested in anything more than friendship right now. The mayor was sensitive and thoughtful. The murder of a young college girl, especially so soon after Spradlin's release, must be killing him. Besides, the FBI was in charge of the investigation, and any release of information would be tightly controlled and might not extend to the mayor. What Baldwin knew was probably limited. With the announcement of the school closing, she had something to give Norm, so this truly would be breakfast with a friend, not a working one. "Yes. You've been a friend to me since I got here. It's my turn."

"Julia, that means a lot to me," he said, relief in his voice. "I'd love to then. I'm starving."

She hung up the phone, her attention returning to the screen in front of her. She went over her notes from the students' conversation and mulled over what she would report to Norm. While it would be unethical to report the possible name of the victim without confirmation, she would tell him about the lead on the missing sorority girl and campus security. She would include the information she might have been missing since the previous evening. Key to her report would be the action taken by campus administration. Sending the kids home sent a clear message. Her phone buzzed again. It was a text from Spradlin.

Are you still reading?

Chapter Forty-Seven

"HE WASN'T THERE." Talbot shoved his phone in his pocket as the two men walked to the car. The campus was quiet, the specter of the dead coed keeping many students in their dorms.

Cancini's steps slowed. "Any sign he'd been there this morning?" Throughout the first investigation, Spradlin had never run away, but met everything head-on.

"Coffeepot was still warm. We've got a team parked outside the house and a second one searching in town. Best we can do without a warrant."

"Why not get—"

"Don't start, Mike. We don't have enough to get a warrant. The official line is we're asking questions—that's it. After we find him, we can decide if a warrant is justified."

"You won't find him if he doesn't want to be found," Cancini said, reflecting on the man he'd known during the first wave of crimes. He hadn't changed.

Talbot slid into the driver's seat. "You don't have much faith."

Cancini closed the passenger door. "Spradlin's not your average guy. He's smart, really smart."

"Maybe. But he hasn't been in the real world in a long time."

"Doesn't matter. He'll be found when he wants to and not before."

"How can you be so sure?"

"I went to see him yesterday."

The FBI man froze. "I see. Should I even ask?"

"I didn't break any rules. I was only paying my respects."

"Your respects. Ri-ight."

They maneuvered through the police blockade, leaving the large bluestone buildings and manicured grounds behind. In town, the trees burst with red and gold leaves, the fall colors dazzling under the brilliant sun. Main Street had been subtly revitalized in the years since Cancini had been gone. Thriving shops and charming stores stood where buildings had once been run down. Anyone driving into Little Springs could not fail to see the beauty. It was picturesque, pure.

Cancini opened the door, breathing in clean, crisp fall air. The heat of the Indian summer had finally waned. He looked at the FBI man over the roof of the car. "Something about the body, the death, is different this time."

Talbot's face was grave. "The beating?"

"Yeah, that and the way her neck was broken."

"We don't have an official cause of death." They walked toward the squat brick building on the corner. "I think we need to wait for the coroner."

"Fair enough." Cancini looked down the street. A black and white was parked at the corner, and another Little Springs cop strolled the sidewalk. "Things are escalating."

Talbot looked at Cancini. "Okay. Let's say I agree with you. Things are escalating. Knowing it doesn't help anyone stop it from happening."

They climbed the stairs to the second floor. Cancini filled two mugs with coffee and brought them into the office. He set the steaming mugs on the desk and pulled up a chair. "Do you know what always struck me as odd about those first murders?"

"No," Talbot said, folding his hands together on the desk. "But I'm sure you're going to tell me anyway."

Cancini blew on his coffee and stretched his legs. "In every case, the cause of death was spinal shock, a broken neck. They were clean breaks, done in such a way that each of the girls died quickly. The M.E. said it was two to three minutes max."

"So?"

"So a broken neck doesn't guarantee death. It doesn't always kill a person. You could break your neck and be paralyzed but still live or even recover if the spinal cord wasn't injured. That's not what happened. Cheryl Fornak and the others, they died almost instantly with minimal suffering." Cancini set his coffee on the desk. "For that to happen, the neck has to be broken in precisely the right way, and it didn't just happen once. It happened five times."

Talbot fingered his tie, his eyes on Cancini. "What are you suggesting?"

"The old murders were cold and calculated. Maybe even an afterthought. He knew exactly how to break their necks to kill them. They weren't crimes of passion."

"I see." Talbot opened a file on the desk and tapped the thick stack of pages inside. "If I remember correctly, those girls were also beaten. That would imply crime of passion—if you want to use that description."

"Okay. How about this? Let's assume those beatings occurred during the rapes when the girls were still fighting. After the rapes, his emotions were spent. That's why the murders were quick, almost efficient. Maybe in his own sick way, he thought he was doing them a favor."

"A favor." Talbot shook his head and tossed the pen on the desk. "Mike, even if you're right, what does any of this have to do with today, with either of the recent murders?"

"I think it means that whether it's a copycat we're looking for—or someone else—they're growing more violent, more out of control. The violence isn't contained to the sexual assault." Cancini held up his hand and ticked off one finger. "First, Geri Hallwell didn't die of a broken neck. Instead, for whatever reason, he hit her in the head. But after she was dead, he put his hands around her neck. Why? To tell us that's what he meant to do? To make it look like a copycat?"

"What do you mean by make it look like a copycat?"

"All I mean is it wouldn't be that hard to make it look like a copycat killing without actually being a copycat. You could throw suspicion away from yourself by changing your M.O. just enough."

Talbot groaned. "Are we back to Spradlin now?"

"Hear me out. I know we need to wait for an official cause of death, but it was nothing like the original murders." He held up a second finger. "Second, Amanda Thompson was beaten badly. Worse than the other girls. Her face and upper body looked as though he used her as a punching bag. Three, he nearly ripped her head from her neck. Even if the cause of death was the same, how it was done was different. There was nothing clean about the way her head was hanging off that bench."

"Because with the other girls, it was quick?"

"Right."

"Copycat but not copycat."

"Right again."

Cancini sipped his coffee. "Our man is extremely angry. The violence is getting harder to control."

"Is that your medical opinion?" Talbot's face was grim, his voice tight. "Dammit, Mike. This is about Spradlin again."

"Maybe. Maybe not."

Talbot tapped the pen on the desk and stared at Cancini. "Fine. I'll bite. What are you thinking?"

Cancini shifted in the chair, pulling in his legs. "Spradlin was in jail a long time. That couldn't have been easy in a place like Red Onion. And all that time in solitary . . . he was already difficult, manipulative, maybe even a sociopath."

"You don't know that. He isn't guilty of anything."

"That we can prove." Talbot shook his head, but Cancini ignored him. "He plays with people, Derek. That press conference wasn't only aimed at the locals, it was scripted for the media." Julia's face came to mind. He suspected Spradlin was playing with her, but he didn't know how or why. "Maybe waiting twenty-odd years to die in a maximum security prison made him angrier than he's letting on. Who knows what kind of man he is now? His mother died while he was locked up. No one in this town will have anything to do with him. You saw that at the press conference. He's alone. No friends. There's anger—something—I know it." He paused, giving voice to one of the theories that made his head pound and his shoulders ache. "Think about it. Outside of us, nobody knows the details of this case better than Spradlin. If someone wanted to play at copycat, who better?"

"Revenge? You think he's getting even?" Talbot asked, lines etched between his brows.

The question was not an easy one to answer. Spradlin was

smart and manipulative. That hadn't changed. Prison hadn't broken him. But it could have brought violent tendencies, long repressed, back to the surface. It could have done things to him they didn't understand. Cancini ran his hand over his face, rubbing the dark stubble on his cheeks and chin. "I wish I knew, Derek. I wish I knew."

Chapter Forty-Eight

JULIA HAD KEPT her promise. It had taken all her willpower not to bombard Ted with questions, but he'd left after only a few minutes anyway. He was shaken, pale and jittery. Sipping decaffeinated coffee, he ate little and left quickly. She was packing up her laptop when Nikki slid into his empty seat.

"Who was that?" the young girl asked.

Julia smiled. She liked the girl's direct nature. "Already practicing to be a reporter?" Blushing, Nikki apologized. "It's okay," Julia told her. "That was Mayor Baldwin. He's mayor of Little Springs."

"Oh. That's why he looked familiar."

"Probably. He's also the great-grandson of the guy who founded Blue Hill. His family still has a large house on campus. He doesn't live in it, though. He lives in town. I think the house is used for visiting professors or something." Nikki said nothing. Her eyes shifted from Julia's to the door. Ted was long gone. "So, will you go home tomorrow?"

A shadow passed over the girl's face. "No. I'll stay."

"I thought they were closing the campus."

The girl shrugged. "I have a friend I can stay with in town. She's a day student and lives at home. I'll crash at her place."

Julia eyed the girl. "Home that bad?"

"It's not good," she said and slid out the seat. "I didn't know her name before today, but that girl they're saying was killed—Amanda Thompson—she came in here pretty much every day."

Julia nodded. It was the second time the girl had been identified by a student. "I'm sorry."

The girl glanced back at the counter. A handful of kids were waiting in line. "It's okay. Like I said, I didn't really know her." She shifted her weight, wiping her hands across her apron. "She was here yesterday, same time as you."

Julia remembered a few students coming in for coffee, but no faces came to mind. "I'm sorry, Nikki."

Her hands stopped moving and she squared her shoulders. "I don't know if this matters, but she was acting kinda weird. She asked me . . ."

"Nikki," a male voice from behind the counter interrupted. The line at the counter had grown. The young man was waving a towel at the kids waiting in line. "C'mon! Are you here to work or gossip?"

"I've gotta go," Nikki said.

"Wait." Julia reached out and took the girl's arm. "What did she ask you?"

"Nikki! Now!"

The girl pulled away. "I can meet you later. I have a class after I get off work, but I could come to your hotel about five."

Julia nodded as Nikki backed away. Maybe it was something, maybe nothing. Either way, it had to be more interesting than the stack of diaries she still had to read. "Sure," she said, "Five is good. I'm at the Little Springs Inn." As she slid her laptop into her bag, her phone buzzed again.

"What's up, Norm?"

"Wait until you hear this."

Chapter Forty-Nine

"We got two hits on the names from the construction company."

Cancini looked up from the files spread across the worktable. "What charges?"

Talbot read from the notes he'd taken. "We've got a twenty-six-year-old male who served three years for robbery. He's been out two years and has stayed clean as far as we know."

"What kind of robbery?"

"Broke into a neighbor's house and stole some electronics. Tried to pawn them for cash."

"Uh-huh. It's a long way from robbery to rape and murder. What else?"

The FBI man cleared his throat. "The second hit is a man who was accused of rape almost ten years ago."

Cancini leaned forward. "Convicted?"

"No. According to the report, the initial charge was date rape, but the girl backed out. She didn't go to the police until a couple of days later. There was no evidence other than some bruising. She was a student at Blue Hill."

Cancini nodded. Date rape was hard to prove and the emotional toll of a trial a high price to pay. The girl wasn't the first victim who didn't take the risk, even with the growing awareness of college date rape. "Sounds promising."

"Maybe. At the time, the kid lived in Staunton and was visiting a friend at one of the Blue Hill fraternities."

"Okay. Anything else?"

"About a year ago, he moved to Little Springs for the job. Since then, there's been a traffic incident that escalated into a full-blown fight. Witnesses disagreed on who was the first to throw a punch, so both men were arrested. But again, no felony conviction. According to the report, our man had only minor injuries. The other guy had a broken nose and ribs."

"So, suspected sexual assault and a hot temper."

"Looks that way. Both men are being questioned later today."

"Can I sit in?"

"I don't know if that's a good idea."

"I won't say a word."

Talbot hesitated, then shook his head. "Sorry. I'm sticking my neck out already."

There it was again. He was an outsider in the investigation whether he liked it or not. It was more difficult than he'd thought it would be. He changed the subject. "Forensics has the button?"

"Yeah," Talbot answered, relief in his voice. Cancini realized he'd been right not to push to sit in with the construction workers. "Marshall doesn't hold out much hope for prints, though. If she ripped it off his shirt, her fingers would be the last to have touched it. She would have smudged his prints. The best we can hope for is a partial."

Cancini frowned. Although he'd come to the same conclusion,

it was also the only physical evidence they had connecting them to the murderer. The girl had died with that evidence clutched in her hand. As she fought for her life, she was trying to help them. "There's gotta be something."

"There is," Talbot said, reading from his notes. "It's a four-hole mother-of-pearl button, one-eighth inch thick, typically found on custom shirts. Threads found on the button were a hundred percent cotton, high quality. They were light blue."

Cancini picked up his coffee and took a long swallow. "Custom." He had no idea what mother-of-pearl was exactly, but he was pretty sure none of his shirts had those kinds of buttons.

"Which means the button came off a shirt that was tailor-made for the perp."

"Okay." Cancini tapped his long fingers on the table. His ex-wife had tried to get him to a tailor once, telling him he needed to "upgrade" his wardrobe. He'd refused and disappointed her once again, unable to justify the expense on a detective's salary. Of course, not long after that, she upgraded herself, trading him in for his captain. "So our guy didn't buy his shirts at Sears. He liked to dress, and we can assume he wears custom shirts of high quality."

"Apparently."

"Doesn't sound like something a construction worker could afford."

"No, it doesn't."

"That narrows the pool a bit."

"True," Talbot agreed, "but it still includes a lot of people. I have three custom shirts myself. One of them is blue." Cancini raised an eyebrow. "Gifts from the wife."

"Right. Sure." Cancini drained the rest of his coffee, hiding his smirk behind the mug. "Still, there aren't that many people around here wearing expensive shirts. This is a mostly rural community."

"Yeah, maybe a few local businessmen might have them. And some professors I'd guess. Not a huge number." Talbot paused, then said, "We can't rule out that our guy might not be from around here. A copycat can be from anywhere."

"He's from around here. Both bodies were specifically placed. He knows the area."

Talbot seemed to consider Cancini's point. While the first girl was probably not meant to be found immediately, there was no doubt the second was intended as a statement. The courtyard where her body had been left would have been teeming with students by eight o'clock in the morning. Even a casual observer could have figured that out. "Maybe."

Cancini leaned back on the hard wooden chair. "Are there any custom shirt shops in town?" Most of the men in Little Springs wore khakis, jeans, work-style pants, and casual shirts. On Sundays, folks dressed for church, but even then, only the wealthier men in town wore suits or button-down shirts and blazers. On campus, professors ranged from casual to formal. He tried to calculate how many men would fall into the latter group.

"No. A local would have had to go to a bigger town." Talbot tapped his phone. "We've got a short list within a hundred-mile radius. The closest is Harrisonburg. There are several in Richmond, too."

Cancini nodded. Talbot would have each of those stores canvassed. They would match the names of clients with locals as well as customers who might have previous convictions of assault. He had no doubt they would be thorough.

His mind drifted to another man, a man who'd stood on the steps of the courthouse, gazed out at a hostile mob, and offered forgiveness. That man had spoken softly, nearly causing a riot with his words. He'd worn no tie, but the suit and shirt had been well-cut for a man who had just spent half his life in prison. In fact, he'd looked more like a magazine ad than an ex-con. The detective cleared his throat. "Can we find out what kind of wardrobe they gave Spradlin when he left prison?"

Chapter Fifty

"HE'S GOING HOME today," Father Joe said.

Cancini stood near the window overlooking Main Street, his head resting against the glass. Talbot had stepped out, giving Cancini privacy for his phone call. His father's release from the hospital was good news. He knew his father was anxious to get back to his own house, his own space. Like his son, he hated hospitals and the nurses and doctors hovering around him.

"Did you call that number I gave you? The one for the home nurse?"

"Yes, Michael. I've arranged for her to start the day shift tomorrow. A wonderful woman from my parish has volunteered to stay nights at the house. She promises he will hardly even know she's there."

"Good. He's gonna hate having someone in his house."

The old priest chuckled. "Don't I know it? He's weaker than a newborn babe but wanted to know why he couldn't drive himself home. Stubborn as a mule."

"Yeah." Cancini watched Mayor Baldwin walk from his office

to the diner, his gait that of a man carrying a heavy burden on his back. His coat jacket was buttoned up. In spite of the warm sun, the air had turned chilly overnight. "I'm sorry I can't be there."

"Nothing to be sorry about, Michael," the priest said. "He'll be fine. He is fine. He knows where you are."

A few of the locals in town had spotted the mayor and surrounded him. One gestured broadly. Baldwin stood and listened without interruption, then nodded and appeared to say a few words. After a few moments, the other man seemed to calm down, shook his head, and walked away.

"You heard the report then?"

"I didn't, but your father did. He told me. Saw it on TV."

"Oh." Cancini's fingers tightened around the phone. "What did he say?"

"He said he didn't expect you home anytime soon."

The words stung. He wasn't there to help his father when he needed him. He closed his eyes. Growing up, he'd blamed his father for shutting himself off, leaving the young Cancini to navigate the loss of his mother and adolescence on his own. Now the tables were turned, and it was Cancini who wasn't there.

Down on the street, the crowd around Baldwin had grown. A uniformed Little Springs officer moved quickly to break it up. Baldwin, to his credit, did not slink away. Cancini sighed. Whatever the detective's original reasons for coming to this small town, the murders of two more girls promised to keep him there. While his father's health was poor, he needed to see this through. To the end.

"He understands, Michael."

"Sure."

"He does. He's worried about you, and so am I."

The door opened. Talbot entered waving a file folder. The detective covered the mouthpiece on the phone. "Yeah?"

"M.E. wants a word with us. Meet you downstairs in five."

Cancini nodded, grabbing his notebook. "Father, I've gotta go. I'll call you tonight to be sure he got home and everything's okay."

"That's fine," the old priest said. His tone was soft, pleading. "Do what you need to do, Michael, and then come home."

Chapter Fifty-One

JULIA LOOKED AT the words typed across the screen. She'd written as much as she could. The girl's identity had been confirmed, and Norm had broken the news that rumors of a second dead girl were true. She had been found off campus earlier in the week. While the FBI wasn't giving many details, they had verified that both women had been sexually assaulted before they were killed. The similarities to the original cases were chilling.

She'd included these facts along with statements from the university regarding the school closing. Local police and campus police would only repeat the FBI statement. Cancini had not returned her phone call, and Ted was confined to the FBI statement, too. The most she could add to her story was a handful of quotes from students and locals on their reactions to the news. Satisfied she had done the best she could with so little information, she hit send.

The diaries on the table waited. She'd finished the first one in the morning but the stack was still daunting. It looked to be more of the same. She sighed and picked up the second book. Words on the third page made her blink and sit up a little straighter.

I think Leo knows. He won't talk to me and is giving me the cold shoulder. He goes out and doesn't come back for hours. When I ask him where he is, he just stares at me. I'm scared.

Julia read the date for the entry. Leo would have been in high school then. The reporter turned the page.

I don't know how he could know, but now I'm sure. God help me, it was the last thing I wanted for him. I've tried so hard to protect him, but I can see it in his face. He thinks I'm deceitful. He thinks I can't be trusted. He stares at me when I go out, like he doesn't believe me when I say I'm going to work or church or wherever. I'm losing him.

She looked up from the page, her fingers tapping absently. Why would young Leo not trust his mother? Julia thought about what was written in the diaries while the boy was growing up. Brenda's life had seemed to revolve around her son. Other than the one incident in middle school with the bullies, the years seemed to have gone by peacefully. She went to her job at the college and to church on weekends. She didn't seem to have many friends but wasn't a complainer. Was there a boyfriend? Was young Leo angry? Yet, if that was all, his behavior seemed immature and out of proportion. Unless . . . unless it was the identity of the boyfriend that bothered the teenage Leo.

Most of the rest of the diary was limited to Leo's antipathy. He avoided his mother most of the time, but when he didn't, he treated her with derision and scorn. One entry near the end of the book brought Julia to tears.

Today, Leo came to church. I didn't know he was there. I didn't see his head in the crowd. Pastor Williams spoke about the wisdom of choosing a life with Jesus, a life of grace and love. He spoke about our Father's eternal love for us. That we were wrapped in his love even when things were bad, when times were hard, when life was at its bleakest. The Lord our Father would protect us and take care of us. He was eloquent, and I remember feeling a warmth inside at his words. After, I wanted to thank him. I don't usually stop to speak to him, but today, I felt compelled. Only after I got in line did I see him. My son, Leo, was standing behind Pastor Williams, nodding at folks, as though he were there every Sunday of his life. It made me cry when he stopped coming with me after grade school, but he wouldn't budge. "I don't believe in all that stuff, Mom. To me, God is like Santa Claus or the Easter Bunny. Fakes." I told him it was different, that God was visible in many places and in many people if he looked, but he shook his head. "You go if it makes you feel better. I don't need to look for God in the faces of strangers. I already know." He was so matter-of-fact, so sure, I let it go, hoping he would come back to God later.

Seeing him standing there filled me with joy. Once or twice, Pastor Williams turned and smiled at Leo while I waited. When I got to the front of the line, Pastor Williams took both my hands in his. "Good to see you, Mrs. Spradlin. I hope you enjoyed my sermon today." I did, I told him. "It was beautiful. Truly inspiring." Leo had moved right next to the pastor. Their shoulders were touching. I saw Pastor Williams look at Leo, questioning, but Leo kept his eyes on me. "Yes, Mom, it was beautiful. Truly inspiring as you say. It's too bad you're such a hypocrite."

Pastor Williams gasped. Leo said it quietly. I heard it, and the pastor, but no one else I think. "What do you know about truth and honesty? What do you know about anything, Mom?"

He hates me. My son hates me.

Chapter Fifty-Two

"YOU LIED TO me." Cancini stood close to the mayor, his voice low.

It had taken ten minutes to corner Baldwin alone. A cluster of reporters had descended on him the minute he entered the lobby. The mayor had stood politely, saying little, sticking to the FBI script, his face the picture of solemn empathy. Deep lines had appeared around his mouth and across his broad forehead. Away from the reporters, his shoulders fell and he moved with lethargic steps.

Baldwin sighed. His suit jacket hung folded over one arm. His loosened tie and unbuttoned collar gave him the look of a man who'd had a long, hard day at the office. "I'm too tired for games, Mike."

Cancini moved closer, his face only inches from Baldwin's. "But not for playing them." The mayor sighed again but said nothing. "You told me Spradlin called you from prison before he returned to Little Springs. You told me he threatened you. It was your whole story for getting me here. Spradlin never called you. He never called anyone. Ever."

Baldwin's eyes cut to the group of reporters clustered around the lobby. With one hand, he slipped off the tie around his neck and stuffed it in his pocket. "You're right." He stepped back from Cancini and lifted his chin. "Leo didn't call me. I called him."

Cancini folded his arms across his chest. "Go on."

"One of the attorneys on his team was an old law school buddy of mine. He agreed to put me in touch with him. I didn't want him here. I didn't want him in Little Springs. That's why I called him. I begged him not to come back, but he's a cold son of a bitch."

Cancini looked hard at the man he'd once considered his friend. Teddy's eyes were bloodshot and rimmed by dark moons. He rocked back and forth on his heels, all the while jingling change in his pants pocket. "You lied to me," Cancini repeated.

"Yes, I lied to you, and I'd do it again. I lied about calling him because I knew you wouldn't understand. Clearly, I was right. But I didn't lie about him threatening me. That part was true."

Cancini's jaw tightened. "I'm listening."

"When I asked Leo not to come back, he laughed. Asked me if I was scared." The mayor's face reddened. "I told him I wasn't, but I was. And he knew it."

"What were you afraid of, Teddy? Spradlin had been cleared. You said that yourself when you stood at that podium and welcomed him back."

"I never welcomed him back," Baldwin said, his voice shaking. "I stated the facts. That's all." He paused. "Yes, I was afraid. Afraid of what might happen if he did return."

"Of what might happen? What does that mean?"

Baldwin's head dropped, and his shoulders heaved. When he raised his head, he blinked away tears. He reached out a beefy hand and laid it on Cancini's shoulder. "We both know what it means, Mike. Everything I was afraid of is happening, and we both know it. That's why I lied. To get you here. And I'd do it again. When I heard Leo was dead-set on coming back, I knew. Same as you." Dropping his hand, he walked away.

Cancini watched Baldwin move back toward the reporters. With each step, the mayor seemed to bring himself up a little taller. Once among the reporters, Cancini could see only the top of his head bobbing in time with questions he couldn't hear. He knew Baldwin would look each reporter in the eye, would think before answering each question, and would somehow make them believe he was telling them all he could without telling them anything at all. The detective frowned. Whatever his motives, Baldwin would always be a politician.

Chapter Fifty-Three

CANCINI PACED THE room, watching Talbot as he spoke on the phone. Talbot glanced up, scratching out a few words on a notepad. He ended the call, and Cancini sat down across from the FBI man.

"Well? Was I right?"

"Mike, I put myself out there for you."

"Derek, I didn't ask you to—"

"I know you didn't." Talbot held up a hand. "But there are a lot people with eyes on this case. When I ask about Spradlin's clothes on the day of the press conference and where they came from, word gets passed up the line."

Cancini crossed his arms. "It's a valid question."

"I can't have this office look like there's some kind of vendetta against Spradlin." He hesitated, fingering the wire of his spiral notebook. "No one wanted you on this. There are some who want you gone already."

Cancini stood up. "We've been over this."

"Yes, and I'm afraid it's the last time. I can't have you be a wild card. No more visits to Spradlin I don't know about."

"That was—"

"And no more wild-goose chases or you're out."

Cancini placed both hands on the chair and leaned forward. "So, I was wrong?"

"No and yes."

"What?"

"No, you weren't wrong. Spradlin did wear a custom blue shirt with mother-of-pearl buttons the day of the press conference."

"I knew it." Cancini paced the office again, chewing his lower lip. "Is it enough for a warrant?"

"Mike, stop. It's a wild-goose chase. It doesn't mean a goddamn thing."

Cancini shook his head. "I don't understand. Are you saying the evidence doesn't matter?"

"Not at all. What I'm saying is the button is more common than we thought. Turns out that quite a few folks from around the state wear custom shirts, and the majority of those retailers use the same button supplier—including the store where John Shandling's dad buys shirts."

"Who?"

"The construction worker, the one with the date rape charge. His dad wears them. Like I said, you were right. Spradlin does have a custom-made blue shirt, but it doesn't mean a thing. Turns out I do, too. So does the president of the college, the mayor, the lieutenant governor, and hundreds more who live within driving distance of Little Springs."

"But none of those people just got out of prison. It's circumstantial, I know, but it has to mean something."

"Out of prison for crimes he didn't commit." Cancini remained silent. "Look, we'll use the button, but by itself, it doesn't mean a thing. There were no prints or usable DNA." He paused, his tone softening. "We need to follow the evidence, Mike."

"It should be enough for a warrant."

"Based on what? That an innocent man has a shirt with a button that I have and the governor has. He hasn't done anything. No warrant."

Cancini pounded his hand on the back of the chair. "Goddammit! It's the governor, isn't it?"

"Sit down, Mike." Cancini's head shot up and his fingers tightened around the wooden back of the chair. "Don't make it personal." Talbot watched him. "We've known each other a long time. You're a good cop. If Spradlin's done something, fine. We'll get him. But it has to be the right way."

Cancini let go of the chair and nodded. Talbot was right. But he'd been right, too, and it meant something. "Can I see the list?"

"The list?"

"The names of all the people who have one of those custom shirts with the buttons."

"Why?"

"I just want to see it. Sometimes a name will pop out or maybe I'll remember something later."

The FBI man searched his face. "Fine. I'll have it sent to your phone." He picked up a folder from his desk, changing the subject. "This is a stack of student interviews. We talked to as many teachers, administrators and friends of the two girls we could, but we came up empty. Virtually nothing connects them. No classes. No friends in common. Amanda Thompson had only been on campus a short time. There's just nothing obvious linking the girls."

"Except they were both students at Blue Hill."

"Yes, except that." He flipped a few pages in the file. "So far, the little forensics we do have points to the copycat theory. The profile of escalating violence fits these crimes, a first-timer getting off on the power. Our expert also worked up a new profile for us on the original cases."

"And?"

"She believes the killer in the first series of rapes was better able to control his emotions, to disassociate himself after the sexual assault and kill them quickly. You were right. He probably had some knowledge of anatomy in order to break their necks in just the right way. Not so in these recent cases—which, according to our expert, also supports the copycat theory. Our copycat can be provoked more easily, is less able to rein in his emotions." He closed the file. "It appears someone out there wants to be the next Coed Killer."

Cancini nodded. He couldn't disagree with her assessment, and it wouldn't be the first incident of a copycat killer, someone who wanted to latch on to fame, even in the shadow of another. A copycat killer might possess the right homicidal tendencies to carry out the crime but lack any creativity on his own. "It's a logical theory."

Talbot clucked his tongue. "But what?"

"But nothing." He stared at the floor, shifting his weight from one foot to the other. "It's a good theory."

"I'm glad you can see that. Turns out Shandling has no alibi for the Hallwell murder but claims to have one for the second girl. We're checking into it."

He rubbed his chin. "So you're thinking since Shandling has a history of women and temper issues, maybe he snapped."

"Maybe. It's a possibility."

"The part about our guy not being able to control his emotions.

What about in daily life? Would he have difficulties at work? With friends and family?"

Talbot picked up a pen and tapped it against the file. "Good question but hard to answer. As you know, there isn't any one-size-fits-all profile. Ted Bundy was able to fool a lot of people, was smooth and well-liked. He used youth and good looks to lure in a lot of innocent women. Shandling's only thirty. He's a good-looking guy and likes to dress up. You could make a case he would fit here. Of course, history is also filled with serial killers who preferred to fade into the background. They're quiet or different or try not to be noticed."

"Until they want to be noticed."

"Yes, until then."

Cancini cleared his throat. "Will you still talk to Spradlin—even without a warrant?"

Talbot sighed. "Yes. The timing has stirred up a hornet's nest around here, as you know. Spradlin missing is a problem. It looks bad for the governor. Copycat or not, we need to talk to him, cover all the bases."

"He'll be found when he wants to be found."

"You've said that before."

Cancini shrugged. "He knows every inch of the land around here. Growing up, his mom worked, and he was left alone. He wasn't the kind of kid who spent the day sitting in the house. If he wants to hide, he knows how and where."

"Okay, found or not found, we'll continue to build our case, such as it is," Talbot said. "We've got a person of interest in Shandling, we've got the profile, and we've got the nature of the crimes. That's it. That's our case."

"You've got the button."

"Dammit, Mike, weren't you listening? The button by itself is not evidence. Why are you so damn pigheaded?" Cancini bowed his head. The silence stretched over a minute, then two. Talbot rubbed his temples. "I'm sorry. I didn't mean that. It's been two days since Amanda Thompson was found. We're running out of time."

Cancini opened his mouth, closed it again. The case was getting to all of them. "It's okay. The kids have gone home?"

"Yes." Talbot fell back against his chair. "Thank God. That's about all the good news we've got."

"How about the original DNA? Any hits yet?"

"No. Nothing so far."

"So, it stands to reason, the original killer could still be out there?"

"Yeah, it's possible. We haven't finished checking the surrounding states." Talbot's face was drawn. He'd already put in countless hours on the case. The pressure on the FBI man came straight from the governor. And Cancini didn't need to be reminded Talbot was putting his job on the line allowing him around the case.

Cancini laid a hand on his old friend's shoulder. "We'll get him, Derek. We'll get him."

Chapter Fifty-Four

JULIA SAT BACK against the stiff lobby sofa and sipped from a bottle of water. She brushed her hair out of her face and scanned the words on the screen. The noise level in the bar made her look up. Reporters and journalists had been pouring into town since the early hours of the morning and swarmed the bar and lobby. She was grateful Nikki had escaped before she was spotted by some eager young reporter from a tabloid. Smiling grimly, she focused again on her computer.

"Fancy meeting you here." Ted stood over her, a sheepish grin on his face. His sleeves were rolled up to his elbows and he smelled of coffee and nicotine. She pasted on a smile and closed her computer. He slipped into the chair opposite her. "I was hoping you and I could have a drink tonight," he said, tipping his head in a shy manner. "Things have been a little crazy, and it would be nice to catch a few minutes with a friend." He leaned forward and touched her arm. "If you're free?"

Julia bit her lip, his fingers on her arm cold and clammy.

"Thanks, Ted. I would, but I'm not." A confused look crossed his face. "Free, I mean. I'm not free tonight."

"I see." His smile twitched, then faded. "I can't say I'm not disappointed." He removed his hand from her arm and looked at her from under thick lashes. "Is it Spradlin?"

Julia inhaled sharply. Was it that small a town, or was she overreacting? She remembered Ted had been nothing but kind to her and she'd witnessed firsthand how devastated he was by events on campus. Julia felt the tension in her shoulders loosen. Aloud, she said, "Ted, are you jealous?"

The smile returned. "Of course not. We're friends, right? Not jealous." He laughed, holding up two fingers close together. "Well, maybe a little."

She smiled, too. It was hard not to like Ted. He was warm and funny, and eager to please. Nikki could be confused, an honest mistake. Still . . .

"Actually, I'm working on a story," she said, lowering her voice. "It's a girl who says someone's been following her."

"Interesting." He leaned back against the cushions, resting his hands on the armrest. "But if she's being followed, why come to you? Why not go to the police?"

She sipped from her water. He hadn't batted an eyelid. "That's exactly what I said. Seems logical to me, too, but she says she has her reasons."

"Sounds like she might be trying to get her name in the paper."

"Maybe." Julia studied his expression. He seemed unfazed, but his hand dropped to his lap. He picked at the fabric of his wool slacks, pinching it, letting it go, pinching it again. "I don't think so, though. I think she's telling the truth."

"What makes you say that?"

She kept her eyes on his face, a tingle prickling at her neck. "She works at that coffee shop on campus, the one near the park." He pursed his lips. "Yesterday, when she left work, she felt like someone was watching her. She tried to lose him by doubling back and stuff like that, but she knew he was still there."

A tiny vein throbbed at his temple. "How would she know that?"

"She saw him."

"Saw him?" His jaw tightened, but he recovered quickly. His fingers twitched in time with the throbbing vein. His face paled, but he held his voice steady. "Did she recognize the man?"

Julia's forced a shrug. "No. Said he seemed familiar, but she couldn't say why. Didn't know who he was."

"I see," he said after a moment, color returning to his face. "Well, I still think if this story is legit, she should go to the police." He stood, all traces of anxiety erased. The vein had stopped jumping, and his fingers were still.

She flushed under his gaze. "I'll tell her."

"Good. It's just my opinion, of course."

"You're probably right. Maybe she is only looking for publicity."

"Yep. You know how kids are these days." His lips had turned up again. "How about a rain check on that drink?"

"Sure," she said, forcing lightness in her tone. "I'd like that." He squeezed through the packed lobby, stopping once to clap a friend on the back. At the door, he wheeled around, finding her watching him. She raised a hand, then looked away, sucking in her breath. He'd known she was lying. She was sure of it.

Chapter Fifty-Five

NIKKI HAD KNOWN he was there. Years of dodging media and her father's security team had trained her well. She knew Julia hadn't believed her, thought she'd made a mistake or misjudged, and Nikki didn't blame her. She wouldn't have believed her, either.

"Are you sure you're not confusing him with someone else? It's an easy thing to do." Julia had leaned in and touched her lightly on the arm. "Why would he be following you? It doesn't make sense."

That was a harder question and one she'd chosen not to answer. She'd shrugged and changed the subject instead. But she knew it wasn't a mistake. She wasn't afraid, although she knew she should be. What he'd done to those other girls was horrible. This man was evil, with a terrible violence in his soul. She'd seen it before, knew it well. She wasn't like those other girls, though. They hadn't been prepared. They had fought him, but they hadn't known he was coming like she did. She didn't need anyone to tell her. She could feel it.

Nikki wondered if she should have gone home instead of staying with a friend, but she pushed the nagging doubts to the corner of her mind. Home was no better and it wouldn't change anything anyway. Nikki squinted in the dark until her eyes gradually adjusted to the shadowy light in the unfamiliar bedroom. She could just make out the shape of her friend Allison, lying on her side, covers kicked aside, snoring softly. She swung her legs over the side of the bed and set her feet silently on the floor. Grateful for the thick carpeting, she tiptoed across the floor and slipped out of the room. The door clicked shut. She froze, scanning the empty hallway. When she heard nothing, she went down the stairs, toward the study. Gray moonlight shone through the window's sheer curtains. She made her way across the room to the heavy oak desk, moving behind it.

Squatting, Nikki pulled a wooden box from under the desk. Allison, nervous about the campus murders, had told her it was there. She hesitated at the lock on the cover, but she had been told about that, too. Reaching under the bottom drawer, she felt for the key her friend had told her would be held in place by tape. With deft hands, she loosened the tape and used the key to turn the lock. It released, and she lifted the cover. Inside was a pistol, glowing black against the bloodred lining of the case. She picked it up, turning it over in her hands. It was heavier than the guns she'd learned to shoot the year before. Even so, the weight felt right.

She wouldn't be like those other girls. She knew what he was, and she wouldn't give him the satisfaction. People underestimated her all the time, and often, she let them. It was easier that way. But not this time.

Chapter Fifty-Six

CANCINI STEPPED INSIDE, instantly wrapped in a blanket of greasy, smoky air. Ernie stood behind the bar unloading and stacking glass mugs. A half-smoked cigarette dangled from his lips. It was the bartender who'd arranged the meeting, but not without a word of warning. "Don't know for sure what ol' Jerry knows, Mike, but if there's anything, he's the one to know it. I heard some stuff around the bar during the first go-'round, before Spradlin got arrested, some nasty stuff, but the bottle has a way of distorting the truth. Jerry though, he's a newspaperman, the old-fashioned kind. If it ain't a fact, he'll keep his trap shut."

"I understand," he said.

The retired journalist was waiting for him. Heavyset with a shock of bushy gray hair, he stood slowly, extending his thick hand. "Jerry Wilkins," he said. "Mike Cancini, right?" The detective nodded. "I remember you. As I recall, you refused to be interviewed, even after you got Spradlin."

Cancini sat down. "Sorry about that. I'm not too good with the press. It wasn't personal."

The man sipped on a Jack and Coke. "Hell, if I took people turning down interviews as a personal affront, I'd have no friends at all." He grinned. "There were plenty of others who were willing to talk, especially during the trial. Everyone after their fifteen minutes."

"Sure," Cancini said. He remembered. The case was on the front page of the local paper for weeks.

"Seems like history's repeating itself."

"Maybe," the detective said. He pulled out a small notebook and pen. "Do you mind?"

"Why not," the man said with a shrug. "Could be interesting to have the tables turned."

"Well, I think Ernie might've told you I'm doing some background, trying to get a better picture of the past, what it was like here before the trial, before the rapes and murders."

The man picked up his drink, swallowing the rest in one gulp. He wiped his mouth with the paper cocktail napkin, balled it up and tossed it on the table. "That was a long time ago. Little Springs was a pretty peaceful town, I guess." His fat fingers traced the rim of the empty glass. He was in no hurry to answer. "Still had the paper mill then, and the college had started growing. Economy was pretty good for us. Things were looking good." His hand dropped from the glass. "But that's not the stuff you want to hear."

"No."

"You want to hear about the rumors."

"I guess I do."

The man stiffened. "I'm not a fan of gossip, young man. That may be the kind of stuff that gets printed in the papers today, but I believe in facts. Facts are news. Rumors are not."

Cancini held his gaze. "I understand, Mr. Wilkins, but if it's possible there's any truth to those rumors, they could be important."

"Well, I don't see how. Even as sordid as those rumors were, there was never any hint of the kind of violence in the coed cases. It was more sexual harassment type stuff. I don't see how one thing has to do with the other. "

"Maybe it doesn't. I don't know. What I do know is that too many girls have been lost at Blue Hill. I don't know if the past has anything to do with what's happening now, but I'd like to find out."

Wilkins sat back and folded his arms across his chest. A throwback, he reported news. He didn't create or generate it, and Cancini had to respect that. But Cancini knew the retired editor was also a father and a grandfather of girls, and he hoped his appeal would make a difference. The old man's face softened.

"I had a woman who came to the paper once. Claimed she was raped. She was upset and wanted us to do a story," the retired journalist said. "She was a sophomore, only nineteen years old."

"But you didn't do the story?"

A shadow passed over the old man's face. "No, I didn't. I sent one of my guys to investigate, and he came back with nothing. Said she was a girl with an ax to grind. She refused to go to the police, so we had to drop it."

"But you think maybe the girl was telling the truth?"

"I don't know," the man admitted. "Maybe."

Cancini wrote a few things in his notebook. "The reporter you sent. Did he say why he thought the girl was lying?"

The old newspaperman's eyes hardened and the lines around his mouth deepened. "I sent a young man I thought had more ambition than ability. I thought his eagerness would help him ferret out the story, if there was one. I think now maybe I made an error in judgment. About a week after he told me there was no story, he got a new job, a big job, up in Philly." The man's lip curled. "He was more ambitious than I thought."

Tapping his pen against the notepad, Cancini sat back against the hard wooden chair. "Dropping the story and getting the new job. You suspected the two things were connected?"

Jerry snorted. "Maybe I did. Maybe I still do, but there's no way to know for sure. I do know he left me in the lurch on more than one story. Whole staff had to work overtime to get the paper out."

The waitress brought another Jack and Coke for Jerry. She set a frothy mug of beer in front of Cancini. "Ernie sent it over," she said. He thanked her and took a swig. It was cold and tasty.

"What about the girl? Did you ever follow up with her?"

"I tried. Went up to the college myself to interview her, but she'd dropped out and gone home. The school said she left because of poor grades. Her parents wouldn't talk. That was the end of the story."

"I see." Jerry had been right. It was more unsubstantiated rumor. Ernie had warned him, but that didn't ease his disappointment. "Well, thanks for your time, Mr. Wilkins."

"Sorry I wasn't more help. I'd like to see this madness stop."

"Yes, sir." Cancini stood, picking up his mug.

Wilkins gestured for Cancini to wait. "Detective, it was a different time back then." Cancini nodded. "Old man Baldwin, he ran the college back then, and he pretty much ran the town, too. Seemed like he had a hand in everything that happened around here."

"I remember him." Cancini recalled a man whose authority was unquestioned by those around him, even the chief of police.

At the time, the college president had been absolutely frantic about the rapes and murders, calling the police chief several times a day for an update on the case. Back then, everyone deferred to him. Cancini sat down again, setting the heavy mug on the table. The old man wasn't done.

"Down here in town," the old reporter said, "we didn't know everything that was going on up at the college. So, when we heard rumors, we didn't pay much attention." He ran his large hand over his face and rubbed his chin. "There is one man, a professor, who might know something. He wouldn't talk then, maybe out of grief, maybe 'cause of something else, but those reasons are long gone now. He might be willing." Wilkins gave Cancini the name and number. "Let me know how it turns out." He eased out of the chair, throwing a handful of bills on the table. "I hope you find the facts, young man. Soon."

Chapter Fifty-Seven

JULIA SAT CROSS-LEGGED in the middle of the bed, her hands wrapped around her cell phone and a notebook filled with questions in her lap. She pushed the button illuminating the screen. One fifty-four a.m. Spradlin would call in a few moments. She leaned back against the pillows and scrolled through the texts she'd received and sent in the last few hours.

10:15 p.m. *Have you read the diaries?*

10:25 p.m. *Half, maybe more but not all of them yet.*

10:26 p.m. *Finish them now. It's important.*

What was the point? What could possibly be in those diaries that was so important? Exhausted, she was tired of playing his cat-and-mouse games. She'd spent most of the last two days on the story of the murders, picking up the diaries in free moments. Still, she'd learned nothing more than young Leo was still angry with his mother over something she'd kept hidden from him. Mrs. Spradlin had begun tiptoeing around her own son. Julia disliked them both. She didn't want to read the diaries. She wanted a scotch and a hot bath.

10:35 p.m. *Why don't you tell me what you want me to know?*

10:36 p.m. *Read. Please!!!*

She'd rolled her eyes at first, then looked at the text again. He wasn't just telling her to read. He was begging. She'd picked up the diary. Why was it so important to him that she read his mother's diaries? And why now? He had to know what was going on at the campus and in town. He had to know the FBI was searching for him. Rumors were all over town.

10:42 p.m. *I'll read. Where are you?*

10:43 p.m. *Thank you. I'll call you at 2.*

And that had been it. She'd finished nearly an hour earlier, although a small part of her wished she'd never started. She checked the time again. One fifty-nine a.m. Any second, her phone would vibrate. She held the notebook in her lap. It was filled with question after question.

She flinched when the phone buzzed once, then twice.

"Hello?"

"Do you understand now?"

"I . . . I think so."

"Have you talked to anyone?"

"No."

"Good. Can we meet?" She didn't answer. "It's important that I speak to you. Only you."

Julia shivered. Norm had been more right than he realized. This was the story of the year—maybe the decade. Her fingers had been itching for the last hour. If she wrote the story well, she could win a prize. If she lived to write it.

"Where? When?"

"I'm in a cabin about forty miles outside of town. Do you have a pen?"

When he ended the call, Julia sat motionless, the phone still in her hand. She shivered again, her skin clammy. She must be out of her mind. The realization of what she had just agreed to sank in. She would meet with a killer. She knew it at midnight, the words in the diary leaving no room for doubt. He was not an innocent man, unjustly convicted. No, he was guilty. She took deep breaths to steady her nerves. The story was the thing. He'd promised she would get the story, the whole story. He'd also promised she would be safe. She wasn't stupid. She was well aware the carrot he was dangling was a dangerous one, but still . . .

An hour passed. Two hours. Three hours. She rose stiffly from the bed and gathered the diaries into a pile. From her bag, she pulled out the large manila envelope with her name scrawled across the front and slid the books inside the envelope. She opened her spiral notebook to a fresh page and wrote a message. "These books were given to me by Leo Spradlin of his own free will. They were the property of his mother and should now be used as evidence." Before she could change her mind, she signed her name and added the notebook to the envelope. She dressed and filled her bag with a fresh notebook, pens, and her tape recorder. Goose bumps covered her arms in spite of the heater she'd turned on during the night.

She picked up the envelope and sealed it with tape. With a large, black marker, she crossed out her name and wrote another: Detective Michael Cancini. The journals and her notes were the only insurance she had, especially if anything happened to her. She sat down, her head bowed. If she didn't go, things would get worse. More girls would surely die. If she did go, she might be next. What if this was a trick? What if everything he said was part of another plan, one she didn't want to contemplate? Her heart thumped under her clothes.

She stood and clutched the envelope to her chest. It held the biggest story of her career, of her life. It held the truth. Her fingers prickled and she rubbed them absently on her pants. She had to go. She locked the envelope in the safe and took one more look around the room. There was nothing else she could do. She opened the door. He had promised.

Chapter Fifty-Eight

He pulled the dark curtain aside, peeking out the window. A gunmetal haze hung low over the ground. He sighed. Winter weather would be coming soon. Letting the curtain fall, he rose from the bed and dressed quickly. It was Sunday, the almighty day designated for worship and reflection. The good people of Little Springs would put on their Sunday best and shuffle off to church services. They would sing and hold their Bibles and nod when the preacher told them they were sinners. The man grunted. What God? He hadn't believed in that for longer than he could remember.

He studied his reflection, squinting to make out his features in the shadows. He dared not turn on a light and give any sign of his location. It had been years since he'd needed his safe place, and it was best to lie low. He'd need to keep his senses sharp.

He picked up a cell phone from the table and flipped to the pictures. The first photo showed the blonde, her hair streaked with blood, her long, muscular limbs limp and lifeless. She wasn't so damn bouncy anymore. There were two more of her, then four of the second girl. His heart pounded as he scrolled through them one by one. He knew it was stupid to have taken the pictures and even dumber to have kept them, but he couldn't help it. He looked at the last picture. It was the girl from the coffee shop. Blurry and taken from a distance, the photo could not mask the girl's pluck or beauty. His loins stirred. He sensed something different about her. She wasn't like the others, didn't easily fit a type. She wasn't a sorority girl or an academic. She seemed bright, and she had a handful of friends. But she was more complicated, wasn't she? He imagined she wanted independence—not only from her family but from what was expected. Oh, how he would love to wipe that insolent look off her pretty face.

He'd expected her to evacuate like the others. Spotting her had felt like a sign. She'd walked several blocks, then backtracked, changing direction more than once. She was smarter than most. He'd give her that, but it wouldn't save her. Did she think she was safe? Did she have a young person's misguided confidence in her own immortality? It didn't matter. She would learn no one lives forever. Death always finds you, one way or another. He breathed a sigh of satisfaction. For the girl from the coffee shop, that day was coming.

He left the darkness of the room and went into the bathroom, where he'd covered the window with a large, black plastic bag. A nightlight provided the only illumination. He filled the bathtub and scrolled through the pictures one more time, lingering on the photo of the girl from the coffee shop. He tossed the phone into the water and watched it sink. There could be no loose ends.

It would be finished soon. One more girl, and the hysteria would be unstoppable. A moment of melancholy washed over him. He would miss the girls. It would hurt like hell, but that's how it had to be. He'd suffered through withdrawal before, and he would have to do it again. The memory of this girl and the others would have to last. If only he could stop time and make it last forever.

This girl would be his final prize, and Julia something altogether different. He liked her. She meant well, but she was nosy, like any reporter—always asking questions. At first, she'd been easy to manipulate, her ambition and desperation to get the story obvious. He'd fed her tidbits, and she'd taken it all. But the two dead girls had made her wary. She was a problem now. It was a damn shame. He'd have to use her hunger to succeed to trap her and destroy her. A smile crept across his face. Two bitches. It was going to be a good day.

Chapter Fifty-Nine

Julia stepped out of the hotel. A fog had risen during the night and hovered over the road like a veil, blurring the light of the streetlamps. The horn of a distant train sounded. The air blew cold, and she pulled her jacket tight across her chest. Glancing at her watch, she knew it would take close to an hour to reach Spradlin. By then, she hoped the sun would be up and the gray skies gone.

She took her time. It wasn't too late to change her mind. She still had enough for a great story. No one would blame her. Norm would understand. He always did. She bit her lip. Yes, he would understand, and he wouldn't say a word. But she'd see the look in his eyes. Norm would know she wasn't willing to take the big risks for the big stories. He'd try to hide his disappointment. He'd tell her she'd done the right thing, but he wouldn't mean it. Spradlin had promised her details—everything. The diaries weren't enough. They were hearsay at best. Norm was a newspaperman and Julia knew how it worked. Without the big story, she'd be relegated to fluffy articles about cute dogs for the rest of her life or be forced to quit the paper. No thanks.

She picked up her pace and walked toward the rental car she had parked around the corner. Off Main Street, darkness and close fog enveloped her. A few streetlamps dotted the streets, though not enough to make a difference. The buildings seemed larger and more imposing in the pre-dawn hours. She walked faster to the compact car. Fumbling with the keys, her hands shook as she opened the door. Sliding quickly into the seat, she immediately hit the lock button. She laid her head on the steering wheel and counted to ten until she'd stopped shaking. What was she trying to prove? This was crazy.

Her phone buzzed in her pocket, and she pulled it out with shaking fingers. Another text from Spradlin.

Are you on your way?

She looked out into the darkness. The fog moved across the road, evaporating with each passing minute. The moon glowed, its welcome light cutting through the dark. She exhaled. With steadier hands, she typed her response.

Leaving now.

He answered immediately.

Don't be scared. I'm waiting for you.

She said the words out loud once, twice. "Don't be scared. I'm waiting for you." She turned the key in the ignition, flicking on the headlights. She whispered his words again. "Don't be scared. Don't be scared." She picked up her phone, scrolling quickly through her contacts. She typed out a message to Norm.

Meeting Spradlin. If you don't hear from me by eleven, find Cancini, and tell him to open the safe in my room.

She hesitated, her fingers poised over the keypad. Norm was a good friend, a loyal friend. No matter what, he should know that.

Don't mean to scare you, but want to tell you I love you. Hope to see you soon.

Fingers trembling, she hit send. One way or the other, the truth would be told. Shivering, she turned on the heat, latched her seat belt, and pressed her foot to the gas. It was time to prove what she was made of. "Don't be scared."

Chapter Sixty

CANCINI SAT UP, running his hands through his short, spiky hair. He wasn't sure how long he'd slept, maybe a couple of hours, maybe more. It didn't matter. Slipping out of bed, he took a five-minute shower, dressed, and answered the door for room service. Moving to the desk where he'd left his notebook, he sipped steaming coffee. He reread several pages, his mind racing. The notes were nothing more than stories, unsubstantiated rumors, yet the detective was convinced they meant something. Sexual harassment was nothing new, but was it true? He rubbed his temples, brows furrowed. The old reporter was right. Even if the rumors were true, what did it have to with now? What did any of it have to do with the murders of the last few days? Or the ones from decades earlier? He shook his head. He was getting ahead of himself. He needed to know the truth first.

Finished with the pot of coffee, he shoved the notebook in his jacket pocket. He had an appointment with the professor on campus, the one the old reporter had told him about. Retired, the man still lived in the same faculty housing he'd lived in for nearly forty years. Cancini considered telling Talbot about the meeting, then thought better of it. His friend didn't need the headache. It was better to leave the FBI out of it until he had facts.

Talbot intercepted Cancini in the lobby. "We have a lead on Spradlin."

"Ah. I guess that explains why you're here so early."

"Three independent callers on the tip line say they saw him two days ago in Martinsville. That's about an hour from here to the west. He was buying cases of water and lots of canned food."

"Supplies."

"That's what it looks like. I sent a team to interview the storeowners, see if anyone remembers which way he went. I've got an APB out on his truck for half the state and into West Virginia."

The two men walked through the lobby. Cancini stopped at a coffee stand, buying two fresh cups. He handed one to Talbot. "Full-blown APB? I thought you just wanted to talk to him."

The FBI man sipped the scalding coffee. His eyes swept over the quiet lobby, ignoring the question. "I've been trying to call you since last night."

"My phone was off."

"Bullshit."

Cancini appraised his old friend. They stood for a moment, each holding their cups, saying nothing.

Talbot spoke first. "Shandling's alibi is solid for the Thompson murder. He's not our copycat."

"You're sure?"

"Yeah."

"I'm sorry."

"Me too. The brass wants this solved yesterday, but they don't want us to smear the governor's name in the process. The truth is,

I don't know what I think about Spradlin. The full APB is insurance. Maybe it is some kind of revenge. Who knows? But it doesn't make sense. He's finally free. Why risk it?"

Cancini opened his mouth to comment, then shut it again. There was nothing he could say that Talbot hadn't already thought of, hadn't turned over multiple times in his head.

"Spradlin going underground—if that's what he's doing—looks suspicious. It's possible he's going underground to avoid being targeted. People around here don't exactly like the man." Talbot's pale face flushed, and his arms dropped to his sides. His voice cracked when he spoke. "Dammit, Mike. I keep thinking about my daughters. I can't imagine . . . I want whoever did this behind bars. I don't care how many people have to be brought in to help on this case. I just want it solved. I want these kids to come back to school and feel safe here."

Cancini bowed his head, lost in thought. It's what they all wanted. All murder investigations carried with them a certain amount of responsibility, particularly when you identified with the victims, felt the pain of their families. Cancini had met Talbot's two college-age daughters. It was no wonder the man couldn't sleep at night.

Talbot took a slug of coffee. "I want to catch whoever did this no matter who that someone is. But"—he stressed the word, looking down at Cancini—"I cannot arrest a man without any evidence, and no one—I repeat, no one—who is even remotely associated with this investigation will so much as make an accusation without real evidence." He exhaled. "I don't know what good it will do one way or the other, but we'll bring Spradlin in. We have to."

Cancini respected Talbot, trusted him, but Spradlin had waltzed right out of town in front of all of them. Still, if anyone could find him, it might be Talbot. "What's the plan?"

"My search team will interview the storekeepers. Based on what we learn, we'll start a thorough search, widening the radius five miles at a time. If he's still in that area, we'll find him."

"In the meantime?"

Talbot tossed his cup in the trash. "In the meantime, we wait."

Cancini glanced at his watch.

"Going somewhere?" Talbot asked.

Cancini looked at his friend. Talbot would take the fall if Spradlin wasn't found. He would be blamed if another girl was killed. And there was nothing he could do but wait. Talbot needed a break. "I've got an appointment up at the campus. It might amount to nothing, but then again, it might be something."

"Another wild-goose chase?"

"Maybe. Probably."

"What's it about?"

Cancini hesitated only a moment. "Mostly rumors about some stuff that might have been going on before the first rapes. Might be a lead. Might be nothing, but there's a professor who's willing to talk about it."

"But not connected to the current case?"

"I don't think so," he said truthfully. "But if we can solve the first set of rapes, maybe we'll find something. I know it doesn't look like it, but somehow, the old and the new cases have to be connected in some way, maybe some way we can't see."

"That your gut talking?"

Cancini shot a look at Talbot. There was something or someone connecting the cases. He knew it. Gut instinct may not have been exactly right, but it was as good a reason as any. "Something like that."

They walked together through the oversized double doors of the hotel.

"Still not sold on the copycat theory?" Talbot asked.

It was a logical theory, and Cancini knew it. But too many things bothered him. Spradlin's disappearance. The uncontained violence in the assaults. The rumors. The button. "No. Sorry."

Talbot scratched his head. "I can't believe I'm going to say this, but hell, I'm not so sold anymore, either."

Cancini shot a look at Talbot. They'd known each other a long time. He knew Talbot had hoped Shandling was the perp, the copycat. Not because he wanted to be right, but because he wanted it to be over. He was a good cop and a better man. "I'm meeting the professor in a half hour. Want to come?"

The two stepped onto the sidewalk into cool, heavy air. Talbot raised his face to the bleak sky. Dark clouds in the distance promised strong storms later. "Why not?"

Chapter Sixty-One

Julia gripped the steering wheel. She focused on the road, her eyes scanning the signs for Route 539. It came up suddenly, and she made a right turn before bringing the car to a stop. She studied her handwritten directions, the paper shaking in her hand as she read. After another mile, she would take a left and follow a dirt road to the end. He would be there.

Julia's hands dropped into her lap. He'd been clear. Come alone. It was the only way he would tell her the story, the whole story. What she already knew was enough to get everybody's attention and potentially turn everything on its head, but it wasn't the whole story. Not for the first time, she questioned her motivation, her willingness to meet a man she knew was a killer. It was a fact now, one he had given her when he placed the diaries in her hands. What she didn't understand was why.

Leo has done the unthinkable.

The words on the page had barely been legible, the handwriting spidery.

He hasn't told me why, but I think I know. After the first girl, I suspected, of course, but I didn't want to hear. After the second, though, I couldn't stay quiet. He told me it was true. He wasn't always this way—so distant, so cold. He told me he did his best to make it as painless as possible for the girls. God help me, I believe him. I don't think he planned to kill them, but it doesn't matter now. He did. My son is a murderer.

She rubbed her arms. What did Brenda know about why Leo killed those girls? What did he mean when he said he tried to make it painless? Julia blinked at the colorless sky. Thick clouds had rolled in, low and heavy. She needed to hurry to get there, before the rain. She pulled out a tape recorder from her canvas bag. It held a fresh tape, almost two hours of time. It would have to be enough. She slipped the machine into her jacket pocket.

Turning left on the dirt road, she slowed to avoid deep ruts and heavy brush. Trees lined the road and hung low over her car. Newly cut branches lay on each side where someone, Leo maybe, had recently cleared this old road. It took almost five minutes to reach the end, where a small, wooden structure, barely bigger than a shack, stood. The cabin's one square window had been covered by something dark, blocking any view inside. A stack of two-by-fours lay near the door. New wood had recently replaced old and rotted pieces.

Leo stood in the doorway, waiting. He watched as she climbed from the car, his eyes darting over her shoulder, down the dirt road. He cocked his head slightly and appeared to listen. Canvas bag thrown over her shoulder, she walked slowly toward the run-down cabin. Once inside, he closed the door behind her.

She took in the compact room. The rising sun provided the

only light. It streamed in through the cracks and chinks in the wooden walls. The window was covered with black plastic; underneath stood a single bed. A table stacked with canned goods and two chairs was pushed against the far wall. Several cases of bottled water were piled in the corner. A small woodstove provided heat and a place to cook.

"Did anyone follow you?"

"No," she said, shaking her head. She shivered in the cabin's dampness.

"Did you tell anyone where you were going?"

Julia could feel his eyes on her and raised her head to meet his gaze. "I haven't spoken to anyone since you asked me to come here." He nodded, satisfied. Julia exhaled.

Julia touched her hand to her pocket, feeling the outline of the tape recorder. "Nice place you got here. Did you build it yourself?" She pressed the record button as she spoke.

"I was always good with my hands. Learned how to fix things, build things. Kids with no dad have to do that." He looked away, his voice husky with nostalgia. "I found this place in high school. It was abandoned, so I rebuilt it. I used to come here to be alone. It's been a long time since I've been here."

His words reminded her she was in a remote location with a man who had already spent years in prison, who had murdered women with his bare hands. Her breathing became shallow and ragged. Her skin screamed with the pain of unseen pricks, and she had to fight the urge to run. Concentrating, she closed her hand around the tape recorder and turned the microphone upward toward Leo. "You said if I came here, you would tell me the truth." She struggled to keep her voice steady. "Everything about what happened back then."

He stared at her. "I like you, Julia." She thought she saw his light eyes glisten, but when he blinked, any emotion she'd imagined was gone. Leo went to the table, pulling out two chairs. He moved with a pantherlike grace, a quality she'd noticed the first time she'd seen him. He'd looked like an aloof movie star at the press conference. Jesus, she'd even found him attractive. Not now. He was remote and cold and maybe something worse. She shivered.

"Yes, I promised you the truth." He hesitated and gestured to the empty chair. After she sat, he said, "I've done terrible things." His voice was matter-of-fact but tinged with unexpected sadness. "I killed those girls. You read the diaries. You know that now. Soon, everyone will know."

"Bu-but why?"

"I had my reasons. Reasons my mother couldn't understand, wouldn't understand."

The words spilled out then, every detail. He didn't spare her feelings or stop when she gasped in horror. He kept talking in a measured and detached tone. She didn't want to listen, but she did. After an hour, he finished and a chill stole over Julia's body. He'd laid it all out, told her everything. She sat perfectly still.

"You understand you can't be allowed to live?"

Her lips moved, but she couldn't speak, nodding instead.

"I'm sorry." He stood slowly, his eyes glowing in the gray light. Julia gasped at the heavy rope in his hands. "I'm so sorry."

Chapter Sixty-Two

He drove east, sipping convenience store coffee. He passed the exit for Little Springs and the next two for the college. A few miles later, he pulled off, turning onto a narrow route that led to the hunting and fishing lodge on the mountain. Julia's compact four-cylinder strained at the incline, and he pressed the gas to the floor. The road was narrow and bumpy, well suited for trucks and SUVs, not cheap rental cars. He pulled into the gravel parking lot, which was less than half full. He parked at the far end, farthest from the lodge and near the tree line.

He got out of the car and looked down the mountain, his eyes following the path of the water. The first girl, Cheryl Fornak, had been found there, at the bottom of the trail, on the banks of the Thompson River. He remembered her well. They'd met at a college bar and dated briefly. She'd been pretty and energetic in a chirpy, singsong way that at first had seemed pleasant but turned grating after a short while. Still, he hadn't anticipated the way it would end. Even when he'd seen the life slip from her eyes and felt her body relax under the pressure of his hands, he'd felt almost nothing. A life ended seemed like no big deal. Later, he'd thought maybe it wasn't nothing he'd felt, but rather the absence of anything. Was he was trying to fill an emptiness? It didn't matter now. He'd long ago accepted he wasn't normal. It wasn't an excuse. It was a fact. The emptiness could never be filled. It had grown until it was the only thing. It was part of him. He gazed down at the trail lined with tall trees. In another few weeks, the trees would be bare, their gnarled branches shorn of leaves. He'd be gone by then. He had to fix everything now. It was the only way.

He opened the trunk and removed a fishing rod, a tackle box, and a large black backpack. He slung the pack over his shoulder. The weight of it pressed into his back as he reached in to grab another jacket. It would grow colder as the day wore on, and it was not a short hike down the mountain. He raised his face to the sky, glad to see the clouds moving in. Rain would suit his purposes well. A couple of men came out of the lodge. Baseball hat pulled low, he spun around and busied himself inside the trunk. When he heard the engine rev and the men drive away, he slammed the trunk closed. He stood for a moment. Both Little Springs and the college were barely visible in the haze. He turned toward the thick trees and the trail signs. He would stay on foot.

He took the blue trail, the most difficult and least traveled. He pulled out the cell phone he'd purchased shortly after his release. He'd stored only a few numbers, but they were the ones that mattered. Julia's name appeared near the top of the short list. He shook his head. He didn't want to think about her. To clear his mind, he breathed in and out, pushing away everything that could distract him. A frigid wind blew across the mountain, ruffling the branches. He threw his head back, letting the wind blow his jacket from his shoulders. He put the phone back in his pocket and picked up his pace. It was time.

Chapter Sixty-Three

"ARE YOU SURE you don't want to come with us?" Allison asked.

Nikki shook her head, loose curls swinging. "You know I'm not big on church, what with my dad and all. Besides, you should spend time with your parents without me tagging along." She lay on the twin bed, stretching her long arms and legs under a quilt. She glanced at the clock. Services would start soon. Allison wore a dark brown dress, brown boots, and her hair pulled back into a tight ponytail—just right for services at St. Benedict Catholic Church. "You look nice," she said.

"Thanks." Allison hesitated. "I know this is going to sound crazy, but I wish you wouldn't stay here alone."

Nikki smiled. She'd known Allison since their first day at Blue Hill, one of the only friends who seemed to understand her issues with religion and her famous father. She didn't treat Nikki like a freak or a celebrity. Best of all, she didn't want anything from her. A thoughtful and quiet girl, she rarely voiced her opinion, but when she did, Nikki listened. This time, however, she wasn't concerned. The gun she'd taken was in her book bag, loaded, and she knew how to use it.

"You'll be gone for what? An hour? I'll be fine. I promise to lock all the doors. Anyway, no one knows I'm here, remember?" Allison did not look convinced. "And if you want, I'll make pancakes for you and your parents while you're gone."

"Geez, Nik. Why do you always have to be so stubborn? You shouldn't be alone."

"I'll be fine. I promise."

"I don't know. It doesn't feel right."

"I may be stubborn, but you're a worrier." Nikki sat up and tossed a pillow at her friend's head with a laugh. "I'll make blueberry. Your favorite."

Allison smiled then. "Oh, all right. You win. I'll tell my mom and dad."

When they'd gone, Nikki went down the stairs to the kitchen, her backpack on her shoulder. She welcomed the extra weight of the gun, grateful to have it nearby. He'd followed her before, she was sure. He'd been watching her. Maybe he knew she was there. She'd read up on him. He was a smart man. He could even be watching her right now. A shiver shot up her spine, and she tightened her grip on the bag. Then she shook her head. She was being ridiculous. He couldn't possibly know where she was. Allison and all her worries were getting to her.

She let her hand drop and checked her cell phone. Frowning, she saw four new messages, one from her mother and three from her dad. She clicked on her mother's first, read it and responded.

I'm fine, Mom. I'm sorry I can't come home.

She paused, then added,

I love you and hope you understand. Don't worry.

She went back to the list of texts. Squaring her shoulders, she read her father's messages.

I'm thinking you should come home. Let us know when we can expect you.

An hour later, he had typed:

Haven't heard from you. Phoned President Sinclair. I know they've evacuated campus. You should be home by now. Don't let me down.

And then:

You are making me look bad. Everyone knows what's going on there. A loving daughter would be home with her family. You're hurting your mother, you know. Get home NOW!

She almost laughed at his desperation, using her mother that way, but her amusement faded. Nikki wasn't afraid anymore. She did feel badly about not being with her mother, but not for the reasons he implied. Her mother could leave at any time. Nikki had begged her to more than once. She silenced her phone and tossed it on the counter. No way would she give him the satisfaction of a response.

Searching the cabinets, Nikki found a large bowl and pancake supplies. She flipped on the TV that stood perched on a corner of the counter to cut the quiet. The first station was televising a religious service. She changed the channel twice more. Groaning, she recognized a preacher on the third station, a long-time friend of her dad's. Apparently, Allison's family did not have cable in the kitchen. She hit the off button and put her headphones in her ears. The music lightened her step around the kitchen. Relaxing, she slipped the backpack from her shoulder and laid it on the counter near the bowl. She unzipped it and pulled the gun to the top, leaving the bag open. She smiled. Allison wouldn't be so worried if she knew Nikki had a gun only an arm's length away.

She heated up the griddle and mixed flour, eggs, and milk. She added vanilla and folded in a cup of blueberries. When the batter was smooth, she dribbled water on the hot pan. When it popped, she spooned on batter and waited for the bubbles on top before flipping, the way her mother had taught her.

Nikki sang along with the song playing in her ears, waving the spatula in the air. Wiggling her hips, she tapped her foot in time with the beat. A moment later, her feet were taken out from under her, and the spatula flew across the room. One strong arm held her at the waist. She screamed, but a large hand over her mouth muffled any sound. Wild-eyed, she reached for her backpack. He jerked her body upward, and her fingers found the edge of the mixing bowl. It skidded across the counter, landing on the floor in a puddle of batter and broken glass. She picked up her right foot and brought it up hard against his knee.

Her headphones were ripped from her ears and the music player clattered to the floor. She brought her foot up again, but before she could make contact, he picked her up and threw her to the floor, her head slamming into the tile. In the seconds before she lost consciousness, she reached up, her fingers clawing at empty air.

Chapter Sixty-Four

PROFESSOR SIMON POURED three cups of coffee. Steam rose and fogged his thick bifocal glasses. He wore his starched, button-down shirt tucked neatly into his pressed pants and his snow-white hair combed close to his head. He carried himself like he used to stand an inch or two taller, his broad shoulders now hunched.

"Cream? Sugar?" he asked. He set the cups and saucers on the table and sat opposite Cancini and Talbot. "I don't know what I can tell you gentlemen, but," he said, "if it helps in any way, so be it. I probably should've said something before." His voice trailed off. "Maybe I didn't think it mattered then. But, what the hell? I'm an old man now, and I can say whatever I like."

Cancini knew the old man had taught for many years at Blue Hill, even chairing the math department for more than a decade. Whatever his reasons for not talking before were his own. Cancini cleared his throat. "Why don't you tell us what you remember, and we'll ask questions as they come up?"

The old man looked at him through the thick lenses, his eyes clouded and opaque. He nodded, then spoke again. "Leo Spradlin was in one of my freshman math classes. Quite possibly the brightest mind I've taught, but it was wasted. I don't mind admitting I didn't like that kid. He had the audacity to correct me in class, in front of the other students, just to show them how smart he was. I could have put up with that, but when it came to tests and exams, he would sign his name and leave the whole thing blank. He thumbed his nose at it, at us." The man spread his hands wide on the table and stared down at his wrinkled, gnarled fingers again. "He was only at Blue Hill because of his mother. From what I knew, she was a good woman, better than he deserved." He paused then added, "And because of Baldwin, I guess, too. The man took a special interest in him. God knows why."

Cancini's pen stopped moving. "Mayor Baldwin?"

"No, no. President Baldwin, Teddy's daddy. For some reason I could never understand, he took an interest in the kid. Maybe it was because he was a friend of Teddy's. I don't know. When Leo was failing my class, President Baldwin strongly recommended I give him a passing grade. I refused at first. But he made it clear that I would not be failing a kid who could show me a thing or two. I tried to argue his test grades were zeros, but he didn't want to hear it. Said I should give the kid a break." Simon's pale skin turned pink. "It went against everything I believed in, but I passed him. Gave him a D. Turns out, there were other classes, other professors with the same issue." He shook his head. "We figured Baldwin was trying to do Leo's mom a favor, trying to keep him in school. I'd heard she wanted him to graduate. She seemed like a good person, and I always got the impression she was a smart lady. There was something, though. She seemed beaten, sad. The entire faculty knew Spradlin was Teddy's best friend. The two were always together, even after Leo dropped out. At least until, well, you know."

Cancini remembered the friendship between Spradlin and Baldwin as tight even when he'd first arrived in Little Springs. Old high school friends, they were part of a fun group back then, a bunch of young men in their twenties who liked to fish, and hunt. Most of them were in school at the college. Although Spradlin seemed to be the unofficial leader of the group, Teddy, already in his first year of law school, was the oldest. Cancini wondered when the friendship between Spradlin and Baldwin had begun to wane. Was it before the murders or after?

"Spradlin didn't care whether we passed him or not. He didn't give a whit about anything as far as I could tell. Not like Teddy. That young man wore his heart on his sleeve. Always felt bad for him, you know. He had a tough time with his dad."

Cancini remembered some of the Baldwin father-son issues. When Teddy's father wanted him to play baseball, he chose football. When his father wanted him to go into academia, he chose law school. They were minor issues really, but Cancini remembered the antagonism on Teddy's face when his father addressed him and the sarcasm that tinged Teddy's words when he answered him. Locked in his own struggle with his father, the young Cancini hadn't thought much of it at the time. Now he wondered if it was more than just a young man's rebellion. Was that why Teddy's father gave Leo attention, to gain favor from his only son?

Tapping his pen against his notepad, Cancini said, "I know it was a long time ago, but I never got the impression that Teddy and his father were that close. Why would President Baldwin take that kind of interest in Teddy's friends?"

"That is the question, isn't it? It's true Teddy and his father weren't close. Not at all. When Teddy was young, he seemed like most boys, you know, seeking his dad's approval. But after his mother died, that changed." The old man gave a shake of his head. "When she was alive, there were rumors, but later . . . you could say that as a widower, President Baldwin was not a discreet man." His mouth turned down. "There were stories, some of them quite unsavory. I'm sure Teddy heard his share."

Cancini glanced at Talbot and saw the same question on his face. "What do you mean by unsavory?"

The man sighed. Sad and tired, he looked past the men at the table to another time. "Most of the faculty lived on campus back in those days. That's not true anymore, but it was encouraged then, especially for those like me who weren't yet married. I was given a faculty apartment, fully furnished. A nice perk actually. The Baldwin family lived on campus, too, of course. They had that big house at the end of Blue Hill Drive. I think it's empty now."

He folded his hands in his lap. "This was a Christian college when I came here. President Baldwin had a national reputation. He preached about God and education and how the two should be joined together. I was mesmerized the first time I saw him speak. Even when he dropped 'Christian' from the school's name, he made a pledge to keep the Christian spirit of the college intact. Most of us didn't like it, but we understood it was a business decision to get the young people here. I loved teaching. I loved the kids." He took off his glasses and wiped the lenses with a cloth napkin. He half smiled. "I'm sorry. I digress. You wanted to know about the unsavory behavior of President Baldwin."

Glasses on again, Simon continued. "As I said, when his wife was alive, rumors circulated. Baldwin was a busy man, a religious man, and I admired and respected him. I put little credence in the talk, but after Marian died, gossip was more frequent and outlandish—or so I thought at the time." A shadow passed over his face. "But then there was what happened with Lilleth, my Lilleth." His voice dropped to a whisper. "He killed her. Baldwin killed her."

Chapter Sixty-Five

DIZZY AND UNSURE, she blinked, trying to clear the haze, her only awareness a thudding noise and blinding pain. She groaned.

"Good," a man's muffled voice penetrated the confusion. "You're awake. I like it better that way."

Nikki's eyelids fluttered, and she slipped away for another few moments, this time waking to fingers pulling at her clothes and body.

"No," she tried to say, but the word sounded strangled. He rolled Nikki on her side. "No," she said louder, struggling to escape his iron grip. She was no match for his size or his strength. She kicked and bucked, head throbbing, until she was spent, muscles burning.

When she lay still, he brought his face close. "Finally with me? Good."

Moaning, Nikki couldn't answer, the pounding in her head overwhelming everything else. She thought it might explode. Cold fingers reached under her shirt and touched the bare flesh of her stomach. His hand moved down to the waistband of her leggings. The throbbing subsided a little, and she tried to knee him but missed. "No," she said, whimpering.

"Don't worry." He laughed softly. "We're going to be friends now, very good friends." Twisting and writhing, she tried to fight off his hands, but he pinned her legs down and pulled at her leggings. She tried to shift, but he had her trapped under his shoulder and hips. She wanted to claw him, scratch his eyes, but he had her wrists locked in a tight grip. He kept tugging until the leggings were around her ankles. Panting, he tore her underwear from her body.

The tile floor was cold against her bare skin. She twisted her head away. The strap from her backpack dangled over the side of the counter, in sight but out of reach. The gun. He fumbled with his pants, his weight shifting. She inhaled and slid backward. He grabbed her leg. She kicked hard, catching him in the thigh. He grunted but held on. She kept kicking harder against his overwhelming strength, sliding still closer to the backpack. His power seemed to grow the more she struggled.

He pulled his hand back and slapped her face. Her head snapped back, exploding in pain. "Be fucking still!"

Ignoring the sharp sting and ringing noise, she wrenched her wrists from his left hand. She tried to scoot farther away, but he yanked her back again. His erection strained the fabric of his linen trousers. His nostrils flared and his eyes reminded her of a wild animal, a predator. She froze. She knew that look, the crazed look of a man who liked the fight, who got off on his strength and absolute power. With every ounce of self-control she had, she let her body go limp.

He awkwardly pulled down his pants while still keeping her in his grasp. She locked on his eyes, watching and waiting. Naked from the waist down, he slid her legs apart, bending over her. His flushed face was close, and sweat from his brow dripped on her forehead.

She fought her panic, desperate to distract him. "I know who you are," she said, her voice soft.

He paused, half smiling. "Yeah, I guess you fucking do. Would be hard not to, now wouldn't it?" Crouching, he dropped on top of her, immobilizing her with his weight. His naked, sweaty skin pressed against her legs. His hot breath smelled like stale coffee and cigarettes. She turned away, fighting the bile rising in her throat, and focused on the upturned mixing bowl and dangling strap.

He stroked her hair with his fingers and whispered, "You're mine now." His breath burned her ears.

Everything about him repulsed her, and every ounce of her being wanted to fight and fight hard. But she knew that wouldn't save her life. "Yes," she whispered, tears rolling down her face. "I'm yours."

He blinked. Then his eyes narrowed to slits. "That's not the way it goes."

"I'm doing what you want. I'm yours." She did not move a muscle. He seemed to soften. Was she imagining it?

"This is bullshit."

"No."

"This isn't how it's supposed to go," he said again. A vein in his forehead pulsed, and his face reddened. "Fine. Let's see how you fucking like this." With his eyes locked on her, he balled one hand into a fist and punched between her legs. White light and hot pain flooded everything. Her body bucked, but she managed to swallow the scream, releasing only a small, guttural cry. He punched again, but Nikki braced, ready this time. She welcomed the pain; she was alive. "You bitch," he said, his jaw clenched. His penis lay flaccid against her leg. Joy and a sense of power rose inside her. "You're playing games with me."

"No, I'm not. I wouldn't," she said, the words pouring out in a rush. "I'll do anything you want. I swear." She tried desperately for a neutral tone. If he was the man she thought he was, he would enjoy her begging almost as much as her fighting. She had to be careful.

"For fucking cryin' out loud," he muttered, scrambling to his feet. His erection gone, he hurried into his pants. "Have it your way then. We're gonna have to do this the hard way." He pulled a thick rope from his pocket and threw the leggings in her face. "Get up and put your pants on."

Exhaling, she moved slowly, the pain in her head and between her legs almost knocking her down. With each movement, she focused on the book bag, just a few feet out of her reach.

"Hurry the fuck up," he hissed.

With one leg on, she pretended to stumble toward the countertop, reaching out to catch herself. Her fingers landed on the cold granite inches from her bag. Pulling herself up, she kept her eyes on him and slowly put her right leg in her pants. His gaze drifted to the large kitchen window, drawn by the squawk of crows.

This was the moment. Sliding her hand across the counter, she found the hard, cold metal on top of the bag. When his eyes came back to hers, he stared down the barrel of a gun.

Chapter Sixty-Six

TALBOT SAT FORWARD. "Killed her? What do you mean?"

A single tear trailed down the old man's wrinkled cheek. "What he did to her—what he did to us—it killed her." His voice shook. "God forgive me, I've never spoken of it."

"Take your time," Cancini said, the words soft. The professor took several loud, noisy gulps of air. When the man calmed, Cancini leaned forward. "When did this happen?"

"1991. Before the attacks. But I should have said something then . . ."

"It's okay. You're telling us now."

Simon nodded. "Lilleth and I were engaged to be married. She was so beautiful, so lovely." He paused. "She'd only been teaching at Blue Hill for two years when we decided to marry. I was older, but she swore it didn't bother her. We laughed about it sometimes . . ." The tears flowed now. "A few weeks before the wedding, Baldwin asked her to join one of his research teams. She was thrilled to be noticed and didn't mind the extra hours. I didn't think anything about it." He stopped, his words muffled through the sobs.

Cancini and Talbot waited, silent. After a few moments, the professor spoke again. "One night, she didn't show up for dinner. At first, I assumed she'd had to stay late to work with Baldwin on the project, but when she didn't call, I went to her apartment. The windows were dark, but her car was in the parking lot. I knocked and waited. I knew she was home. I could hear her crying through the door. I knocked some more, but she wouldn't let me in. I didn't know what to do. I waited for close to two hours, but when she still wouldn't let me in, I had no choice but to go home."

Cancini's shoulders tightened and he swallowed. Next to him, Talbot cleared his throat.

"The next morning, I went to her apartment again. I knew she wouldn't have a class until ten. At first, she refused to see me. I said I wasn't leaving and told her I'd canceled all my classes for the day. Eventually, she opened the door." He shuddered as he spoke. "Her eyes were swollen and red and I knew she'd cried all night. There was a bump on her head and bruises on her arms. I asked what happened, but she wouldn't answer and shook her head. I tried to take her in my arms, but she backed away from me. 'I'm dirty,' she said. I had no idea what she was talking about." He paused again, his old hands tightening into fists. "It took hours to get it out of her, but—" He raised his eyes again. "Baldwin forced himself on her." His tone hardened. "They were alone in the lab and he told her how lonely it was being a widower, how he had needs. Lilleth wasn't like that. She was a virgin. But he wouldn't take no for an answer. She fought as best she could, but . . ." his voice died.

The old man hung his head, his slight shoulders rocking. The minutes ticked by until Cancini asked, "What happened after that?"

Simon shook his head again, sniffling. Finally, he said, "Lilleth was so ashamed. She gave me back my ring, told me she was unworthy of marriage. She blamed herself. I told her I loved her, but nothing I said made any difference. A few days later, she swallowed a bottle of pills and she was gone."

Talbot spoke then, "And Baldwin?"

"He denied it. Said Lilleth had fallen in love with him on the project, but he'd refused her for my sake. He said she was angry and hit him over and over. She lost her balance and hit her head. He made it sound so logical." He twisted the napkin in his hand.

"And you never told anyone?" Cancini asked.

The professor blew his nose and wiped his eyes. "Who would have believed me? You don't know how convincing he could be. God forgive me, I almost believed him myself." His shoulders seemed to sink further into his chest. Cancini looked away. Professor Simon wasn't the first man to make such a mistake, to lose a woman he loved. But the depths of his sadness and guilt were his alone.

Cancini had the truth, though he didn't know which truth. The professor's story didn't add up to evidence, at least not the kind the FBI could use, but it did paint a picture of the past. And it framed the present, an ugly and twisted picture of the present, and possibly, the future. The old man had no reason to lie. Lilleth was long gone, having taken her own life only days before their planned wedding. The professor, immobilized by grief, had done nothing. When the shock had faded, still he'd done nothing, his grief matched by fear. Now, he was near the end of his life, that time when men with regrets seek redemption and forgiveness. It was sweet relief to speak the words he'd kept inside so long.

Cancini stood, pushing back his chair. Simon needed to be alone with his memories. "Thank you for your time, Professor."

The old man nodded but did not raise his head. He sat still, knotted hands folded in his lap, his heavily lined face wet and tired.

"Thanks for the coffee," Talbot said. They left the man in the kitchen and walked back through the spotless house, letting themselves out. Neither said a word as they got into the car. Cancini gazed out the window at houses and yards slipping in and out of view. They passed through the campus, the bluestone buildings fading into gray sky.

Talbot turned onto the highway and headed back to town. He broke the silence. "Simon's an old man, Mike. Maybe . . ." His voice trailed off. Cancini understood. Finding certain truths was the worst part of the job, and what did it really tell you? Where could it lead? The answers were sometimes the worst part of all. "You knew Baldwin's father. Do you believe him?"

Cancini rubbed at the edges of his notebook. The stories carried some truth after all. They both knew the man wasn't lying, but knowing and wanting to know weren't the same thing. "Yeah, I believe him."

Talbot was quiet a moment. "Yeah, okay, I do, too. There was more going on in this town than I would have thought." He clucked his tongue. "Strange to think about the president of a Christian college being . . . doing the things he did." Cancini said nothing. "But President Baldwin is dead. I don't see how it ties in now."

It was a good question. The past and the present. Cancini didn't know how they were connected, but he guessed Teddy had learned what his father was like, particularly as he got older and the rumors spread. According to the professor, the father-son relationship had been strained after Mrs. Baldwin's death and Cancini knew this to be true. He just hadn't fully understood the reasons until now. And Simon was right. Teddy had always worn his heart on his sleeve, always struggled to rein in his emotions. Cancini's neck ached and his head pounded. Teddy hadn't changed.

"Maybe it doesn't," he said. "But Teddy's father, the things he did. It means something. I know it does. I just can't put my finger on it yet."

The men rode another couple of miles in silence.

Talbot pulled the car onto Main Street, finding a spot near the hotel. The lobby teemed with reporters, many of them nodding toward Talbot and Cancini as they entered. Cancini scanned the crowd. Julia wasn't there.

Talbot shifted his weight, keeping his eyes on the reporters. "I'm heading to the office. Coming?"

"Yeah, in a minute. I've got something to take care of, and then I'll be right over."

The old church bell chimed ten times, echoing down the street. The early services had ended. Cancini wasn't a man of faith, at least not the way most people defined it. Still, he understood many locals in Little Springs were, and, as the professor had reminded them, the college was founded on religious principles. When the sounds faded away, he went to the front desk.

"Could you ring Ms. Manning's room, please?"

The clerk nodded. After a moment, he shook his head. "There's no answer, sir."

The detective looked around the lobby. "Have you seen her this morning?"

"No, sir." The phone on the desk rang. "Is there anything else I can do for you?"

"No," Cancini said, frowning. He walked toward the elevators, staying out of sight of the reporters. He pulled out his phone and dialed her number. It rang five times, then six, then seven. Walking through the lobby again, he checked the street outside. He checked the bar and the business center. He dialed her again. Still no answer. She'd called him several times over the last two days, and now she didn't pick up. Something was wrong.

Chapter Sixty-Seven

HE INHALED SHARPLY but didn't panic at the sight of the gun in her hands. Instead, he smiled. She was a smart little thing, a convincing actress, and the realization sent another surge of excitement through him. She was fucking good. He'd almost believed her. Her fight was different, but it was a fight just the same. Pleased, he stood up straight, tucked in his shirt, and straightened his belt. He wrapped the rope around his hand. Keeping his eyes on her face, ignoring the gun, he said, "The folks will be getting out of church soon and be wanting some breakfast." He nodded at the griddle smoking on the stove. "Unfortunately, they will have to make it themselves. I can't leave you here now."

Nikki stood in front of him, both hands gripping the gun. Eyes round in her pale, tear-streaked face, she licked her lips. "I'm not going anywhere," she said. Waving the gun toward the back door, she promised, "Go on. This is your chance to get out of here. If you go, I won't tell anyone. It will be between us. I promise."

He raised his eyebrows. She stared back and ignored the smoke billowing up toward the ceiling. She tightened her grip on the gun and struggled to hold it steady. His eyes flickered to the weapon. She knew how to hold it, but it seemed heavy in her hands.

"I don't know if I can take that chance, Nikki." His words were soft, tender. He held up his hands in a gesture of helplessness. "We're in this together now."

She shook her head. "No. We're not together. Ever." She breathed hard. Her arms had dropped an inch, the gun aimed now at his stomach. "You're going to leave, or I swear to God, I'll shoot you."

Time was running short. The clock hanging on the wall told him the church service would be over in ten minutes. The congregation would slowly rise from their pews, gathering first in the lobby, then again on the steps and across the manicured lawn. They would shake the hands of Father Donahue and nod about the good sermon, and then their faces would take on somber expressions. "It's a terrible thing that's been going on." "We're praying for the families of those girls." And on and on it would go—the good people of Little Springs wearing their piousness on their sleeves. But when church was over and Sunday had passed, he knew the truth. He'd seen the bruise marks on Mrs. Orion's arms. He'd seen countless men stumble home from bars. He knew about the wives who did not honor and obey their husbands. He'd witnessed the drug deals on the high school campus. They were fucking hypocrites—all of them. He considered the girl standing in front of him. In spite of her fear, she remained relatively calm. She might actually shoot him. The girl had spunk.

He slowly unwound the rope from his hand, putting it back in his pocket. "I guess you win." He raised his hands again, palms up.

A car horn sounded down the road, and the girl flinched. He lunged toward her, grabbing at the gun with one hand and reaching for her with the other. They fell together, bodies crashing to the floor, the gun between them. His elbow slammed into the hard tile floor, and he grunted, the gun slipping from his grip. The girl tried to point the gun at him but was no match for his strength. They rolled once on the floor until he pinned her, the gun wedged between them. She spit in his face, the saliva landing on his lower lip, dribbling down his chin.

"Bitch." With one hand on the gun, he punched her with the other, his fist smashing into her face, the crack of her jaw breaking loud and sharp.

His admiration for her grew. Even after the crunch of bone in her jaw, she wouldn't let go of the gun. She tried to head-butt him and wriggle out from under his weight. He hit her again, this time connecting with her right eye. He felt her weaken. Time was running short, and he knew he couldn't risk any more time with her. He twisted the pistol until the tip was pointed at her, the butt of the gun pressing into his abdomen. He looked into her wide eyes as he pressed the trigger, watching her accept the inevitable. The gun blast obliterated all other sounds. When its echo faded, the only noise left was the ticking of the clock on the wall.

Chapter Sixty-Eight

HER RIPPED SKIN bled where the rope cut into her wrists and ankles. Ignoring the pain, Julia struggled against the restraints. He'd tied her hands together, securing them to a wooden pole in the small cabin. He'd tied her at the ankles, as well. She rubbed the rope against the wooden pole, hoping to wear it down. She screamed in frustration, the sound dying in the empty cabin.

Her eyes welled, and she swallowed a sob. No one could possibly hear her. It was no wonder he hadn't bothered to cover her mouth.

"I'm sorry," he'd said. "I don't want to do this, but there's something I have to take care of first. This is the only way."

She'd tried to argue with him. "But I won't tell anyone where you are. I . . . I won't tell anyone anything. I promise. I'll be careful."

She'd fought back tears when he shook his head. "There's no time." He'd stared into her eyes, unblinking. "You know too much."

He'd taken her keys and left. The tires of her rental car had rolled over the gravel and dirt road, the sound disappearing with the car. She'd been left lying on the floor, alone. She blinked, forcing herself to look around the cabin. She had to get it together and find a way out. She had to get out before he returned.

Tipping her head back, she looked up at her burning wrists. The rope was tight, probably even tighter as a result of her struggles. But maybe if she could twist her hands a little, she might get free. The minutes ticked by. Beads of sweat hung on her forehead, and blood dripped from her wrists. She twisted more. Finally, she touched the edges of the rope with her fingers.

It was no use. The tips of her fingers oozed blood, every fingernail ripped off, and still she was no closer to loosening the knots. Tears streamed down her face. Chin quivering, she gave in to the sobs that wracked her body. Fear and exhaustion took over; she hung her head.

I'm going to die here. The thought pressed in, and she had trouble breathing. Would he come back, or would he leave her there? Spradlin had told her everything. He'd started at Cheryl Fornak and left nothing out. When he'd spoken about his hands around the girls' necks, she hadn't been able to look at him.

"Cheryl wasn't a bad person," he'd said. "I didn't plan it. If you'd asked me that morning, or even earlier that night, if I was going to murder her, or anyone, I would have said no."

It had been difficult to ask questions, but she'd fought her feelings of revulsion. "Then why? Why did you do it?"

"I had no choice. I couldn't let her talk about being raped. I don't think she expected me to hurt her." He'd paused. "It was easier than I thought it would be, taking a life. It was that night when I knew something was wrong with me. Something was missing."

Every nerve in her body had told her to run then, but she'd

stayed in the wooden chair, listening as he talked about each girl, providing details that left no doubts in her mind.

"Death is only a state," he'd told her at one point. "People are afraid of it, but I don't know why. There's no pain after you die."

She hadn't wanted to listen anymore. She'd wanted it to stop, but he kept talking. When he was quiet, she'd asked the one question that scared her most of all. "Why'd you come back? Nobody would have ever known the truth."

His hands had curled up into fists. "To finish what I started." Her heart beat wildly with his words. Cancini had been right to warn her about Spradlin after all. Lying on the wooden floor, she had no more tears. He was gone now, but the words and thoughts of death hung in the air. It all made sense now, in a sick way.

Had he been gone an hour? More? She couldn't be sure. The only window was covered, and the light was dim. Her fear gave way to anger and eventually, frustration. There had to be something she could do. With nothing to lose, she started screaming. She screamed over and over again until her throat burned. She strained her ears but heard nothing, only the sound of her own breathing. Fresh tears pricked at her eyes. And then she heard it. Buzz. Buzz. She jolted. Buzz. Buzz. It was coming from her canvas bag. Her cell phone. Someone was trying to reach her. Ignoring her bleeding wrists, she felt fresh energy course through her aching body. There had to be a way.

Chapter Sixty-Nine

"GODDAMMIT," HE MUTTERED, crossing the backyard and hurrying to the car he'd parked on the next block. It wasn't supposed to happen that way. She'd ruined everything. God, he'd wanted her so bad. The thought of having her thrilled him, but it wasn't to be. Shit. He'd had to fucking shoot her. It was her own damn fault.

The shock of the gun exploding between them had frozen them both for an instant. Had he missed? Blood spread across her white T-shirt and spattered his own. Her fingers were still wrapped around the barrel of the gun, her mouth open. Her eyelids fluttered, then closed. He hadn't missed. He grabbed a kitchen towel, loosened her fingers, and wiped down the gun. He replaced it in her hand. Grabbing another towel, he wiped down all the surfaces he'd touched. Stuffing the towels and her underwear into his pockets, he washed his hands and slipped out the door. Three minutes had passed since the shooting.

Back at his car, he pulled on a jacket and ran his fingers through his hair. He drove away, obeying the speed limit, keeping his ears open for sirens. After a few miles, he turned onto the highway, then turned again onto a narrow country road.

"Goddammit," he said, smacking the steering wheel. Church services would be over by now, and she would be found any minute. The police would swarm the house. He'd done what he could to eliminate any trace that he'd been there. A grin spread across his face. Maybe this was a good thing. Another dead girl. She wasn't naked like the others, though, and had no marks around her neck. That could make things interesting. How would the FBI reconcile this new event? What would the great Cancini do?

He stopped the car and laughed, sure he couldn't have planned it better if he'd tried. The confusion would buy him time and, more importantly, the opportunity to clean up a few loose ends. Hell. He was looking forward to it.

Chapter Seventy

"HER NAME IS Nikki Stephenson." The Little Springs cop directed his report at Cancini, ignoring Talbot. "She's a student at the college, staying here with the Walshes because of the evacuation." He nodded toward the couple and young woman huddled outside the kitchen. "That's them. Their daughter and this girl are classmates. They say her dad is Senator Stephenson, you know, from Alabama."

Cancini and Talbot exchanged glances. Cancini had seen the man on TV a few times. He was a talker. "Why didn't she go home to her family?"

The cop stole a look at the Walshes. "They said she didn't get along with 'em—especially not with the dad."

"Have they been contacted?"

"No, sir. Not yet."

"Okay. What happened here this morning?"

The cop read from his notes. "The family went to church, left the house about eight forty-five for a nine o'clock service. Solid alibi. The Walshes are a good churchgoing family." He cleared his throat. "Ms. Stephenson stayed back saying she didn't want to go." He gestured at the broken bowl and spilled batter on the floor. "Apparently, she promised to make pancakes while they were gone. Family returned a little after ten and found her. We had just gotten a call about a loud noise in the neighborhood and were sending a car, so it couldn't have been more than a few minutes before we got here."

Talbot nodded once, then stepped out to speak to the family. Cancini stayed, assessing the crime scene. The house was probably thirty or forty years old by the look of it, but the kitchen appeared newer. It had shiny new appliances and granite countertops. The refrigerator was covered with family photos and mementos. Several cookbooks stood perched on a shelf near the stove.

A door at the back of the kitchen led to the side yard. The top half was glass, giving a clear view of the yard and the neighbor's house. No panes were broken.

"Did the neighbors see anything? Hear anything?"

The cop's eyes followed Cancini's. "No. Most were at church, too. We're still canvassing the rest of the street."

Cancini checked the door again. "Any sign of a break-in?"

"Nothing obvious. Couple of scratches on the lock. Coulda been picked, but might be nothing."

"Okay." An open backpack perched near the counter's edge. Closer to the stove, a bag of flour and a carton of eggs had been left out. He moved closer, pausing at the cooktop. His hand warmed over the griddle, the heat still coming off the pan.

"That was still on when we got here," said the local cop. "It was pretty smoky for a while. It's better now."

Cancini nodded. The burnt smell almost masked the metallic odor of the girl's blood. He crouched, resting his hands on his thighs. The floor was smeared red, and while the emergency unit had been careful, it was difficult to determine if any evidence had been disturbed.

"What else?"

"There was a gun in her hand. Mr. Walsh says it looks like the one he kept locked in a box in his study. His is missing."

"I see." No obvious break-in. The only sign of a possible struggle was the broken bowl and batter on the floor. Did the girl know her attacker? How and when did she get the locked gun from the study?

Cancini stood up, his knees cracking. "Where's the gun?"

"Forensics has it."

Walking to the kitchen window, Cancini saw a large yard that opened to the adjacent neighbor's back lawn. Only a handful of yards were fenced. It would be easy to skip across to another street and disappear.

"Were you here when the medics took the girl?"

"Yes, sir," the young cop said.

"Any idea whether she'll make it?"

"I don't know, sir. It looked pretty bad."

Cancini gripped the counter's edge. Was it the same guy? And if it was, why was he taking chances, entering a home?

Talbot came back into the kitchen. "I've got what I need for now. I think we should head over to the hospital. See if the girl can talk."

"Right." They walked to the front door and stepped outside.

Cancini spotted at least a dozen reporters hovering across the street. A handful of neighbors stood in their yards watching, a new fear on their faces. This was different. This wasn't a campus crime. This was their neighborhood. He got in the car, shutting the door. The cameras turned their focus from the front of the house to them, snapping pictures as they pulled away. The journalists shouted questions, but he heard nothing. Cancini searched the faces for Julia, his skin growing clammy and his mouth dry. Where was she?

Chapter Seventy-One

SPRADLIN REACHED THE bottom of the trail a quarter mile from the campus and close to the oldest block of dormitories. Only a few cars sat in the faculty parking lot, even fewer on the street. Ducking behind a building, he dropped the fishing rod and tackle box he'd carried down the narrow trail. He removed his backpack and pulled out a hardhat and work shirt. Slipping on both, he cocked his ear for sounds of large equipment. There. As he'd suspected, while the students were away, the construction company worked to make up for lost time.

Circling the park near the cafeteria, he turned in the direction of the old faculty housing. Keeping his head low, he ducked behind an academic building, walked through the parking lot, and stepped into an alley behind the buildings. After two blocks, the alley ended, and he stepped back onto the sidewalk. Muffled construction noises from the other side of campus drifted his way. He replaced the hardhat with a baseball cap and kept walking along the empty street. Then he saw it, up ahead, past a row of dark buildings. The Baldwin house.

He stood, taking it in. For a brief moment, the years fell away, but he pushed the memories from his mind. Coming here was risky, but he had to do it. He had to follow it through to the end. Like most of the buildings on campus, the house stood dark, every curtain drawn. More mansion than house, it sat perched at the top of a small hill. Stone steps led up from the street to the front doors. The wide porch boasted heavy white columns and a white railing that ran the length of the house. The imposing windows, like the house itself, loomed over the rest of the campus. Exhaling, he walked toward it.

He'd been there a few times with Teddy, when old man Baldwin and his wife were still living. The front rooms had been formal, unlike the rustic house he'd grown up in. Teddy told him they were reserved for elaborate dinners and parties meant to impress visiting dignitaries and to placate the underpaid faculty. He'd never been invited, but Teddy had described the events in detail.

He remembered a back door that led to the kitchen and servants' quarters. Turning left at the end of the road, he walked to within thirty yards of the house, then looked in both directions. No one was around. He ran across the lawn, turned, and sprinted to the back of the house. Out of view, he leaned against the brick and stone wall, catching his breath. The back lawn sloped downward toward a smattering of trees. Colorful flower beds lined a large patio. Outfitted with wrought-iron sofas, lanterns, and round tables, it stood waiting for guests. The small lake Teddy's grandfather had built shone through the trees. Fully stocked, students used it to fish, canoe, or jog along the path that skimmed its banks. Today, however, it was as deserted as the rest of Blue Hill College.

He moved toward the kitchen door. With long fingers, he

touched the heavy steel and the bolt lock. Dropping his hand, he jiggled the handle. Locked. From his pocket, he pulled a lock pick and tension wrench. Crouching slightly, he held the doorknob with one hand and worked the lock with the other. Done, he stood and picked the deadbolt. Glancing around one more time, he slipped inside, closing the door, careful not to make a sound. He stood in the semidarkness and listened. If he'd tripped an alarm, it was silent. He moved inside. He wouldn't be in the house long enough for it to matter.

The house had changed. Shiny stainless-steel appliances and black countertops replaced the old. A rack laden with sparkling silver and copper pots hung from the ceiling. The old oak table where he and Teddy had eaten leftovers and drunk milk was gone. A massive bank of cabinets stood in its place. He stared at the spot where the table used to be. Mrs. Baldwin would sweep in, pile a plate with cold cuts, rolls, and cookies, and insist the boys eat every bite. A quiet woman, overshadowed by her more effusive husband, she doted on Teddy and any friend he happened to have around, even young Leo. She'd seemed nice, but Spradlin had long ago learned that no one was exactly as they seemed. He blinked. Twin dishwashers and double refrigerators occupied an entire wall. Whatever bit of warmth and coziness that once filled the large kitchen had been erased. It was strictly a workspace now.

He moved toward the back staircase, climbing the steps quickly and quietly. Bypassing the second floor with its large master bedroom and perfectly appointed guest rooms, he headed to the third floor. He hesitated on the landing, listening. Sure he was alone, he walked to the end of the hall. The door was closed. The old "Keep Out" sign that Teddy had hung as a teenager was still taped to the door. The grown-ups had never used the third floor. It was always Teddy's domain. Although his bedroom was downstairs, he'd been given this large room as a young child. Once a playroom filled with plastic toys, it morphed into a teen hangout fitted with a TV and refrigerator.

He turned the doorknob, opening the door. In spite of the darkness, he dared not turn on a lamp. Switching on a small flashlight, he panned the room. He'd been right. The room was being lived in. Empty water bottles and a couple of food cartons had been tossed in the trash can. Heavy black drapes covered the windows, shutting out the world. On the bed, the sheets were rumpled.

He trained the light on the open closet doors where a small pile of clothes lay in a heap. A yellow shirt with a brownish stain caught Spradlin's eye. He crossed the room and pulled the shirt out from under the other clothes. Several small stains spread across the shirt as though someone had dropped something that had spattered across the fabric. With his finger, he touched one of the larger stains. At the surface, it was slightly crusty, but underneath, still damp. He sniffed the residue on his finger. Blood. Peering closely at the shirt, he saw no tears or holes. Giving no thought as to whose blood it might be, he balled up the shirt and stuffed it in his backpack.

He stood up and swept the flashlight across the room again. A computer tablet peeked out from under the bed. He walked over and picked it up. Clicking it on, he tapped a few icons, navigating his way through a handful of files. "Idiot," he said, slipping it in the backpack with the stained shirt.

The rest of the room looked clean. He pulled the backpack up on his shoulder and switched off the small light. He was tired of playing games, tired of everything. "Goddammit," he said to the empty room. "I warned you, Teddy. I warned you."

Chapter Seventy-Two

"SHE'S UNCONSCIOUS, AND there's a lot of internal bleeding. We're doing everything we can," the doctor said. He glanced from Cancini to Talbot. "Has Senator Stephenson been notified?"

Talbot nodded. "Yes, her parents are on their way."

The doctor straightened his shoulders. "Right. I don't have anything more to add at the moment. I need to get back."

"Wait. One question, Doctor," Cancini said, stepping in front of the doctor. "We need to know. Was Ms. Stephenson sexually assaulted?"

Dr. Charles scowled and his thick white eyebrows seemed to grow above his narrowed eyes. "Detective, we're trying to save that young girl's life. No one has had time to do that kind of examination." He raised his chin. "Now, if you'll excuse me," he said, brushing by the men.

They watched him walk back into the critical care ward. Cancini didn't blame him. The man was under a lot of pressure. The girl's father was not only a senator, but a well-known evangelist and large contributor to the college. Blue Hill Hospital was a teaching facility, and news of Nikki's identity had spread quickly among the hospital staff and to the national media. Cancini understood, but none of that changed his need to ask the question. Whether she lived or died, the question of sexual assault would have to be answered.

Cancini shoved his hands in his pockets. He sighed, looking back at Talbot. "What did you learn from forensics?"

"There was only one set of prints on the gun, and—" He stopped, cut short by Teddy Baldwin coming toward them. In spite of the well-fitted suit and finely combed hair, the mayor wore his fatigue on his face. He brushed past the small throng of reporters to find Cancini and Talbot.

"What the hell is going on in this town?" He threw his hands in the air, shaking his head. "First, we've got what you tell me is a copycat rapist, and now we've got a shooter." Red in the face, the mayor grew louder, his finger aimed at Talbot's chest. "You pushed my police out of this investigation, and what've you got? I'll tell you what you've got. Nothing. Nothing but complete chaos and a whole lotta people who are goddamn terrified to leave their homes. Hell, people can't even go to church anymore without being scared half out of their minds." He dropped his hand when he caught Talbot's glare and shifted his focus to Cancini. "Please tell me you've got something. Anything."

Talbot stood ramrod-straight, eye to eye with the large man. "We've got something."

Teddy swung his attention back to Talbot. "Okay. What is it?"

"I can't tell you."

Red blotches colored Teddy's already florid face. "Wh-what? Are you kidding me? I have a town full of people who have a right to know something."

Talbot folded his arms across his chest. "Fine. You can tell whomever you need to tell that the FBI has several leads and"—he lowered his voice—"a person of interest."

Cancini repressed a smirk. He knew it wasn't exactly true, but the partial bluff couldn't be directed at a better guy. Talbot didn't need the mayor's interference. He already had the governor, and now a senator, on his back.

The mayor snorted. "A person of interest? That means nothing. You've got nothing on the campus murders, and nothing on this. You should've picked up Spradlin from the beginning, like I told you. I don't know why you're protecting him. Now he's hiding out somewhere, laughing at all of us. In the meantime . . ." He shook his head, his eyes shifting between the two men. "It's a goddamn mess. What am I supposed to tell people? Wait, folks, they'll get him after the next dead girl. Christ."

Pink spots appeared on Talbot's cheeks. Cancini shifted to face Baldwin. "If the girl lives, she can identify her attacker."

Baldwin looked away with another shake of his head. "The girl has a hole in her belly. I've been told she's in a coma and isn't gonna make it."

"How do you know that?" Talbot asked. "We haven't released any information."

Cancini watched the mayor's face. His lips twitched for a moment before he turned his anger on Talbot. "How do I know that?" His voice shook. "How do you think? I'm the mayor of this town, for God's sake. I've known every person, every law officer, and every goddamn doctor and nurse in this town for years." He waved a hand toward the lobby and the long white corridor. "These are my friends." Baldwin's eyes slid from Talbot to Cancini. "I expected more from you, Mike. I thought you cared about the people here and about the truth. I even warned you about Spradlin coming back. I thought you would help us, protect us. Ha! You're not the detective you once were." He spun on his heels, pushing his way back through the reporters. He delivered a terse "no comment."

"Goddamn hothead," Talbot muttered.

Cancini's head shot up. His eyes followed Baldwin until the mayor emerged from the mob of shouting journalists. With reporters trailing, he pushed through the glass doors.

"How'd you ever stand him?"

"Huh?"

"How'd you ever stand that asshole?"

Cancini stared after the retreating mayor, his mind racing. Baldwin was more than a hothead. His emotions still swung wildly. "He's worse now."

"Yeah? Guess politics will do that to a man."

"I guess." The reporters returned to the waiting room. Whipping out their notebooks and phones, they huddled together, but none of them was Julia. Cancini's shoulders tightened. It was odd that she wasn't here, large bag on her shoulder and microphone in her hand, angling for a snippet of information.

"Hey, you all right? You seem a million miles away." Talbot touched Cancini on the shoulder.

"Yeah, sorry." He cleared his throat, turning his back on the reporters and thoughts of Julia. "I was thinking about Baldwin and Spradlin. They were best friends once. Now, I think Baldwin would flip the switch on Spradlin himself if he could. Strange, don't you think?"

"A little, but friendships don't always last. Maybe Baldwin decided being friends with a convicted rapist and murderer didn't look good anymore."

"At the trial, Baldwin testified for the defense. Remember? He even had some half-assed, cockamamie story giving Spradlin an alibi."

Talbot nodded. "That's right. It was a bit of a bombshell, wasn't it?"

"You could say that." The detective remembered the day Teddy came to him about testifying. He remembered his shock and his anger.

"The defense has called me as a witness," Teddy had said. "I'm gonna testify about seeing Leo in Harrisonburg the night Cheryl Fornak was murdered."

The news had stunned Cancini at the time. Teddy had never mentioned seeing Leo Spradlin in Harrisonburg on that night or any night of the murders. "What are you talking about? We've been putting this case together for weeks. You've never said a word about this."

Teddy hadn't been able to look him in the eye. "Yeah, well, I'm telling you now."

"You're lying for him."

Teddy hadn't denied the accusation, only apologized. "I thought you should know," he'd said.

During the trial, Teddy's testimony was easily discounted. It was late, the lighting had been poor, and he'd only been passing through the town. No one was with him when he saw the man who resembled Spradlin. No one could corroborate his story. He wasn't accused of lying or charged with perjury. It was too hard to prove. Folks around town assumed he'd made a mistake or had testified out of some misguided sense of loyalty. Cancini hadn't cared about Baldwin's misplaced loyalty. He'd cared that Baldwin had lied. Their brief friendship over, Cancini hadn't spoken again to Teddy Baldwin until after Leo's release.

Cancini bristled still at the memory. "His testimony wasn't credible."

"But as I recall, no one could prove he was lying."

"He was."

"Fine. Baldwin was lying." Talbot frowned. "But he was in law school, right? He had to know what committing perjury would do to his career before it even started. Why do it?"

It was a question Cancini hadn't considered back then. He'd been young and wholly focused on seeing the case through to trial. In hindsight, Teddy had taken a huge risk. "I don't know. I don't understand a lot of what Baldwin does."

"Yeah. He talks big, like he hates Spradlin, but I don't know. I mean, that pension he gave Spradlin's mother? Why do that?"

Cancini's brows drew together. "What pension?"

"After Spradlin's mother lost her job." Cancini shook his head. "Sorry. I thought you knew." Talbot buttoned his jacket, his eyes on the growing cluster of reporters. "When Spradlin was convicted, the college let her go. Not surprisingly, she couldn't get work anywhere in town and she couldn't afford to move. She was broke. The lady had used every penny of her retirement to send Spradlin to school before he dropped out."

"And?"

"She stayed. Had money for groceries and electricity with no obvious source of income. I couldn't understand it at first, so I had our financial forensic team go through her statements. Turns out when she stopped working, she started receiving a monthly check to her savings account until the day she died, deposited directly into her account at the college. I'm not sure if she even knew where it came from."

"And you traced it to Teddy?"

"Well, yes and no. It was actually Dr. Baldwin who initiated the original transfers."

Cancini said nothing, but found himself wondering why a college president would authorize money to Mrs. Spradlin, her son a pariah in town.

"After Dr. Baldwin died, Teddy continued the payments. He took care of her until her death, I presume, for Spradlin."

"Did Spradlin know?"

"I don't know. I doubt it," Talbot said, shrugging. "You're right though. That friendship, or whatever you want to call it, was strange. Is strange."

Teddy was full of surprises, and supporting Spradlin's mother out of loyalty to a long-dead friendship was just another in a long string of surprises. Teddy had made no secret of his feelings for Spradlin now. He'd lynch the man if given the opportunity. "Yeah," Cancini said, "very strange."

Chapter Seventy-Three

BLOOD DRIPPED FROM Julia's wrists. Her phone had buzzed several more times, but she'd been unable to reach it. She'd screamed in frustration. She'd fought until her arms lost all feeling and her legs were like rubber. Dried tears stained her face. She had no idea how many hours had passed since he'd gone.

Car wheels crunched gravel in front of the cabin. Julia jerked, every nerve firing. The car door slammed. He was there, standing in the doorway, gray skies behind him.

"It's worse than I thought," he said. Spradlin came close and pulled a knife from his pocket. Reaching up, he cut through the ropes, and her arms dropped to her sides. She wiggled her hands until the feeling returned, pinpricks from the tips of her fingers to her elbows. He walked her to a chair, arm around her shoulders, and helped her to sit. Grabbing a water bottle, he opened it, handing it to her. "Drink this."

Julia gulped the water, watching him move about the small cabin.

"I didn't want it to come to this," he said, dragging a cardboard box out of the corner. He brushed away the dust and sliced it open with the knife. Spradlin tossed some crumpled newspapers to the floor. He pulled out a rifle, about three feet in length, the long steel barrel widening to a wooden butt. Julia stifled a gasp, her heart and mind racing. He held the gun in both hands, turning it over several times. He brought it up to his shoulder and looked through the viewfinder. "Looks like it's still in good shape," he said.

He reached back inside the cardboard box and pulled out several small boxes. He opened the chamber of the rifle and pulled out a tube. She watched him wipe each part of the gun with a cloth. He loaded the brass bullets one by one. "I never liked hunting," he said. "You'd think I would. I never missed, but there was no fun in it. I always liked this gun, though." His fingers trailed the length of it, resting on the trigger.

Her chest pounded. "What are you going to do?"

Spradlin sighed. He lowered the gun until the barrel was pointed at the ground. Shadows hollowed his face when he raised his eyes to hers. "Something I should have done a long time ago."

Chapter Seventy-Four

THE DOCTOR'S GRIM face told the story, the long hours at the hospital evident in the dark circles under his eyes. "I want it on record that I don't like this. I don't like it one bit." He wagged a finger at the FBI man. "But her father is insisting if there's any chance she can speak or communicate . . ."

"I understand," Talbot said, his tone somber.

"I don't want you upsetting her," Dr. Charles warned. "She's stabilized but still in critical condition. We can't be sure of the extent of the internal bleeding. She's not out of the woods."

"I understand," Talbot repeated. "We were—"

"When can we see her?" Cancini interrupted.

The doctor shifted his gaze to Cancini, not hiding his resentment. "She's only been out of surgery a short while. She should wake up soon." He looked from one man to the other. "When she does, you will have five minutes. That's all. Am I clear?" He didn't wait for a response, turned his back on them both, and left.

Talbot spoke first. "She might not be able to tell us anything."

"True."

"And even if she can, this might be unrelated. A shooting in a residential home. Doesn't fit with the M.O. This could be a crime completely apart from our case on campus."

"It's not," the detective said.

Talbot, who'd been pacing the hall, stopped, looking back at Cancini. "How can you be so sure?"

The detective hesitated. "I can't," he admitted. "But it doesn't feel like an attempted robbery. Nothing was taken. No evidence that anything even happened outside of the kitchen."

"Maybe the girl surprised an intruder. Someone who knew the Walshes go to church every Sunday like clockwork. I mean, the girl wasn't supposed to be there."

"True again. Like I said, I can't be sure."

A young FBI agent came down the corridor, handing some stapled pages to Talbot. "It's from the priest at the church," he said. "A list of the people he remembers seeing at the nine o'clock service this morning. There are several witnesses who can verify the Walsh family was there the whole time. Father and daughter sat in the second row, and the mom sang with the choir."

"Okay, thanks," Talbot said to the young man. He scanned the pages and handed the list to Cancini. "Looks like fifty or so folks including your buddy, the mayor."

The detective looked up. "Baldwin? Are you sure?"

"That's what it says."

"Interesting."

"Okay. I'll bite. Why is that so interesting?"

Cancini scanned the list. "Denomination. The Walsh family is Catholic. There aren't a whole lot of Catholics around here, so I know the church. St. Benedict's, right? That's Catholic." He'd gone inside once, during the first series of rapes. Back then, the tragedy of the girls' murders had nearly overwhelmed him. He'd been driven to find the killer, but the reality of it had scared him more than he was willing to admit at the time. Not long before Spradlin had emerged as his most obvious suspect, he'd found himself inside the sanctuary, sitting in a pew. A cluster of candles burned at the altar, the scent drifting to the back rows. He hadn't prayed or sought out a priest. He'd sat, letting the quiet seep into his bones.

Cancini folded the list. "The Baldwin family is Baptist. There's a huge church up at the campus; most of the churches around town are either Baptist or Methodist. Baldwin isn't Catholic."

"So, he isn't a member of this church?"

"Doubt it."

"Oka-ay. Then why was he there?"

"That's a good question."

The door to the private waiting room opened. "Gentlemen," the gray-haired doctor said, his voice nearly a growl, "she's awake."

Chapter Seventy-Five

"I DON'T UNDERSTAND," Julia whispered.

"I won't let anything happen to you. I promise," Leo told her, wrapping strips of torn sheet around her wrists. "But you need to be here. You need to hear everything. I'm trusting you." He sat facing her, wiping away blood and dirt. "When he gets here, he won't be expecting you. You will be under the bed. I'll get him talking."

Julia shuddered, but he was right. She'd come to get the story; she had no choice but to comply.

"He won't even know you're here."

"What about my car?"

"I'll hide it in the brush behind the cabin. He won't see it. There's only one way in, and that's to come down the dirt road. I'll see him before he sees me."

She nodded. He taped the bandages in place and handed her a fresh washcloth. She wiped the rest of the grime and dried tears from her face.

"I'll need my tape recorder."

"Is there any room left on the tape? I don't want you to copy over what we talked about before."

Her mouth opened and then closed. She knew the worst of this man, yet she didn't understand him. After a moment, she said, "I have an extra in my bag."

"Good. Get it."

She found the extra tape and put it in the tiny recorder. She was ready.

"I'm sorry about earlier," he said. "But I couldn't risk you leaving. He doesn't trust you anymore. He won't let you live."

She knew Leo was right. Ted had seen the question in her eyes. She'd done her best to cover up her suspicions, but he hadn't been fooled. She blinked back fresh tears. Damn. She was so stupid. She'd liked him. Trusted him. Then after she'd met with Nikki in the hotel, there'd been doubts. She shouldn't have ignored them.

Leo moved around the cabin. He pulled a single chair to the back and placed it in the shadows. He picked up the rifle, wiped it again, and placed it on the chair. She watched him gather her bag and the bloody cloths. He tossed them into a cabinet, slamming it shut. Outside, the rain thudded against the thin wooden roof. She stood frozen, her heart racing.

He gestured to the bed. "It'll be cramped, but you should be able to hear everything. Stay back against the wall, and no matter what you hear, no matter what you think is about to happen, do not look out from under the bed. Do you hear me? Do not look out."

She inhaled, her fingers tightening around the tape recorder. "You're going to kill him, aren't you?"

"He's given me no choice," Leo said, his face impassive. "I have to."

Chapter Seventy-Six

"NIKKI?" TALBOT SPOKE softly, standing as close to the bed as possible without touching it or the girl. Her eyelids fluttered, then closed again. "Nikki? We need to ask you a few questions."

Her eyes opened. She blinked, moved her head a little, and seemed to take in the hospital room, the shiny equipment next to the bed, the plastic bags and tubes. A crease appeared between her brows. She closed her eyes again. Talbot stepped back, standing shoulder to shoulder with Cancini. "Why don't you give it a try?"

Cancini studied Nikki's battered and bruised face. One eye was swollen and puffy. Her jaw was wired shut, and she'd lost a great deal of blood. The girl was fighting for her life, but they needed to ask questions. What if she knew something? What if she could identify her assailant? What if her attacker was the rapist? Cancini understood the doctor's anger. Under different circumstances, he might feel the same way, but these were not other circumstances. He moved toward the bed and leaned in close. "Nikki, my name is Detective Cancini."

Her eyes opened again, the crease between her brows back.

"I need to ask you a couple of questions about what happened at the Walsh house."

For a moment, she lay still, blank-faced. Seconds ticked by. Her eyes glistened and tears slipped down her cheeks, as the memory of the attack seemed to return.

"I'll try to be brief, but I need your help to find the person who did this to you. Do you think you can help us?"

Blinking back the tears, she tried to speak. Cancini leaned in close, but her words were unintelligible. He shot the doctor a questioning look.

"We had to immobilize her jaw. Between that and the swelling, she might have difficulty talking."

She tried to speak again, but her words were garbled. Cancini put his face close to hers, but he still couldn't make out what she was trying to say. He looked at Talbot, and shook his head. Fresh tears sprang to the girl's eyes.

The doctor spoke, his attention focused on the screen with the green lights. "Gentlemen, I think that's enough. Your questions are causing her stress and discomfort. We need to keep her calm."

"Can we come back later?" Talbot asked.

Dr. Charles was quiet. "I don't think so. The next several hours are critical, and you're not helping."

Cancini stayed close to the bed, studying the girl. She knew something. He could see it in her battered face, in the way she seemed desperate to communicate, but she was weak and would be lucky to make it through the night. Nikki reached out, searching until she found Cancini's hand. Her wet eyes pleaded with him. She tightened her grip around his hand and didn't let go.

Cancini nodded at the girl and raised his free hand. "Just one more minute, please." She was weak, but her grip was strong.

"Let's do this a different way. Why don't I ask you a question, a yes or no question? Squeeze my hand once for yes and twice for no. Do you understand?"

He felt one squeeze. "Good girl." This could be the break they were looking for, but he needed to do it right. "Was the person that attacked you a boyfriend or a friend?"

She squeezed twice. "No," he said aloud. "Had you ever met your attacker before?"

Two squeezes. "Was he a fellow student?" No. He paused. He asked the obvious question, the one he'd been thinking about since the attack on the first girl. "Was your attacker Leo Spradlin?" The beeping increased on the machine. Nikki grew agitated again, but this time the doctor said nothing, his protests momentarily forgotten. She squeezed his hand. Once. Twice. "No?" he said aloud. "No."

Talbot exhaled. The doctor intervened then and called for a nurse. He put his hand on Cancini's shoulder, pulling him away from the bed, but Nikki would not let go. She struggled again to speak.

"Please," Talbot said, shooting a look at the doctor. "One more minute."

"It's okay," Cancini said to Nikki. "It's okay. I'm not giving up. I'm with you." He peeked at the monitor. This girl was fighting for her life, but she wanted to help. She wanted them to find their man. He hesitated. He knew what he wanted to ask, but he wasn't sure he wanted to hear the answer. The girl's eyes, unblinking, never left his. He swallowed. The name had been bouncing around his head, nagging at his brain for days. If he was right, it would change everything.

"Nikki, the man who attacked you," he said, his voice soft, "was it Teddy Baldwin?"

Cancini heard the gasps behind him but kept his eyes locked on Nikki's. The beeping from the monitor slowed, and Nikki's face softened, the crease between her brows disappearing. She squeezed his hand. Once.

He stood up straight, and her hand slipped from his. "Yes."

Chapter Seventy-Seven

AFTER THE SECOND attack, Spradlin had disappeared. Word had gotten around town. Anyone who hadn't already been sure Spradlin was guilty couldn't help wondering after that. Teddy had taken every opportunity to fuel the fire. "Why would an innocent man, one who made such a public show of returning to his hometown, suddenly disappear during a fresh wave of rapes and murders?" he'd asked. "I'll tell you. Only a man with something to hide." Even the skeptics had lapped it up. Teddy had shaken his head and hidden his smile. Leo was playing right into his hands.

The FBI hadn't been able to ignore the disappearance, either. They'd put out an APB on the man, and he'd been informally elevated to a person of interest. Baldwin had even heard the governor's office was trying to launch a new investigation into the DNA evidence to find out if it had been tampered with. Everyone was trying to cover their tracks. Teddy smiled as he drove north along the interstate.

Cancini had made it easy, too. His ego had blinded him. He couldn't let go of the past or Spradlin. He'd been the hero once.

If things went according to plan, it would be Teddy's turn, and Cancini could play a supporting role. What a laugh. The girl was a complication, if she lived. He would have to make sure that didn't happen. And then there was Julia. She'd stuck her nose in where it didn't belong. If only she'd never met Nikki or met with Spradlin in the library. Who knew what he'd been saying? Either way, she knew too much.

When he reached the narrow western route, Teddy turned off the highway and pulled the car over to the side of the road. The sky was spitting rain, and he could see swollen clouds in the distance. A full-blown storm was fast approaching. The dirt road wasn't far now.

We need to meet. I'll send you the directions in one hour.

Almost forty-five minutes had passed since he'd received that message. No way Leo would expect him yet—not without having sent directions—but Leo had underestimated him as usual. He'd known about Leo's little cabin since their high school days. Leo had to be there. He had nowhere else to go.

He pulled a pair of plastic gloves out of his pocket and snapped them on. He reached over to the passenger seat and picked up the handgun. Leo's handgun. He'd been able to get everything he needed from Spradlin's house a few weeks before his release from jail: the gun, a pair of shoes, and a couple of old T-shirts. Cocking the pistol, he checked the bullets. It was loaded and ready. He set it on the passenger seat, next to a pile of plastic bags. Inside each bag were two strands of hair. The girls hadn't minded when he pulled the strands. They'd been dead when he took what he wanted.

He switched on the wipers and pulled back onto the road, running through the plan in his mind again. The shoes he'd taken were in a brown paper bag in the trunk, covered with dirt and leaves from the woods where he'd left the first girl. He'd swabbed the insides of the other girls' mouths with the T-shirts; they held precious traces of saliva. Everything was ready. He would plant the evidence after he cleaned up the loose ends. It would be overwhelming and irrefutable.

He came to the dirt road and turned slowly, searching for a place to hide the car. After a short distance, he parked in a small clearing, still out of view of the cabin. The winds blew, and the sky was about to open up. He hauled old branches from the side of the road to cover the rear end of the car. It wasn't perfect, but it was the best he could do before the storm.

Opening the passenger door, he reached in and grabbed the gun. He stuck it in his waistband, then pulled his jacket closed and zipped it. Leo was going to commit one more murder, and then, overcome with guilt, he would take his own life. Teddy looked to the sky, letting the first, heavy drops hit his face. He'd never imagined it would end like this. They'd been such a great team once. Fuck Leo. There wasn't any other way now. Leo had made that perfectly clear.

He wiped his arm across his eyes, blinking away the rain. Careful to walk inside the tree line, he crept toward the cabin, stepping over rocks, roots, and broken branches, the uneven ground slick with fallen leaves. Crouching under some heavy branches, he eyed the small wooden structure and a compact car parked in front. He smiled. He knew that car. Julia's car. He'd been right again.

His phone buzzed, and he glanced at the screen. It was Janie from the hospital, the surgical nurse who worked in critical care. A plain woman, overworked, she welcomed his attention, his questions about her family. People didn't realize how far you could get with just a few kind words. Teddy did. Those kind words often yielded a few favors now and then. Protecting the phone from the rain, he opened the text.

I'm sorry to give you the bad news, but your friend's daughter didn't make it.

Teddy licked his lips. The girl was gone. And Julia was with Leo. Neither of them was expecting him yet. It couldn't be more perfect.

Chapter Seventy-Eight

"BALDWIN HASN'T BEEN seen since he left the hospital. Being a Sunday, his office is closed." Talbot turned the corner. He drove up to the white house with the blue shutters and parked on the street.

Cancini craned his neck to look back at the two-story Colonial. The driveway was empty, and no activity was visible through the windows. The house appeared vacant. "He left the hospital almost two hours ago."

Both men got out of the car, Talbot with a search warrant in hand. "Yeah, and you should know the priest at St. Benedict's confirmed he only saw Baldwin at the beginning of the service in the back row. No one remembers seeing him after that."

"So, we think he went to the service and slipped out after a few minutes."

"Right. The Walsh house is about three miles from the church. He could have been there by nine-ten at the latest."

Cancini and Talbot walked up the sidewalk, pausing as a team of agents circled to the backyard. Talbot drew his gun, pointing the barrel upward. Cancini rang the bell. After several minutes and no answer, Talbot's men opened the door and spread out among the rooms.

Cancini headed upstairs where he inspected the three bedrooms one by one. He guessed the first was a guest room, furnished with only a double bed and single nightstand. A second bedroom held a treadmill, bike, and TV. The hall bathroom was clean except for one towel crumpled on the floor. Slipping on a pair of gloves, Cancini picked it up by the corner. It appeared used and smelled musty. He dropped it back on the floor. The master bedroom was also empty. He stood in the doorway, scanning the room. No books on the nightstand. No television set. No pictures on the walls or framed photographs. The bed was haphazardly made, but otherwise, the room was clean. The walk-in closet held rows of suits, shirts, and shoes. A clothes hamper stood against the back wall of the closet. Cancini lifted the lid. It was empty.

He found Talbot in the kitchen.

"All the trash has been emptied," Talbot reported. "There's a thin layer of dust on the countertops and bookcases. I'd say he's been living elsewhere for the last few days."

Cancini opened the refrigerator. It was mostly empty except for a couple of take-out cartons, some bruised fruit, and a half-empty carton of milk. The date on the milk had passed. "I'd say you're right." The Baldwin family owned several properties. It seemed reasonable that Teddy would have access to all of them. "How many other residences do they own?"

"Four. One is at a ski resort in West Virginia, about two hours from here. One is in Virginia Beach. And there's a house in Florida. I've got people checking out those places."

"And the fourth?"

"The big house on campus. It's usually reserved for visiting professors, guests of the president, people like that. But with the evacuation, it's been sitting empty."

Cancini followed Talbot back to the car. They rode in silence to the campus. Cancini leaned forward, rubbing the base of his neck. The dull ache that had started at the hospital had grown to a pounding throb that spread over the back of his head. He recognized the pain as penance, as a physical reminder of the evidence he'd missed, the mistakes he'd made. How could he have missed Baldwin for so long? How could he have he have missed the shifty eyes behind the amiable, good ol' boy politician? He slammed his palm into the dashboard. "Goddammit. He was right in front of us the whole time!"

"Maybe," Talbot said, his tone noncommittal.

"What do you mean maybe? Nikki identified him as her attacker."

"Yes, she did, and we can get him on that when we find him, but as of now, we can't link the other attacks to Nikki. The evidence we have in those cases is still circumstantial, like it or not. It no more incriminates Baldwin than it does Spradlin or me. No matter how you look at it, the return of Spradlin and the new attacks is still suspicious. No one has pointed that out more than you."

Talbot was right. Spradlin was hiding something back then, and he was hiding something now. Why make a show of coming back and then disappear if you have nothing to hide? The road was lined with thick trees and bramble and he rolled the window down. The colors had changed in the last several days. Green had turned to gold and rust and red. Spradlin and Baldwin. Baldwin and Spradlin. Cancini had once thought he'd understood them both. Now, he wasn't so sure.

Cancini's mind returned to the girl lying in the hospital bed, struggling for her life. "How many guards do you have outside Nikki's room?"

"Two. He can't get in, but just to be sure, I took an extra precaution."

"Oh?"

"Baldwin got a message from a friend. She told him the girl didn't make it."

Cancini nodded. "Good move."

"Yeah, one of the few lately."

They pulled onto Blue Hill Drive, parking in the long circular drive. They piled out and circled the house. One by one, the agents checked in with Talbot on their walkie-talkies. Cancini looked up at the grand house. It struck him as immodest, hardly the type of house he envisioned for a servant of God. He thought of Father Joe's small parish apartment, the one he'd lived in for more than thirty years. It didn't have columns or sweeping lawns. It wasn't grand in any sense. This house was everything Father Joe's apartment wasn't.

Loud static erupted from the walkie-talkie in Talbot's hand, and a deep voice boomed from the speaker.

"Sir, there's someone on the line from the *Washington Herald* for Detective Cancini. He says it's urgent."

Talbot handed the walkie-talkie to the detective.

"Cancini here."

"Detective, this is Norm Jensen. I'm from the *Herald*, Julia Manning's editor." His voice shook, the words rushed. "She's missing, and she said she loved me and—"

"Slow down, Norm. Start at the beginning."

"Oh God," he sobbed. "I hope we're not too late."

Cancini's heart skipped a beat. "What do you mean?"

Norm struggled to speak. "Julia. She's not the melodramatic type. That's me," he said, stifling another sob. "Look, she sent me this text message." He read it to the detective.

"There's a package for me in her safe?"

"Yes, but she's not there. I've had my assistant call the hotel three times. They found some clerk who said Julia left the hotel before the sun came up. Why would she do that?"

"I don't know, Norm."

"You've got to find her. That message . . . I've got a bad feeling."

"Okay." He waved for Talbot. "Stay on the line and let one of these officers get your information. We'll get back to you as soon as we know something."

Cancini spoke quickly, his right hand on his gun. "That was Julia's editor. She's the reporter I told you about, the one who's been meeting with Spradlin."

"And?"

"And she's missing. I need you to send someone to her hotel. There's a package addressed to me in her room safe."

"I'll send someone now. Where will you be?"

"I'm heading west in the direction Spradlin was last seen," he said over his shoulder. "How fast can you trace a cell number?"

Chapter Seventy-Nine

EVEN THROUGH THE noises of the storm, they both heard the snap of branches outside. "He's here," Leo said, cocking his head toward the door. "I don't know how, but it doesn't matter now. He's trying to catch me off guard." He pushed Julia away from him. "Get under the bed. Hurry."

She nodded and dropped to the floor. The dust under the bed stuck to her sweaty skin. Stifling a sneeze, Julia pulled her blouse up over her nose.

A chair scraped the floor near the back of the cabin. Leo would wait in the shadows, the rifle in his lap.

Footsteps sounded on the wooden steps. She clicked record and inched backward, pressing the small of her back into the wall. The front door slammed open, then shut again. "I'm here, Leo. What do you want?"

The silence stretched out until Julia didn't think she could hold her breath a moment longer.

"I want things to end. It's got to end," Spradlin said finally.

Baldwin snickered. "Jesus, Leo, how many times have I heard

that before? That's what you always fucking say." He moved forward in the cabin. "Why don't you come closer so we can talk? We haven't been able to do that since you got back."

"Where were we going to talk, Teddy? In town? At the diner? I'm a pariah in this town, and you know it." Baldwin found the chair Leo had placed near the front door. The legs creaked. He must have sat. She pictured the two men facing each other, seated on opposite sides of the room. "We both know being seen with me wouldn't be good for your image."

"I'm sorry about that," Baldwin said with a sigh. "I'm sorry about a lot of things." Spradlin snorted. "Believe what you like. Look, I did the best I could. I tried to help you." Another snort. "I made sure you had the best lawyers available."

"It was the least you could do. You were walking around on the outside. You got elected mayor. You got to live. What did I get?"

The rain came down harder, beating on the roof. "If the truth had come out, we both would have been in jail. Is that what you wanted?" Baldwin answered.

"When? Then or now?"

"Leo, it doesn't have to be this way. I don't want to be enemies, not now, not after everything . . . you're free, aren't you?"

Lightning cracked in the distance, and the thunder that followed made the cabin shudder. The winds had picked up and blew through the old boarded walls.

"I'll never be free, Teddy, and you know it. Neither of us will ever be free."

"You need to fucking lighten up, Leo." Silence. "Where's the girl? The reporter?"

"Gone. She knew too much for her own good."

"Really? Now you're sounding like the man I used to know."

"I don't want do this anymore, Teddy. Why'd you do it? Why'd you start again? I warned you, didn't I?"

"Yeah, you warned me. So what?" A match sizzled, followed by the distinct odor of cigarette smoke. "You don't get to fucking tell me what I can and can't do. Don't you get it? No one has ever suspected me, Leo. No one. And there've been others. In Florida. Out West. I wore a mask those times. I had to be careful. They were usually whores, and nobody gave a crap about them anyway. They weren't as good as the college girls, but I needed them. They were my prizes for good behavior."

"Did you kill them, too?"

"No. I could've, though." His tone wistful, he added, "I should've."

Julia's heart pounded, thumping so loudly she was afraid Baldwin would hear it. She willed herself to be still and quiet.

"So, what changed? You used to be squeamish about that sort of thing." Leo's voice sounded flat, almost bored.

Baldwin chuckled. "Yeah, I was, wasn't I? Leo, let's sit over at that table where we can talk—like old times."

"No." And then, "Did you enjoy it?"

"Enjoy it?" Baldwin said the words slowly as though the idea was new. "Not at first. I was going to do it your way, you know, with the first girl. I was gonna break her neck in one clean stroke, like you, but then someone was coming. I had to improvise."

"You hit her."

"You could say that. I fucking bashed her head in." Julia bit down on her lower lip to keep from crying out. "The second one, I did her neck. Wasn't as clean as yours, but it was good. It was damn good."

"So now you think maybe you do enjoy it?"

"Yeah, I guess I do." Julia detected a smile in his voice. She swallowed hard, blinking back tears. "Maybe we're even more alike than you thought, Leo. Maybe I'm the stronger one now."

"I never enjoyed it, Teddy. I did what I had to do."

"Really, Leo? Are you trying to convince me or yourself? I am so fucking sick of hearing about how you protected me." Scorn tinged his words. "I can't let Teddy get caught. Teddy's gotten himself into a mess again. I can't let that happen. I can't let Cheryl or Theresa or Marilyn talk. And there was only one way to keep them quiet, wasn't there? Poor you. You got to wrap your hands around all those fucking little necks and snap them in half like twigs. You showed 'em, didn't you? Don't try to tell me you didn't get off on it. You got off as much as I did." His voice grew pensive. "God, I loved putting those stuck-up girls in their places."

Julia held her breath, her eyes wide in the darkness under the bed. She recognized Ted Baldwin's voice, but she didn't know him. Was he mad?

"You're wrong." Leo said.

"What? So, now you're trying to tell me you felt bad when you killed those bitches? Oh, please."

"No," he said. "I'm trying to tell you I felt nothing. I didn't feel guilty, but I didn't enjoy it, either. I just did it."

"For me?"

"I guess."

"But not anymore."

"No."

A minute ticked by. The wind whistled, and the rain thumped. The storm almost drowned out their words. Careful not to make a sound, Julia pushed herself away from the wall a few inches, straining to hear. She held the recorder closer to the voices.

"Okay, so what happens now?" Baldwin asked.

"It's got to end."

"Sure. Okay." He spoke as though he were thinking out loud. "The FBI doesn't have anything anyway. I've been keeping tabs on the whole investigation. There are a couple of loose ends I need to tie up, but after that I'll stop for sure. Then, after a couple of weeks, maybe months, everything will go back to normal." The front shadow shifted, and the chair legs moved. Baldwin stood now. "Sound good?" he asked.

Leo stood, too. "No, that's not how it's going to end." A click let her know he had cocked the rifle. "Turn yourself in, or you die."

Baldwin laughed, braying like a hyena standing over his prey. "You're out of your fucking mind, Leo."

"Don't do it, Teddy."

Julia's hands and legs shook and she held her breath. The silence gave no clues to what was happening and then, "The jacket stays on, and leave your hands where I can see them."

"Sure. Whatever you say." Julia slid forward until she could see the room and the backs of Baldwin's legs. He shuffled forward a few steps. "But you've gotta know I'm never going to turn myself in. Why the fuck should I? I've been the mayor of this town for a long time, and I plan to keep it that way. Believe it or not, I'm pretty damn good at it. Besides, you would never kill me, and we both know it. You might not be willing to protect me anymore, but you won't kill me. I'm your brother."

"I can, and I will."

Baldwin snickered again. "Goddammit, Leo. Why do you have to be such an asshole? Let me walk outta here, and I promise it will be done. I'll stop."

"I can't do that."

"Leo, you're not fucking listening to me. I'm never turning myself in. I'm not going to prison. That is not fucking happening. Put the rifle down."

"No."

Rain lashed against the tiny window and roof, popping like firecrackers on the Fourth of July.

"Okay, Leo. This is how we're gonna do it. Forget your ideas. This is much better for both of us." Teddy took one step backward. "I'll turn around and walk out of here. You let me go back to my life, and I'll help you go anywhere you want. I'll set you up, make sure you have money, make it so you can disappear. You're an innocent man according to the law. You can spend the rest of your life on an island somewhere, living the good life." He took another step back. He was halfway across the room.

Lightning cracked over the cabin, throwing a hazy light across the floorboards. Baldwin froze. Thunder boomed, the sound echoing in the small room. When the rumbling faded, Cancini stood in the doorway, gun in hand.

Chapter Eighty

"WELL, WOULD YOU look what the cat dragged in. Everyone's favorite hero, the great detective." Baldwin raised a finger, pointing toward Spradlin. "It's about time you got here," he said, his tone turning serious. "He was about to shoot me."

Rain dripped from Cancini's spiky hair onto his nose. He wiped it away, blinking in the semidarkness. Baldwin stood in the center of the old cabin, his arms hanging at his sides. Leo stood at the back, rifle trained on the mayor.

Baldwin gestured toward Leo a second time. "Turns out you were right to question his release after all. We were both right."

"Oh?" Cancini asked, looking back and forth between the two men.

"I've been doing a little investigating, too. I had to. You know how I feel about my town and all the good folks here. It's my responsibility to protect them. I had to find out who'd been hurting those girls."

"I see." Cancini scanned the cabin. No sign of Julia, her bag, or her phone. "And this is where your investigation led you?"

Baldwin nodded. "Exactly. I came out here to confront Spradlin. Good thing you got here when you did. As you can see, he was going to shoot me."

Cancini glanced back at Spradlin. He held the rifle up at his shoulder, gripped the barrel with one hand, and touched the trigger with the other. He had not moved since Cancini entered the cabin. "Is that true, Spradlin? Were you going to shoot him?"

"Yep."

"See," Baldwin said. "I told you. Thank God, you're here now. It's police business now. You take care of him, and I'll wait outside." He took two steps toward Cancini.

"Stop." Leo's toneless voice interrupted. "I told you there was only one of two ways this could end, Teddy."

"You wanted it over, Leo. Now, it's over. Like last time."

"You leave me no choice," Spradlin said, taking aim at Baldwin's heart.

Cancini raised his pistol. "Don't do it, Spradlin."

"He won't." Baldwin smiled. "He can't." He took another step and then another.

The explosion shook the cabin, the blast nearly drowning out the second, sharp thwack. When the shots faded, Julia screamed and screamed.

Chapter Eighty-One

"JULIA." CANCINI RUSHED to the bed and dropped to the floor. "It's okay. Shhh. It's okay." He tried to calm her, speaking softly, until her screams petered out. Reaching under the bed, he took her hands. They shook in his careful grasp. Slowly, she crawled out, her bandaged wrists still bleeding. Sitting on the floor, her head to her chest, she took deep breaths, exhaling slowly. He stayed crouched next to her, one hand resting on her back, the other holding the pistol, still pointed at Spradlin.

"Is she okay?" Leo asked. He sounded tired, his voice strained.

Spradlin sat in the chair, one arm in his lap, the other dangling toward the floor. The rifle lay at his feet.

"I'm okay," she said, her voice ragged.

Cancini stood slowly, staying close to Julia. Baldwin lay crumpled on the ground, his blood spreading across the floor. Cancini shifted his stance to block her view. With his free hand, Cancini pulled out his phone, dialing quickly. He requested an ambulance with backup. Nodding toward Spradlin, he asked, "What about you? Is it bad?"

"It hurts."

"Sorry."

"No, you're not."

"You're right. I'm not. I'd do it again. You shot a man in the back." Cancini looked down at Julia. She still sat against the bed, her body shaking. He touched her shoulder with his hand and squeezed. His eyes swept over the dead man and back to the Spradlin. "Why? Why'd you do it?"

Spradlin shrugged. "I had no choice."

"That's a load of crap. You always have a choice, Spradlin, like Baldwin had a choice. If he hadn't started up with the college girls again, you'd both be free men. He had a choice, too."

"He made the wrong choice." Spradlin grunted, his breath raspy. Red drops dotted the wooden floor underneath his arm. "When did you know?" he asked.

"I didn't for sure, until today." Cancini hesitated before admitting, "The old case kept bothering me. In spite of the DNA evidence, I knew you were involved. It finally came to me. You didn't rape those girls. That was someone who couldn't control their emotions. You only killed them. Once the idea got in my head, I knew there was only one person who could've been the rapist, but I didn't have any proof."

"Baldwin."

"Right. You guys were always together back then. And his testifying at your trial . . . that never sat right with me. I came across some stories about his old man. The tendencies were there." Julia got to her feet; Cancini steadied her, taking her arm. Her face pale and her legs unsure, she stood only a moment, then sat on the bed. "He made a mistake this time. He attacked a girl this morning, but she didn't die." Julia gasped. "She identified Baldwin. You didn't need to shoot him. He was going away anyway."

Spradlin shook his head. "It doesn't matter. It needed to end."

Cancini sighed. "Look, I'm not gonna say I like it, but you were a free man. You couldn't have been retried on the first series of murders. But now?" He turned his palm upward. "You shot an unarmed man in the back—a man who would have gone to prison anyway. You could have walked away. Why?"

"You said it yourself. I killed those girls. I don't deserve to walk away."

Cancini frowned. "C'mon, Spradlin. Since when did you start having a conscience? You just killed your best friend. Hell, for a while, he was your only friend. You had the same choices any of us have." When Spradlin said nothing, Cancini felt the urge to cross the room, grab the man, and shake him. "Whatever," he muttered, repressing the urge. Distant sirens broke the heavy silence hanging between the two men. Cancini steadied his gun. "Okay, when they get here, I'm going to arrest you for the murder of Teddy Baldwin. They'll take you to the hospital, and then it'll be up to the locals and the FBI."

"That's fine." Spradlin nodded at the cabinets against the wall. "Julia has some documents for you and some audiotape. There's a tablet in my backpack I took from Baldwin. All of that may help." She drew in her breath. "You can use them however you want."

Spradlin was helping him? He'd shot the one man who could have guaranteed his freedom. He might've been an unwanted man in Little Springs, but he would've been free. The sirens came closer. His fingers tightened on the pistol. Spradlin hadn't moved since the shooting, but he couldn't take any chances. Not with Julia.

"There's something wrong with me, Mike," Spradlin said, breaking the silence. "You're right. Nothing means anything to me. Life. Death. Meaningless. It wasn't hard to kill those girls. It meant nothing. I felt nothing." Cancini looked into the empty eyes of the man in front of him. He'd recognized the deadness even when they were young. It was one of the reasons he'd initially suspected him. "Feeling nothing. That's not normal. I didn't know it at first, but, later, I did. I couldn't change it, so I accepted it." The sirens blared louder, only a few miles from the cabin. "Teddy. He was the opposite. Whatever I lacked in emotion, he had, and then some. When we were young, he couldn't control them. I think he got better at it maybe. But he was sometimes manic. It wasn't his fault."

Cancini's eyes narrowed. What the hell was Spradlin talking about? "It wasn't his fault? The rapes? Is that why you killed those girls? You were protecting him because it wasn't his fault?"

"Yes."

"But you didn't protect him this time?"

"No."

Cancini stared, then shook his head. "I don't understand."

The bumping of cars on the narrow, dirt road rumbled the cabin's windows. The sirens were almost upon them.

"I think I can explain," Julia said, looking between Cancini and Leo. Spradlin nodded at her. She turned to Cancini. "When Leo went away to prison, he was worried about Ted, but Ted promised he'd get help. He promised he wouldn't attack any more girls." She spoke louder over the sirens. "As far as Leo knew, he'd kept those promises. The rapes stopped. But at some point, he realized Ted hadn't stopped. He'd only gotten more careful."

Julia stood. She was nearly shouting now. "Ted had snapped. He was mad. Leo warned Ted he was coming back and that he wasn't going to pretend anymore. Ted begged him to leave the past alone. Leo agreed if Ted promised to stop. But Ted lied. He used Leo's release to start again. All Leo wanted was for everything to stop—all of it. They had to end the line with them. It was the only way."

Cancini watched Spradlin. Outside of the piercing eyes, his face was impassive, his features as set as those in a mask. "What do you mean 'end the line'?"

Julia moved close. She placed her hand on his arm and her lips near his ear. Brakes and slammed doors nearly drowned out her words. "Bloodline," she said, her breath warm. "End the bloodline. Leo and Ted were brothers."

Chapter Eighty-Two

CANCINI PUT THE newspaper down and reached for his coffee. He glanced out the diner window. The sun barely over the horizon, folks streamed out from the subway station on the corner. Women and men, young and old, political types and bankers, all starting another day in downtown D.C.

"Julia did a good job on the articles," Talbot said, scooping up a mouthful of scrambled eggs.

Cancini returned to the paper he'd set aside. Baldwin, wearing a suit and a smile, stared out from the front page. His picture was that of an average man, not unlike many of the men plodding from the subway to their offices. He might have a two-story house in the suburbs, a wife, and 2.4 kids. He looked normal, not like a rapist or killer. Then again, what did one look like? They didn't all come with warning signs or tics or strange behavior. Maybe that's what made the truth so hard to see.

He had read the other two articles Julia wrote in a three-part series about the Blue Hill crimes. She had pulled from Mrs. Spradlin's journals and from the tapes she had made in the cabin. The rest came from interviews and old files. She deserved the three days of front-page coverage. The newspaper brass must have thought it had prize-winning potential. He agreed.

"Yeah," Cancini said, and took another swig of coffee.

"Are you gonna see her?"

He set the cup on the table. It was the same question his father had asked him the night before.

"You like her, don't you?" the old man had asked. "I'm not trying to push you, but I don't want to see you end up alone, like me. Your mother wouldn't have wanted that."

"Dad," he'd said, swallowing a lump in his throat. "There's no rush. It's not like you're going anywhere." His father was alive, but the doctors were only prolonging the inevitable. His breathing was better, but a nurse would now come in every day to take care of meals and baths. The old man hated it. Cancini felt sorry for the nurse.

"Maybe. Maybe not. Are you going to ask her out or not?"

"Not right now," he'd said, sighing. "She needs to figure things out. Her husband wants to reconcile. And everything that happened in Little Springs was a lot for anyone. She needs some time."

He repeated the same answer to Talbot. He did like her, though. A lot. But chances were, she didn't have room in her life for a cranky, hardheaded detective. He understood. Probably better than most. Besides, he'd been alone a long time. He wasn't sure he knew how to be anything else.

Cancini changed the subject. "What happens next?"

Talbot pushed away his breakfast. He wiped at his mouth and tossed the crumpled napkin onto the plate. "The evidence, such as it was, has been recovered, logged, and filed. Baldwin's car contained quite a bit of usable DNA evidence. Presumably, Baldwin was planning to plant that evidence in Spradlin's house. We were also able to confirm the men were brothers; they shared the same father. Apparently, Mrs. Spradlin was one of President Baldwin's victims. She married William Spradlin when she found out she was pregnant."

"And she kept that secret from Leo?"

"Yes. It's not clear how Leo discovered the truth, but it explains President Baldwin's interest in him. Unlike his son, the old man did feel some guilt and remorse for his actions. Particularly after Professor Simon's fiancée committed suicide."

"So he tried to clean up his messes, right a few wrongs."

"Maybe. According to a few sources, the male side of the Baldwin family struggled with a history of violence, mostly sexual assault as far as we can tell. Theodore Baldwin, Teddy's great-grandfather who built the college, was a religious zealot, used his religion as a shield, maybe justifying and covering his own weaknesses. Who knows for sure? Either way, since the shooting at the cabin, the locals have been coming out of the woodwork, happy to share." He rubbed his hands together. "It's taken weeks, but the statements are finally finished."

"That's longer than you thought."

"Yeah, well, everyone who ever knew Baldwin wanted to come in and give their two cents. Most of it's useless, except for shedding some light on the family history. With all the testimony, the journals, and the tape, both cases are closed."

Cancini nodded. His captain had insisted he return to D.C. shortly after the shooting in the cabin. Not that the detective had minded. Baldwin was gone. Spradlin had confessed. All that remained was the bureaucracy. A waitress slipped by their table, refilling their cups.

"And Nikki? How is she?"

"Good. Doctors say she's fine." Talbot grinned, his eyes crinkling. "She came by my office yesterday. Bit of a surprise."

"Oh?"

"Wants to be an agent." He shrugged, smiling broadly. "She's got some fire, that girl."

"You'll help her then."

"Sure. Why not? She's smart enough."

Cancini agreed. She had determination and spirit, in spite of her father's best efforts.

"And Spradlin?"

The smile faded from Talbot's face. "No trial, of course. He's already waived any future appeals, requesting the death penalty as soon as possible."

Leaning against the bench seat, Cancini frowned. He should be glad. The man was guilty of horrible crimes. No matter his motives, he had murdered innocent girls, calmly snuffing out their young lives. He hadn't flinched when he shot his brother in the back. He hadn't shed a tear. Now he was pleading guilty. Did he feel guilty? Cancini doubted it. By his own admission, he was incapable.

"Everything will be expedited. His admission to the previous murders makes it a slam-dunk. It's somewhat rare, but I've been told the execution could be slated for as soon as spring." He sipped the steaming coffee. "And the governor has officially entered lame-duck status. The party won't touch him."

Cancini's eyes wandered back to the front page of the paper. Smaller pictures of the dead girls ran underneath the larger shot of Baldwin. The case of the Coed Killer had come full circle. Cancini hoped the town and its people could find something approaching peace in the aftermath. Maybe now, there could be closure. Outside, the sun shone down on the city from a cloudless sky. "It's over now."

"Yes. It's over."

Epilogue

April First

Cancini pulled into the half-empty parking lot, squinting into the bright sun. Studying the boxy, gray building in front of him, he ran his fingers through his short, dark hair. Located in southwestern Virginia, Red Onion State Prison was a supermax facility. The majority of its inmates spent twenty-three hours a day in isolation. It was filled with lifers and those like Spradlin, men whose death was already ordained by the courts.

He got out of the car, shading his eyes. The sun had risen high in the sky and time was running short. He still had to go through security, empty his pockets, and hand over his gun. From there, someone would escort him to the viewing room. On this day, he would watch Leo Spradlin die.

A short, beefy guard said little as he led the way through halls that smelled of bleach and sweat. By the time Cancini entered the last wing of the prison, he had been searched three times. While most of the employees had been polite, none had been friendly. They each wore the same expression of disinterest, their dull eyes and slack mouths as identical as their prison guard uniforms. They didn't care that he almost didn't come. They didn't care that he was tempted to turn around and leave, that he'd seen too much of death already.

Stopping in front of a black metal door, the escort asked, "Do you have any final questions about the rules?" Having been briefed, Cancini shook his head. "Okay. Ten minutes until time," the guard said, opening the door.

Julia jumped to her feet as soon as he entered the room, hand at her throat. "Mike. I didn't expect to see you."

Cancini stepped forward slowly, swallowing hard. He hadn't seen her since they'd returned to D.C. She'd written her series, returning to both the paper and, he heard, her husband. Cancini had stayed away. He swallowed again. She was more beautiful than he remembered. Her auburn hair was pulled back from her face in a loose bun at the base of her neck. She wore a black pant-suit and pearl earrings, accentuating her alabaster skin and the cinnamon freckles that seemed to have exploded across her nose. Her eyes, her robin's egg–blue eyes, searched his, waiting.

"I didn't expect to see you, either." It was the truth. The viewing room was small, walled on three sides, the fourth a single large pane of glass. Spradlin would be on the other side soon. Another uniformed guard stood in the corner. He looked once at Cancini, then back at the wall over the detective's head.

Julia reached out, as though to touch his arm, and then dropped her hand again, shaking her head. She stepped toward him, stood on her toes, and pecked him on the cheek. He stiffened, as uncomfortable as she seemed relaxed and friendly. She waved a hand at the viewing chairs. "I think this is us."

He sat down. It was difficult not to stare at the one-way glass. On the other side, a shiny silver table covered with a white cloth had been placed next to a single chair. A flat-screen monitor on a rolling pedestal sat blank in the corner. Cancini's eyes were drawn to the chair where Spradlin would receive the injection. Its shape and black cushioning reminded him of the chair he sat in when he had his teeth cleaned, only that chair didn't have straps.

"Congrats on your nomination," he said, breaking the silence. "I heard you've been nominated for some kind of prize. I'm sorry. I don't remember what it was."

"The Guggenheim. It's for criminal justice reporting." She looked down at her hands.

"Yeah. That."

"Thanks." Turning to face him, Julia asked, "Why are you here, Mike? Is it a closure thing?"

"No. Not like that." Cancini's attention was drawn back to the glass and the empty chair. "He sent me a letter. Didn't say much, asked if I would be a witness. And you?"

"Same. I got a letter, too."

He nodded. "Not official capacity then? For the paper, I mean?"

"No." She raised her chin. "I left the paper."

He glanced at her ring finger. It was bare. "I see."

"Some things aren't meant to be, I guess."

"Yeah." He didn't know what else to say, so he said nothing.

On the other side of the glass, a man in a white coat came in and placed several items on the white-covered table, then exited.

"I'm glad you're here," she said, her voice soft. "I almost didn't come today. Watching him die . . ." Twisting her body in the seat, she looked into his eyes. "I know what he did. All those girls. I know this is what he deserves. I know this is what he wants, but . . . God, this is hard." Her voice trembled with emotion. She stopped and took a deep breath. "There has to be some tiny bit of him that isn't all bad. He kept me away from Ted. He could have killed me himself. He could have shot you and then Ted." Her words came faster and her face closer. "He could have walked away, like you said that day in the cabin. He could have disappeared. He could've done all of those things, but he didn't. Instead, he told me everything. All of it. He says he didn't feel anything, but I think he wanted to. He wanted so much to feel something, anything." Her voice faded. "Do you know what I mean?"

He did. She wasn't entirely wrong. In a way, Spradlin was giving up. He couldn't find a reason to live, so it was time to die. But Cancini couldn't feel compassion for the man, even on the day of his execution. He'd seen the twisted, brutalized bodies of girls who would never have careers, or get married, or grow old. He knew the man who had banished his mother from his heart. He knew the man who had allowed Teddy Baldwin to assault women over the course of decades.

Everything she'd said, he'd already thought. Spradlin could have walked away. Was it a crisis of conscience? Had all those years in prison changed Spradlin after all, even in some infinitesimal way? He understood the pity in Julia's eyes but couldn't share that sentiment. Just because Spradlin couldn't feel anything didn't make him less guilty or less evil. There was nothing innocent about Leo Spradlin.

Movement on the other side of the glass brought both of them back to the present. Spradlin, hands and ankles cuffed, was led in by two guards who helped him into the chair. They strapped him down, further restricting his movement. The man in the white coat returned along with a second doctor or nurse. The doctors hooked Spradlin up to the monitors, checked the readings, and made notes in their charts. The guards stood stone-faced near the door.

Cameras angled down at Spradlin would capture everything on videotape, the official record. The door to the viewing room opened, and the prison warden and an elderly man entered. The old man nodded at Cancini and sat on the opposite side of the room.

Behind the glass, Spradlin waited. He lay back in the chair, his eyes closed as though resting. The heavy beard he'd worn for years was back, and the orange jumpsuit hung on his lanky frame. He appeared tired, older than he had only a few months earlier.

Julia sniffed, and out of the corner of his eye, Cancini saw her wipe away a tear. Everyone waited. After what seemed like an interminable amount of time, the first doctor picked up a syringe. "It's time," he said. Speaking to the prisoner, the doctor explained there would be a succession of shots. The combination of drugs comprised the lethal injection. "Do you have any questions?"

Leo opened his eyes. He looked directly at the doctor, who seemed to visibly shrink under the intensity of the prisoner's gaze. "Are they here?"

"Who?" A brief look of confusion passed over the doctor's face.

Spradlin was still, looking at the two-way glass.

The warden rose and walked to the glass. He pressed the intercom button. "Both of the invited witnesses are present."

Spradlin tried to lean forward, straining against the straps. He stared at the glass as though he could burn a hole through it by looking hard enough. One of the officers moved quickly to the chair, pushing him down again. Leo let him, his eyes glittering under the glare of fluorescent lights. The doctor stepped forward, his fingers finding usable veins. One by one, he emptied each syringe. Spradlin's face and body were still at first. Then his fingers twitched and a leg jerked. His face remained impassive. Minutes slipped by, and the instruments on the monitor registered the slowing heart rate. The warden shifted in his seat. The doctors waited. Still, Spradlin's eyes remained open, his body not yet succumbing to the drugs.

Julia sat with her head bowed, silent tears flowing. Cancini reached out, took her hand, and squeezed. She held on tight. When the monitor beeped and the heart rate flatlined, she flinched. The doctor stepped forward and closed Spradlin's eyes. He was gone.

The warden and the other man stood, shaking hands. "You okay?" the warden asked.

The man nodded, shaking wisps of snow-white hair. "It's finally over." Deep wrinkles were partially masked by thick glasses. Only then did Cancini recognize the man. It was Cheryl Fornak's father.

The warden glanced at his watch and then at Cancini and Julia. He waved a hand toward the door. "There's going to be a brief press conference. Formality really. Would you like to come?"

"I don't think so," Julia said. She'd wiped away the tears, but Cancini could tell she was still a little shaky.

"No, thanks," Cancini said.

The old man walked toward them, reached out, and clapped a hand on Cancini's shoulder. Behind the lenses, his eyes were wet with unshed tears. "It doesn't bring her back, does it?" he said.

"No, sir. It doesn't." It never did. Not a conviction. Not prison. Not even execution. None of it brought back the dead. But it did help. Cancini knew he would never understand a man like Spradlin. He'd said he had no choice. He was wrong. There was always a choice. With young Cheryl Fornak, and every woman after, he'd made the wrong choice.

Mr. Fornak squeezed Cancini's shoulder, his hand stronger than it looked. His eyes cleared. "Thanks," he said.

Watching the two men leave, it occurred to Cancini that Spradlin had made one right choice after all. The final one.

He took a deep breath and his eyes found Julia. She'd moved close enough for him to smell the vanilla scent of her hair. "I spotted a coffee shop about fifteen minutes up the road. If you want, we could stop and get coffee."

She smiled. Tiny moon-shaped lines appeared at the corners of her mouth. "I'd like that."

Acknowledgments

I CAN'T REMEMBER when I first started loving books. I just did. I tore through them whenever I could, wanting to be Nancy Drew or Laura Ingalls. By high school, I was reading everything from historical romance to thrillers to horror. Stephen King kept me up many a night during my teenage years. Even now, I have so many favorite writers, it would be hard to put together a list. What hasn't changed is that I'm still thrilled to discover a new writer, try a new genre, or meet a character I can't forget. Thank you to all those writers who continue to mesmerize and inspire.

Writing may be a solitary job, but publishing a book takes a whole slew of talented people. First, thank you to Chloe Moffett, my amazing editor at HarperCollins Witness Impulse, for loving this story and for believing in the Cancini series. Thank you for all your input and hard work and thank you to the entire Witness team. Thank you to Rebecca Scherer, my wonderful agent at Jane Rotrosen, for being in my corner and for all your support.

From the earliest draft through the final edits, I've had incredible support and help. Thank you to Donna McGrath, James

Larsen, Helen Larsen, Kate Hamson, Lisa Wood, Julie Ehlers, Maria Gravely, Roberta Sachs, and Beth Rendon for your honest feedback—especially when the subject matter was sensitive and timely. Each of you offered constructive criticism that made a difference to the story. No writer could have a better "street team." Thank you also to Ginger Glenn, Virginia Glenn, and Ann Horowitz for their enduring support, and to Mary Mitchell, who is missed by so many.

Thank you to Joni Albrecht for helping me take this story and make it better. Because of you, I feel I've done justice to Detective Cancini and *Stay of Execution*. Thank you to Guy Crittenden for your support and beautiful vision. You will forever be a part of this story.

Thank you to Gram and Pop, always fans no matter what I do. Thank you to my four wonderful children for letting me be distracted (Mom. Mom! MOM!) and understanding. Thank you to my gorgeous daughter, Cameron, for politely listening to more than your share of "book" updates and for taking the time to write out editing comments and notes. And a special thank-you to my husband, David, for always encouraging me and still making me laugh every day.

Finally, I want to thank all the readers of *A Guilty Mind* who let me know they wanted more Cancini. It's been my pleasure to write the second book in the series for you, and I can't wait to write the third.

About the Author

K. L. MURPHY was born in Key West, Florida, the eldest of four children in a military family. She has worked as a freelance writer for several regional publications in Virginia, and is the author of *A Guilty Mind* and *Stay of Execution*. She lives in Richmond, Virginia, with her husband, four children, and two very large, very hairy dogs. She is currently working on her next novel, *The Last Sin*. To learn more about the Detective Cancini Mystery series or future projects, visit www.kellielarsenmurphy.com.